WHITE SANDS, RED STEEL

WHITE SANDS, RED STEEL

A HE-DOG ADVENTURE

KEITH C. BLACKMORE

Podium

WHITE SANDS, RED STEEL

CHAPTER 1

Blue sky.

A bowstring of cloud stretched across it.

Some birds coasted into He-Dog's vision, black specks below a summer sun. He squinted against the fiery brightness, eventually looking away with a gnashing of teeth and a curse. Down his gaze went, seeing the dark rise of mountains days away. He pawed at the sweat coming off his ugly head and cursed. He scratched at the long scar splitting his wreck of a nose. He hated stinking of sweat. Not even shaving his head to the skull stopped him from sweating, though Balless had once told him it would. Balless had probably only said it to see if he would actually do it. He-Dog bared his bad yellow teeth.

Heat.

He hated the heat.

He stood atop a ridge overlooking a vast plain of sand and glare. A ring of mountains capped the horizon. Below the mountains stabbed the highest of the city's spires, dipped in copper, and the flash they threw back made him squint again. Who put copper on their rooftops in this day and age? It seemed like a huge waste to him. Those high towers stood behind a thick fence of menacing stone guard towers. No copper there, but plenty of action. He-Dog watched the tiny figures swarming the battlements. The besieged had kept the attackers out, so He-Dog supposed they were winning, but by the barest of margins. The battle raged back and forth without either side really gaining an edge, but with plenty of dying. That much was obvious.

All to the tune of beastman war drums being pounded upon somewhere unseen, and their Seddon-damned screaming.

The city walls were perhaps forty or fifty feet high, that was his guess, and he guessed he was probably wrong.

He-Dog hated being wrong.

Being wrong in such heat made him grind his teeth.

There was lots of movement along those walls. Like red ants, those men were. But then, if what was camped outside the walled city of Foust was at his door, He-Dog might just be moving, too. His gaze lingered on the battlement heights for a moment more before dropping to the teeming horde laying siege to the city. He ignored the sporadic sleet of spears, bolts, and arrows being traded between the defenders and the attackers. He looked to the east and saw nothing but screaming beastmen. To the west, even more screamers. In fact, Foust was rotten with the damn brutes. Siege towers, the tops of massive tents, and a rippling mass of bodies spread out around the city like the blackest of banquets.

Man and beastman killed each other until evening.

With the sun dropping, a frustrated horde pulled back from their siege, giving up a respectful distance to the archers, spearmen, and catapults of Foust. The mass of unwashed beastman hides drew back from the walls like a living, swearing rug. And He-Dog had thought *he* smelled bad.

The retreat revealed a white beach marred with catapult shot and the recent dead, leading all the way up to the front gates. Long, dark shadows marked the land, and He-Dog wasn't sure what was blood and what was shadow.

Beaten for the day but not defeated, the beastmen pulsated with a fury that made He-Dog snort in disgust. Beastmen.

He hated killing beastmen.

They were *messy*.

They screamed constantly, believing no doubt that it whipped up their juices for battle. They screamed when they charged, they screamed when they hit, they screamed when they *got* hit, and they *howled* when they died.

Scream. All they did was scream.

Then they covered you in beastman blood and guts. The blood, in particular, took forever to wash off, and it stank as bad as beastman shite.

He-Dog *truly* hated fighting beastmen. If you didn't die yourself, you ended up stinking or just deaf. Sweet Seddon above. He'd rather just slap his own balls and have done with it.

But there was no other way. He-Dog sighed, letting some steam off his growing fury. He should never have taken on the task of delivering a message scroll to the surrounded city. Worse still, he and his boys should never have spent the wages, paid in full upfront nine days ago, before setting out for Foust. He doubted they would be able to spend it all, but when you believe you are about to perish, you will throw coin at just about anything.

He-Dog looked down at his feet, feeling his sweat abandon him for the earth. He massaged the back of his head, touching the long, single war braid he allowed to grow at nape of his neck. He scratched at his left palm, which had once been crushed under a catapult boulder. It was a wonder the thing had healed at all. He was a big man, V-shaped, and presently naked from the waist up. Scars latticed his muscular frame like curses written in an angry tongue. Dark hair grizzled his chest. He wore heavy boots and breeches of rough cloth, both as dark as his nature, or so he liked to think.

The screams of the beastmen didn't unnerve him. Their drums didn't bother him. And the frenzy they worked themselves into did nothing to sway him from examining his palms. He took his time, frowning at the throaty noise rising from the field. He slapped his hands together.

Damnation. They were noisy.

But they were only beastmen.

And he was going to run straight through their bloody works.

Slapping his shaven head, He-Dog half-turned on the rocky cliff and looked back the way he had climbed. He regarded the armored koch, well hidden from the carnage the plain. It was a heavy, ugly beast, brutal in weight and design, behind a team of six horses. He'd nailed the koch together himself, and damn Chop and Balless for saying otherwise. It was *his* creation.

Well, the armored parts were, anyway.

There were plenty of rusty sheets of iron covering the wheels, windows, and just about any place He-Dog could pound a slab into the transport's hide. If he was good at one thing, it was pounding things. It was big enough for perhaps six smaller people, or four fools wearing armor. An iron housing bruised and dented by battering rams encased the driver's seat. The small space was barely big enough for the driver, Borus. He-Dog ignored his grumblings. As long as *he* didn't have to drive the thing.

Short sword blades protruded from the wheels, and the roof bristled with spikes. He-Dog had run out of materials when he replaced the roof. Balless had crashed through the old one while doing one of his drunken jigs in full battle dress. He-Dog refused to let Balless on the top of the koch ever again. Balless had called him a dance hater for that.

The sides of the transport were a mess of overlapping planks and armor plating, outfitted with sliding panels. There was so much metal, He-Dog wondered how the damn thing never tipped on its side, but Chop had weighted it and built it on a wide chassis. Nothing rocked this koch. And six horses, every bit as cranky as Borus without his grog, hauled the entire miserable lot along, six horses that made just as much noise as any of Balless' victims. Big horses. The biggest team of beasts He-Dog had ever seen. They had to be to haul the weight of the koch and their own barding. *Barding.* They probably wore more steel than a damn army. And then there were armor plates on the sides, rising up from the same heavy poles that kept the animals in line. The plates were thin, but afforded some protection to the horses if someone attempted to stab them. That was if He-Dog didn't take it in his mind to do it first. He would have built the armor plating higher to almost cover the beasts, but it was too heavy and costly, and he didn't want to appear as if he actually *cared* for the six monsters.

He didn't.

He-Dog had ridden inside that miserable, uncomfortable hunk of wood and iron stinking of man and horse flesh for nine days. He hated the horses and vowed to eat all six the moment he found a big enough fire pit.

He-Dog hated the expense of the horses. He hated feeding the things.

Hated the koch.

Hated the business.

He stopped at the spiked log mounted on the front of the koch. The weapon looked like something from the abyss. It stuck out a good two feet in front of the lead horses—far enough so that it couldn't kill the beasts—held a foot off the ground by the same armored poles. He-Dog picked at a dark-stained tip on one of the many blades sticking out of it and flicked the piece of dead flesh at the ground.

This, now.

This he *liked.*

He liked barrelling down anyone who tried stopping him. He relished running them down, rolling them under rust-specked blades and hooves, and firing them out from behind like the shite from some sick cow after a bad feed. He liked the *whump* and jump the koch managed when bodies went under a wheel. He liked seeing the fear in whoever's eyes when they rolled into town. The ram was a meat maker. A crowd divider. And He-Dog loved strutting around unobstructed in it, feeding off the attention the ram demanded.

"We going?"

Half of He-Dog's face hitched up when he looked over at Balless. Lords above, the man was ugly and big and, once in armor, built like one of Foust's guard towers. Balless held a long, spiked mace in his paw of a hand. The man routinely toughened both fists by punching wooden planks.

"Aye," He-Dog growled as if it pained him to talk. "We're going."

"How many down there?" Balless ground his jaw, eager for the smashing to commence.

"A few," He-Dog said, hoping to disappoint him.

"You're lying." Balless grinned, showing the remaining shards of his dental capacity. The mace he held had done that to him. He-Dog still hadn't convinced him that it was his own drunken swing that gave him that winning smile. Balless was only good for one thing, and neither of them had a clue as to what it might be.

"Aren't you?" Balless asked, doubt suddenly in his eyes. The man had small, piggish eyes that almost seemed perfectly round. Where He-Dog only had scars, it looked as if someone had taken a war-pick to Balless' features. Pieces of the man's face were gouged out and had regrown in a collage of trenches and valleys. Next to Balless, He-Dog was a handsome devil.

He-Dog shook his head. "Aye." He liked confusing the big man. "Hear that?" He jerked a thumb back toward the seige. He looked at his other companions, every bit as loathsome to take in as Balless.

The smaller man called Chop was inspecting one of

two short swords he wielded in battle. His crown was bald, the skin and gristle there a dirty shade of red from where a Paw Savage had once scalped him, and black, from where Chop had burned himself to stop the bleeding. Chop had lost most of his face in the blaze that followed. His lips were burned away, too, so most of his words were mangled and unrecognizable, which was too bad. Chop's melted face was a thing of fascination for He-Dog, and he still snuck glances at its devastation. No matter how bad Chop's face was, Balless was unquestionably uglier. Although neither of them would admit it, both Balless and He-Dog believed Chop to be the smartest of the group. But the man spoke as if his brain were addled. He-Dog believed Chop's inability to communicate through simple speech was slowly driving the man mad.

Borus drove the koch. Tall and lanky, he had also been an archer, serving in the rear lines of old man Reven's Helldogs. He could loose an arrow though a keyhole at a hundred paces and a man's peehole at fifty. He-Dog figured that even if Borus ever missed the peehole, the scream of the bastard being skewered in the pisser would still impress. Borus often boasted of medals he had won and wenches he had bedded, just before he vomited and passed out from too much grog.

Borus liked to live in his past.

Except the part of his past where old man Reven's Helldogs were routed and a rampaging line of Dezer horsemen had rolled up the exposed archers like a house rug covered in bright jam. Borus had taken the edge of an axe across one of his prized eyes and woke up, screaming, in a pile of corpses with dirt being flung on him. He had also discovered he was missing most of the fingers on his right hand.

Since then, Borus only glared ahead when he was sober.

He-Dog never looked into Borus' one eye. And he thought it bad luck to look upon the black empty socket.

Borus was a man who had had it all but, because of another man's mistake, lost everything. He was full of hate to the core, lava red and spitting. One could feel the air temperature rising simply by standing beside the man. He-Dog was only too glad to have Borus driving. He wouldn't want to have him somewhere behind his back, and he *certainly* didn't want the man against him. Where He-Dog only thought he hated most things, Borus actually did.

Of the four companions, Borus was perhaps the least amusing. Where He-Dog thought of himself as dangerous, Chop as pitiful, and Balless simply insane, Borus kept his one eye fixed murderously ahead, as if he were fixated on the very gates of Saimon's Abyss in the distance… and looking to smash them.

"They're down there, all right," He-Dog said loud enough for all of them to hear. "And they're getting hot. You all ready?"

Chop and Balless nodded. Borus only stared in the direction of the noise.

"Koch's ready." Balless hefted his mace.

Like hyenas after a kill, they grinned at each other. Except for Borus. His eye still stared ahead.

"What's your plan?" Balless asked.

He-Dog regarded Balless with loathing. They all knew they needed a plan to reach Foust. And to get through an army of raging beastmen, that plan would have to be a brilliant one. A *smashing* one.

He-Dog was not one to deliver plans like that.

Chop might, possibly, but no one could understand the bastard.

"We drive right through them," He-Dog growled as if speaking through a muzzle. "Right through the damn works. Right up to Foust's door and damn any of them in our way."

"In our *way!*" Balless growled back, a sound strained with building pressure.

"They won't expect a thing," He-Dog said and felt it to

be true. Who would expect a lone koch, even one looking like something from Saimon's nightmarish Abyss, to come up behind an army and just cut its way through?

Chop smiled. It made He-Dog uneasy to see those burned lips draw back in a smile. It looked as though he were about to bite someone.

"*Ahhhlieiiii*," Chop said.

Borus was already climbing aboard the koch, disappearing in the armored sheath of the driver's seat. It was heartening to see such support from the boys. He-Dog felt like a real leader instead of the misshaped piece of meat he usually passed himself off as.

"Saddle up, then." He reached for his helm and armor.

And they did.

CHAPTER 2

Well back from the sands of the dead and dying was a vast gathering of tents made from cured animal hides, bones, and long timbers. Beastmen of the four major breeds strutted, swore, and fought each other there, anxious to be the next to face the high stone walls of Foust. In this veritable sea of beastman pleasantries, one tent dominated. A wall of fierce black beastmen surrounded the huge, mottled pavilion. They were big creatures, bare-chested as they all preferred to be in battle, dog-snouted and tusked. Like all other beastmen, they carried weapons that smashed and hacked and didn't require a great degree of finesse. Their coal-colored muscular flesh shined in the diminishing evening light. The lips of their short muzzles could not completely conceal formidable jaws. The black beastmen were prized among their kind for their sense of order and discipline. They stood, rooted in place, guarding against all—even other beastman breeds which they scorned. Beastmen were not above taking the head of one of their own if one came too close to the War Skull's tent without permission.

Within the great War Skull's pavilion, the beastman chieftains of the twenty-nine united tribes gathered around a huge fire pit. King Blood Skull, leader of the horde, stood while the others squatted or sat. The beastman king stalked around the low-burning blaze, fixing his twenty-eight chieftains with a baleful glare. Blood Skull was a huge black, towering over all others. His muscular girth, terrible strength, cunning, and unholy ability with a war club had enabled him to kill the previous chieftains in bloody succession, absorbing each of the dead beastmen's tribes into his own until he was the sole ruler. Ringing the edges of the gathering were the bare, grinning, and in some cases, broken skulls of the twenty-eight dead chieftains.

Blood Skull stomped around the fire pit, seething with barely suppressed fury. He drew himself up to his full height and flashed a derisive look at the skulls draped in shadow and encircling the living. They all smiled at him, it seemed. Blood Skull bared his yellow teeth and tusks. Superstitious to the core, he felt his rage over the failure to take the walls of Foust armored him against any beastman ghost seeking revenge. The king clenched his hands, which were like massive paws. Blood Skull had adorned himself in rough-shod armor as a symbol of his might and leadership. Under the majestic folds of the pavilion, his full barbaric splendor hushed the gathering. An assortment of worn weapons hung from his frame, including the war club that had claimed the lives of the twenty-eight chieftains.

The present twenty-eight, those not yet brave enough to challenge Blood Skull for his crown, knew their bony predecessors watched their backs.

Blood Skull ranted at them. He swore vile oaths in the harsh beastman tongue that would enrage any breed of worth, yet these blood bastards sat rooted to the spot and took it with lowered eyes. Spittle flew from his tusks. His eyes drenched his minions with poison. He lashed out, shaking fists and cursing the chieftains' failures. He droned like a thunder storm spitting directly over their sorry heads. Why had they not succeeded in taking the walls?

Blood Skull gnashed his teeth, stomped and raged, and continued to work himself into a fury that would have made the Lord of the Underworld, Saimon himself, draw back in respect.

When Blood Skull stopped to draw a breath, one of the beastman chieftains spoke. He was a white, known for cunning, slyness, and cruelty. Keeping his eyes lowered, the chieftain suggested they might attempt another attack by night.

Blood Skull froze in his tracks. He gazed down on the seated white. The beastmen next to the white chieftain regarded him. The white again explained his reasoning for a night attack, even though the previous night's assault had proved costly to the horde in both warriors and siege machines. The towers, in particular, were difficult to replace, as there were no trees around for leagues.

"Again?" Blood Skull inquired in a controlled voice. The beastman language bubbled out of him in a series of guttural snorts and barks.

The white nodded.

Blood Skull pulled his war club from his side and brought it down across the head of the white beastman, shocking the gathered chieftains. In one moment, Blood Skull had seemed to be actually thinking and considering the white's words, and then the next, his war club came down and crushed the white chieftain's skull like a rotten egg. The creature's legs kicked as he rolled over, and Blood Skull placed one booted foot on his dead chest. When the king wrenched his weapon free, bone and brain matter bespattered those nearby.

Blood Skull shook his war club at the remaining cheiftains and asked if there were any more suggestions.

There were none.

Perhaps the white chieftain brought out the worst in the king. Perhaps it was the failure of his leaders to take the city, or perhaps it was simply the nature of Blood Skull's black soul. Whatever the reason, War Skull ranted with such fury that the beastmen before him felt as if fiery catapult shot rained down on their heads. He threatened them with death. He threatened them with castration. He threatened sending them back to their individual territories, to keep watch over the young with the females—a vow that made more than one of the cheiftains wince ever so slightly. There was no greater shame to a beastman warrior.The War Skull ranted and roared so much that he was completely oblivious to the approaching sound. A thundering drew closer and louder as the king went on cursing. Shouts and screams erupted from beyond the tenebrous folds of the pavilion. One of the green beastman chieftains sitting near the tent wall felt the ground tremble. He lifted his head in a question, looking at his companion. The other chieftain, a red as mottled as a fire toad, bared his tusks in warning.

Then, the red's expression softened.

Both beastmen turned to the blackness of the tent wall. Above them, three dark skulls, victims of Blood Skull's ambitions, grinned and kept their secrets. The other chieftains did not move, still rooted to the spot by Blood Skull's harangue. After a few seconds, the others dared to look in the direction of the approaching rumble.

A heedless Blood Skull shook his war club. He swore and vowed to kill them all and wear their guts. He didn't see the beastmen behind him inch away from the tent wall. He didn't consider that the growing fear on the chieftains' faces was the result of anything other than his mounting fury.

The ground continued to tremble, intensifying threefold.

Shouts and screams of warning erupted from outside.

The seated beastmen turned in the direction of the commotion. Even Blood Skull paused, finally realizing the sand beneath his feet pulsed with a wrath of its own.

The west side of the pavilion wall burst inward, ripped down from its timbers and chewed up by a flashing whirling thing of blades and bad intentions. Evening light split the shadows within, and the beastmen scurried back from the ruined wall like cats sprayed with water. A great rolling log, driven by a team of six horses, charged into the mass of chieftains and scattered them in all directions. The vehicle roared across the fire pit, sending up a flurry of red embers.

A puzzled Blood Skull turned around, and his jaw dropped.

The koch's spiked log struck the beastman full on, bursting the king like an overripe melon. The black, spun underneath the vehicle by the force of the whirling blades, was trampled by the team of six horses and crushed again by the thick wheels of the koch. The mashed corpse of the king was shat out behind the carriage in a fine cloud of dust, blood, and wrecked armor. The koch bumped and thumped with speed, and the sudden demise of the War Skull prompted the beastmen on the other side of the pavilion, in the direct path of the rolling pin, to get the hell out of the way. They sprawled to the left and right with howls of fright.

The koch burst its way through the opposite wall, chewing up the evening's calm and leaving twenty-eight chieftains staring after the wooden beast in utter shock and awe.

CHAPTER 3

"Damnation!" He-Dog leveled an evil look in the direction of the driver's seat. Borus was born a bastard, and when they were safely through, He-Dog would have a talk with the man about taking them through the camp, and taking them *through*. The koch bucked and jumped in places, and He-Dog was certain that the armored bucket was about to flip. That was unacceptable in his mind. He righted his helmet and gripped the overhead timbers. He wanted to peer through the narrow slit in the shell of the beast, but something told him that it was better if he did not. He glanced around the interior of the koch. Everything was still in place.

He-Dog looked at Chop. The man had put on his battle dress, a worn cuirass with enough scars in its surface that one would think the man had been scratched repeatedly by lightning. Metal bracers with exotic writing fitted over his forearms and lower legs, beneath a crenulated skirt of leather. His twin swords hung from his hips. Chop's burnt features were concealed by a black leather mask that He-Dog knew to be of Nordish origin, but it was useless to ask the bastard where he had gotten it.

Chop's eyes met He-Dog's. Chop thought the same

thing.

Borus wanted to kill them all.

Perhaps this was the day.

He-Dog looked at Balless. The man grinned at him with a mouth full of absent or ruined teeth. If He-Dog didn't know any better, he would have thought the man drunk with joy. Balless was encased in the heaviest of armor, a mix of chain mail and metal plates strapped to his body like bowed planks to a barrel. An open-faced helmet squashed down upon his head. His mighty mace hung within easy reach from a peg next to his right thigh. A wooden shield rolled to his left, and Balless slammed a hand down on it.

He-Dog looked away before he grinned back, in spite of himself.

The koch shook with every impact over masses best left unseen. Borus hunched over in the driver's seat, his shoulders just barely fitting into the space. Ahead, the armor extended like blinders, and he could see the mighty backs of the horses as they pulled the koch's carcass. Borus cracked the reins again and again. Beyond the lead animals, beastmen dove for cover. Some fell sprawling to safety, while others were taken completely by surprise. Those too stunned to move were rolled over and pulped.

Borus did not say much these days, but a smile distorted his one-eyed face. He steered for another tent, evil delight ripping through his person. The koch smashed the animal skin wall, scattering beastmen like grain from a ripped sack. Screams and howls cut the air. A horrible concoction of brutal sounds and curses comprised the beastman language, and he was exposed to the best of it. Unlike his companions in the back, Borus could clearly see the full carnage. He looked to his left, through a slit in the armor no thicker than an arrow shaft, for confirmation of whether what he saw ahead extended to their flanks as well.

It did.

Beastmen.

An *ocean* of beastmen.

Worse, an ocean of beastmen waking up to the fact that they were being attacked from behind.

Borus scowled.

He could not see the walls of Foust anywhere.

Then, the *whok* of something hitting the right side of the armor made him flinch. It was joined by another. Then another. The tip of a spearhead punched through the shell, and the sound made him jerk his head in that direction. With his left eye, he saw that the beastman spear would have taken him full in the ear if it weren't for the armor plating. Whoever had thrown the weapon was *strong*. The thought made him smile, and he hunched lower in his seat. He hoped that somewhere ahead the walls of Foust would reveal themselves.

A downpour of multiple impacts, metal punching metal, filled Borus' ears like the angry rain of a Sunjan summer.

With each impact, the armor dented and groaned and came that much closer to yielding.

Borus cracked the reins again.

CHAPTER 4

A heavy thump hit the right side of the koch, just above Balless' head. The sound made the big man look up, one hand holding onto his helmet. His piggish eyes met He-Dog's. A rain of punches and strikes enveloped the koch's outer shell as if it had just driven under a landslide, causing the three men inside to crouch a little lower.

He Dog looked up at the ceiling. "Faces up, boys."

Things were going to get interesting.

Grinning his ruined smile, Balless hauled himself to his feet and faced the rear of the koch. Chop braced himself on the right side. He-Dog slapped his helmet, cursed himself for luck, and faced left. They positioned themselves in front of the armored panels that would easily slide away when necessary. They eyed the rack of short spears near the covered openings.

Outside, a thunderous tide of sound washed over the thick-skinned koch as it labored through the beastman ranks. Infuriated by the brazenness of the single invader, those who were quickly run over gave their lives for the remainder of the horde to wake them to the threat. Beastmen no longer stood in the path of the beast. They parted for the vehicle, slinging spears and unleashing crossbow bolts at its thick hide. Orders were shouted by sub-chieftains, and beastmen who had been about to partake of the evening meal gathered mauls and maces, great axes and war clubs.

It was one thing to drive through a beastman encampment.

It was another to do so at dinnertime.

The way ahead of the koch parted, the rolling pin of death no longer striking terror into the beastmen, but a grim appreciation for the contraption. Why hadn't *they* thought of something like that? Lifting muscular arms to wave their minions forward, the beastmen quickly sealed the cut the koch had made, and counterattacked. The koch slowed, bouncing over those unfortunate few caught in its path.

And the beastmen jumped.

Some of them flung themselves at the koch's sides, grabbing the roof, only to slip and fall into the whirling blades attached to the wheels. Beastmen were opened up in a shower of gore. Some managed to hang on while their brethren hurled weapons at the moving koch. Axes and spears imbedded themselves into the places between the armor plates. The constant bouncing of the transport made it difficult for the beastmen to aim. With one violent bump, a thrown axe found the back of a white's head. The blade split the creature's skull like a knife cutting hard fruit, knocking the boarder from the side of the koch.

Snarling, the beastmen who had managed to hang on gouged the lower and upper railings and clawed at the armored surface of the koch. They would paw their way into the koch's innards if need be, and each intended to be the first to kill whoever was inside.

The koch panels slid back, obstructed by the huge bodies of the beastmen clinging onto the sides. Spearheads jabbed, puncturing abdomens again and again until death took the boarders, and they dropped. As soon as the carcasses fell, the panels slid back into place.

But the beastmen insisted.

And where the koch had not yet reached, grappling hooks and ropes were readied.

*

He-Dog slammed his window shut and gripped a spear, its tip covered in beastman blood.

"Dog balls." The reek of it wrinkled He-Dog's nose and he held the weapon at arm's length, wishing he had released it when he made the kill.

To his left, Balless yanked his panel open and stabbed at something, his thick arm working to and fro with a terrible energy. If the beastman outside screamed, it was lost in the growing wail of war cries and the relentless thrum of human-skin war drums. Chop opened and closed his own panel with a measured calmness, repeatedly stabbing and cutting beastman flesh.

The koch struck something hard and bounced. It teetered to the left, flinging He-Dog into the wall and almost causing him to lose grip on his bloody spear. His forehead crashed into the wood and his helmet left an impression.

"Borus!" He-Dog shouted, baring bad yellow teeth. "Watch where you're steering!"

Borus did not reply.

He-Dog swore. Borus was going into one of his moods where he would not speak or acknowledge anyone. The koch jarred over something in its path and He-Dog's jaws clapped together. He bit into his tongue. He spat blood and fired a poisoned look at the back of Borus' head. He could see the man hunched over his reins. He-Dog could not see what Borus saw. The picture was too fluid.

In truth, He-Dog did not want to see. It was better for all of them that way. Let mad Borus face the truth of the horde. He didn't care if he lived or died.

Something about which He-Dog was conflicted.

Something crashed onto the roof of the koch, distracting him from the one-eyed man. Balless and Chop looked up. Balless gripped his spear and moved to a panel above them. He gripped a knob and yanked it back. His spear stabbed upward.

Outside, the beastman who had reached the roof of the koch suddenly danced and fell, swallowed up by the enveloping horde. Grappling hooks flew through the air like thick strands of barbed spider webbing. Some bounced off metal plates. Some gouged and held. At the ends of these ropes, angry looking beastmen, their muzzles wide and snarling, held on and readied themselves for the pull.

All at once, three lines of beastmen were yanked off their feet.

The force of the jolt left several of the creatures in the sand behind the koch, cursing stinging paws. Plenty more hung onto the rampaging koch, and the weight could be felt by those inside its tough hide. Spears and axes cut through the air. In one instant, a crude-looking war axe cut clean through one of the ropes and a long string of furious beastmen flailed to a stop.

Inside, the continuing clack and crash of weapons bouncing off the koch's hide didn't distract the men. They felt the drag. A black-masked Chop studied the interior as if searching for a leak. The koch slowly *swerved.* The men struggled to stay on their feet. Balless looked at He-Dog, his grin faltering. Things were going from fun to unfunny.

He-Dog looked at the back of Borus' head.

"We're slowing down, you pissy bastard!"

The once-champion archer did not reply. His one eye narrowed in concentration as he took in what lay ahead. Beastmen were no longer in the way. They adapted to the flow of battle and scrambled out of the path of the meat koch. Catapult shot—rounded stones—and lengths of timber remained in the direct path of the transport. Spears and axes continued to pepper off the armor plating covering the driver's seat, some even split gaps in the wood. Ahead, Borus saw thrown weapons bouncing off the barding on the horses. Some of the beastmen even stood to the side of the beasts and stabbed at them. Fortunately, the creatures were knocked aside by the charging animals.

The beastmen were not entirely stupid. It was only a matter of time before one of the horses went down.

Borus snarled. It would be interesting to see what happened when it did.

CHAPTER 5

The dusty plains surrounding Foust had looked flat to He-Dog when he initially gazed upon the besieged city from the safety of the mountain ridge. He was wrong. The land dipped and rose about the fabled walls. Some of these sandy hills rose to the height of two men.

For the beastman horde, these mounds were important in the placement of certain siege machines. The first thing they did, under the cover of darkness, was to erect walls for the siege machine operators. Then, beastman ballistae, some capable of firing a devastating barrage of multiple spears, were hauled to the hills' heights by sweating and cursing beastmen. Paw over paw, they labored with chains and dragged the weapons on crude wheels until they were in place and pointed at the face of Foust.

As darkness fell, the clatter of battle drew close to one hill in particular. The leader there, knowing that his single spear ballista was mounted on a cranky swivel, barked orders to his operators. The reds jumped to the task. There was no time to spare. Baring tusks, a dozen of the creatures turned the ballista. Curses cut the air.

The red leader tied a thick rope to the loaded missile. He checked the distance. It would be a difficult shot. A damned near *impossible* shot.

With a snarl, he resolved to try.

*

The horde was fully aware of the intruder and its intended path. Beastmen worked to block the koch's way. They hauled and dropped catapult shot in its path. They dragged timbers before it. The skill of the driver infuriated them. No matter how the beastmen concealed their traps with their own bodies, parting only as the koch approached, the driver somehow sensed the danger, and veered to the left or right without losing control. Sand spun from under the wheels. The spiked roller bounced and rattled with mindless fury. Thrown axes and spears found their mark, some deflecting off the metal hide, some sticking.

The koch came on.

Some beastmen tried to board the thing from the sides but were driven back by the whirling blades fixed to the wheels. Behind the koch, like meaty streamers of a festival gone bad, long ropes trailed. Beastmen held on to these ropes, snarling and clinging to the lengths with the strength and sheer stubbornness that made the brutes so dangerous. More of the savage creatures from the sidelines jumped onto the ragtag train behind the koch and, paw over paw, hauled themselves toward the back. One rope snapped from the weight. A grappling hook lost its grip when the koch bounced.

But the last rope became a bridge.

Savage-faced beastmen drew closer to their quarry.

*

Back on the hill, the crew of beastmen placed the ballista exactly where their leader wanted it. A huge spear, iron tipped and gleaming, lay ready in the weapon's breach.

The red leader saw the approach of the koch. It had turned somewhat, but would eventually cut across their line of fire. He judged the distance with a professional air, and barked out adjustments. Lucky for him, the thing slowed down. War drums pounded a harsh beat. The horde pressed in on the tiny transport.

The red beastman kept one eye on the approaching koch. It would be in his sights shortly.

Snarling, the red went for the release lever.

*

The first beastman at the back of the koch almost reached the roof. He had both paws on the railing and pulled himself upward when the armor plates slide across and Balless shoved a length of spear into his chest. Blood flowered in the air. The beastman fell away.

Another was right behind him.

He grabbed for Balless' wrists and held tight. Surprised, the big man regarded the furious creature. Fangs and tusks gleamed in the beastman's open mouth. Balless' smile returned as he yanked backward with all of the strength of his arms and legs, jerking the beastman forward. The creature's forehead clacked off the armored brim of the opening. The beast's eyes grew glassy. Balless yanked inward a few more times, delighting in the beastman's predicament, until he let the unconscious creature drop out of sight.

Balless peered out the window and his grin wilted. There were a *lot* of beastmen out there hanging off the koch's sunny ass. He spied the rope, just out of reach. Unless he stuck out his arm.

Balless did just that.

Eight beastmen, spitting and snarling at the sand flung into their faces, saw a long muscular arm ending in a length of spear emerge from the back of the koch. Axes and spears *pinged* and *panged* off the armored hide, failing to find meat.

Balless cut at the rope, heedless of the deadly rain seeking his arm.

From within, He-Dog bawled at him to get his arm back inside.

Balless declined to obey, focusing solely on the stubborn weave of hemp. He bared his winning smile. The rope was half cut.

He almost succeeded.

CHAPTER 6

On the battlements of Foust's walls, interest in the raucous happenings below grew among the guards of the evening watch. It wasn't unnatural for the beastman drums and war cries to carry on through the night, but this was different. One keen-eyed soldier pointed out the reason for the incessant madness. Gradually, the koch came into view. The soldiers of Foust crowded the crenels, watching in morbid fascination at the hopelessness of the koch churning toward them. As it drew closer, they saw the sheer *vastness* of the horde press in on all sides of the koch, and to a man, they felt their guts twist in despair.

"Think they'll make it?" one soldier asked his companion.

The other man didn't bother answering.

*

A line of beastmen formed up with a bristling wall of spears. They butted the ends of their weapons into the sand and stood snarling in the face of the oncoming nightmare. The battle koch, bad to look upon at any time, was pure evil at the moment. Covered in beastman blood and other fleshy matter, the thing charged forward with Borus cracking the reins as if bearing down on the rosy ass of Saimon himself. The one-eyed archer saw the line of spears and smiled.

The spiked ram snapped the spears and scattered the beastman line. The warriors at the edges of the line escaped with their lives, while those closer had their legs sheared off or slashed at the knees and thighs. The beastmen in the middle went under the log, dead by blade and hooves before the wheels marked them. More spears flew at the koch. More axes thundered into its wooden and iron flesh. Howls of rage perforated the air. Drums pounded.

And the wagon drove on.

*

Seeing enough was enough. The red yanked back on the release mechanism and the ballista shook. The missile sang out over the heads of beastmen, directly on a path to hit the moving koch. The leader *knew* it had hit the target.

It was a near perfect shot.

*

The iron tip of the spear punched through the right side of the koch in a shower of splinters and a crunch that badly scared Balless. The weapon surged forth, two fingers away from Chop's right side and just under his arm. He looked down at the fearsome barb in stunned fascination. He-Dog and Balless stared at the thing that almost took their companion. They exchanged looks. Chop glanced over his shoulder at the pair, his mask covering his expression of wonderment.

In that instant, they all began to laugh.

*

Elation surged through the red leader at the success of his shot. Throaty cheers went up from the ballista crew. Connected to the ballista to his right, a coil of rope whipped out and neared its end. Over the heads of beastmen struggling to cripple the koch, the ballista operators could see the grievous wound they had given the monster. The red beastman bawled orders to ready another missile.

The rope tightened.

Unhindered by the ballista's missile, the koch pushed forward, yanking the rope attached to the spear lodged in its gullet. Its horses, laboring so hard that their hearts could burst before any beastman weapons took them, determinedly hauled the transport closer to the walls of Foust. With a groan of wood and iron, the rope snapped garrotte-straight and jerked the ballista from its perch on the hill. The red beastman and his operators fell screaming from the siege weapon. The ballista itself bumped and rolled down the side of the hill, crushing a knot of beastmen too slow to move out the way.

Where it dragged.

Until it dug in.

*

The moment the ballista halted, the rope and spear ripped an entire section from the koch.

"Dog balls!" He-Dog swore as a chunk of wood and metal, the door to the interior in fact, already weakened by the relentless storm of axes and other thrown weapons, tore away. The jolt in the koch caused all four men to buck in their places. Chop threw himself backward, narrowly avoiding falling out into the paws of blood-craving beastmen.

Up ahead, Borus smiled. He could clearly see the walls of Foust. They weren't so far away.

The wall of beastmen ahead parted. Logs and catapult shot loomed.

Borus' grin wilted. There was no way around this barricade.

He might have shouted a warning to his companions, but a war axe flew out of the horde. It connected solidly with the third horse in the team in a spray of red. The beast was probably thankful for being killed.

Everything happened at once.

*

From the battlement heights, the soldiers watched as beastmen attempted to board the oncoming koch. They saw the killer rain of axes and spears and even arrows fall upon its shell. They collectively gasped when the ballista spear stabbed the transport through its ribs and cringed when the rope snapped taut. They saw the drag upon the koch and cheered when it pulled the terrible siege weapon down from its hill. The beastmen lines split. A chunk of wood and iron ripped from the koch's side. A storm of weapons flew at the exposed guts of the transport.

The koch flew through the air.

The rolling pin hit the log jam and snapped from its moorings with body shaking force. The surviving horses before the koch ploughed forward, screaming and dying as they charged into the ram's blades. The koch pushed them ahead, until beasts and wheel crashed upon the logs. Leather bindings snapped. Inertia shoved the vehicle forward, running over the brave animals that had pulled it so far, crushing them. The transport launched, pausing at a lazy apex, and crashed back down on its ruined side in the sand. A sheet of dust whipped over its carcass, smothering all. Sounds of timbers snapping, bindings tearing, and horses screaming cut through the maddening thrum of war drums. Eventually, a respectful silence spread up and over the plains of Foust.

For a moment, the silence held.

Then, the lands awash in beastmen erupted in one thunderous cheer.

CHAPTER 7

In the aftermath of the crash, a disappointed hush fell over the watchers on Foust's crenelated walls. They had been victims of the siege for some time now, and the distraction below was welcome until it was crushed, along with any hope they might have had.

"Well," one of the soldiers muttered from the heights of Foust, already bored. "That was good."

He turned away.

His companion leaned forward, as if hearing something beyond the monstrous wailing beyond.

Something was happening below.

*

The door flew off its hinges with one mighty kick. The boot that did the kicking lingered for a moment, then withdrew. A massive hand appeared and Balless pulled himself out of the koch, through the small portal separating the driver's seat and the main interior. He barely fit. The shoulders of his armor splintered the edges of the door's frame. The big man crawled over the dead bodies of the horses and the wreckage of poles and wheels. Blood covered him. The lingering dust cloud from the impact clung to his person. Once free of the koch, Balless stood, leaning heavily against a section of the roof bare of spikes.

The beastmen surrounding the crash site slowly quieted as the single armored figure emerged. They watched him fall against the roof of the transport. Snarls and beastman curses filled the air. The beastmen's Gods of War smiled upon them. Here was one to pound into meat.

Balless took deep, steadying breaths. One hand steadied the helmet on his head. His senses had been rocked when the koch left the ground and crashed back down, but he was slowly regaining them. He hefted his long mace in his right hand. The weapon came up with warning. The spiked head was the size of a newborn child.

Balless detached himself from the wreckage of the koch, but kept his back to it. It was one angle he would not have to worry about. He rolled his massive shoulders and held his mace two-handed like a club. He faced the waves of beastmen standing not thirty paces from him.

And grinned.

Infuriated with the insolence of the man, the bravest of the beastmen surged

forward. Reds, blacks, and greens brandishing war clubs, axes, maces, and mauls rushed at the single warrior. Howls and guttural screams stabbed the air.

Balless stepped back a pace. He drew his mace to his shoulder and waited.

The beastmen were practically on top of him.

He went low.

Balless dropped and swung his long, spiked mace at the unprotected legs of the beastman wall. Powered by his mighty arms, his mace smashed through a collection of knees, bursting them like hard plums. The first wave of beastmen collapsed before the big man, writhing on the sand as if hooked from the sea. Those still standing suddenly had to step over a thrashing fence of their brethren. One beastman had his face bashed in when he tried. Another had his shoulder crushed. A third swung an axe at the man and had his weapon's head smashed from its wooden shaft. Balless brained the same beastman with one swipe of his mace. Another beastman jumped over the fence of the fallen and Balless struck him down in mid-air as if the creature were a ball. Blood spattered Balless' armored form and fell like black rain from his person.

The second line of beastmen paused in its attack, sizing up this grim man-thing before them.

"*Balless!*"

Hearing his name, the big man looked. A battered and bloodied He-Dog emerged from the wreckage and rolled a rounded shield toward him. Balless caught it along the edge and quickly fitted its wood and iron frame to his arm. The black mask of Chop squeezed out behind He-Dog. The swordsman got to his feet and adjusted the leather hiding his face so that he could see. Here and there, ugly weeping wounds were visible on Chop, covering his battle dress in blood. The masked warrior beheld the beastman tide before him and pulled out both of his short swords, daring the enemy with a leather look. Steel gleamed in the dusty air.

He-Dog swore under his breath. He hated it when Chop engaged in such theatrics. He also hated that Chop had left him with the task of hauling Borus' worthless, death-seeking carcass from the koch. If he didn't think it would amuse the beastmen, He-Dog would beat the unconscious man to death.

Instead, he set his jaw and pulled his companion from the wreckage.

Balless and Chop took a step toward each other, closing the gap between them and forming a wall. Balless was a grinning bear, beaten and bleeding. Chop was just as frightful. Both men faced the ocean of beastmen.

Another wave of axe and club wielding beastmen charged the overturned koch. They rushed the pair of men in a storm surge of noise. He-Dog looked up, his hands under Borus' arms, and knew they were about to die.

There were simply too many.

But neither Balless nor Chop seemed to realize it.

The pair ripped into any beastmen within striking range. A cacophony of strikes, screams, and moans cut through the air, matching the beat of the beastman war drums. Chop was a fluid streak of black leather and silver. His twin blades seemed to only touch his attackers, but they opened bloody gashes both long and deep. Beastmen fell dead and dying in droves at his feet, and a twitching mound began to rise. Where Chop was pure style and finesse, Balless possessed the subtlety of a maul. Holding his shield before him, the massive fighter broke skulls and crushed limbs with his mace while his shield mashed faces.

The beastmen screamed at the warriors refusing to die. They charged again.

A club crashed into Balless' shield arm, numbing it. Another cracked across the forehead of his helmet, hard enough to break the skin underneath. Blood ran down into Balless' face, partially blinding him. An axe tore a chunk of chainmail from his thigh and a spear gashed it to the bone a moment later. Another axe came down hard on the edge of Balless' shield, splitting it to his forearm. With a grunt, Balless heaved and bashed in the head of the axe's owner. Then he proceeded to kill the rest.

Beastmen crowded around Chop until they began to slow the swordsman. There were simply too many. One beastman clubbed the man's right forearm, denting his bracer and breaking his arm. The sword flew from Chop's tingling fingers while a bolt of pain lanced up his arm. Another beastman slashed an axe blade across the masked man's leather-bound chest, splitting it open to the ribs. Blood sprayed. Yet another axe slashed down, breaking the bone above his right eye, knocking the swordsman back. The mounting pile of dead surrounding Chop saved him as the beastmen struggled to reach their prey. Though his wounds were crippling, the swordsman still managed to slay his attackers as they attempted to reach him.

Other beastmen came.

Taking up his sword, He-Dog switched with Chop. He relieved the man behind the pile of dead and gave him a chance to catch his wind. He-Dog hacked and stabbed, slashed and punched. Beastmen fell. But for every two who fell, one scored a hit on He-Dog. An axe blade licked his jaw, opening a new spitting mouth. A spear punctured his left shoulder, rendering it useless. A club clacked off his helmet, denting it deeply and causing black motes to explode before his eyes. Another club clipped his jaw again, snapping it in a sparkle of pain. Even worse, the beastmen were *bleeding* on him.

Bloodied and snarling, He-Dog swapped with Chop again.

Balless didn't appear to need rest.

They fought for seconds more, the beastmen surging against the pair of warriors and dying in heaps and droves. Then, the tide relented. The beastmen retreated, leaving a mound of their dead. Reds, blacks, whites and greens lay slaughtered at the feet of the two men. Balless and Chop watched them retreat. The warriors' chests heaved, trying to suck in as much air as they could before the next wave. Grime, blood, and sweat covered their flesh.

Balless looked at Chop. The man's mask was half hanging from his face, as was his broken armor. Beastman axes and spears had wrought devastation on him and blood ran freely from a multitude of wounds. He was a mess.

Chop regarded Balless and slowly shook his aching head in wonder. The man was a tree that, no matter how many chops it took, refused to fall down. Even as he watched, streams of blood seemed to bubble from somewhere underneath Balless' helm. Muttering an oath, Balless raked the helm from his scalp and tossed it to one side. He grinned at his companion with stained teeth. Through the tatters of his black mask, Chop's lipless mouth smiled back. If there was one good thing about Balless, he was eternally positive. Chop limped a step and looked down. A spear point had pierced his lower haunch. Grimacing, he staggered to his knees. The rush of battle left him, and the pain of his wounds rushed in.

A battered He-Dog saw Chop fall. He left Borus propped against the husk of the koch. He reached the bleeding mess of Chop and pulled him back, placing him next to Borus. He took Chop's place, giving Balless a determined look. There was still killing to be done, and he wanted to be on the line with his companion still standing

Just beyond the dead, an ocean of beastmen seethed.

CHAPTER 8

One beastman detached himself from the line: a massive red, fearless, and frothing curses at Balless. He waved a huge single-bladed war axe. A jawless human skull crowned the weapon's head.

Balless grinned back, his teeth lined with blood. It would be mace against axe.

The Red took three steps forward and dared Balless to meet him beyond the field of dead. The beastman stepped onto an area of the sand clear of bodies and waited, hunched over and baring tusks.

Shrugging his shoulders, Balless went to meet the challenger.

He-Dog could not believe what was about to happen. He and Chop watched as Balless stepped and stumbled over the wall of corpses. The big man appeared to be at the end of his strength. His armor was nothing but metal rags. His head was a mess. He-Dog grimaced as his companion staggered to the open sands and faced the red challenger.

If the beastman was pleased, he did not show it. Again, he brandished his weapon at Balless. Again, the beastman uttered a long barrage of curses. Teeth and tusks flashed.

The watching beastmen roared in expectation.

He Dog shook his head. "Well, dog balls," he muttered beside a staring Chop. "He doesn't mean to fight him *alone*, does he?"

With that, the red charged, his war axe high. He brought the weapon slicing downward. The creature's upper body rippled with the strength behind the chop.

Balless nimbly stepped out of harm's way.

He cracked his mace across the bare skull of the beastman, braining the creature with one swipe. The champion's head exploded upon contact, brain matter and bone fragments showering the sand. The screams of the beastmen died as abruptly as the life left the red. The human had taken on the strongest among them and killed him easily.

From where he watched, He Dog shook his head again.

That was one *stupid* beastman.

The gathered beastmen watched as the towering man backed up, toward his comrades. None moved to attack as a beaming Balless climbed back over the pile of dead. He-Dog continued to shake his head. He had seen it many times before and often pressed the point upon his drinking companions. It wasn't how hard you hit. It was how hard you could *be* hit. Balless was proof.

Balless was also a monster.

"Dog balls." He-Dog swore again. Balless *looke*d like a monster.

Chop muttered something.

"Shaddup," He-Dog informed him. He didn't have time to try and figure out what the shagger wanted to say. Balless returned, standing guard beside the thigh-high mound of ragged bodies. He glanced at his wounded companions.

And grinned his broken grin.

He-Dog did not smile back. He eyed the beastmen surrounding them. Leaderless they might be for for now, but beastmen were never still for long. The war drums and chants started again. The beastmen were gathering steam and this time, when they came over the dead, He-Dog knew there would be very little fight left in himself or his boys.

The thought made He-Dog boil. He *hated* the thought of dying to beastmen.

Balless shrugged, and walked slowly back to where his companions lay waiting. With a heavy sigh, he plopped down beside them.

"See that last one?"

He-Dog nodded. "Unfit, he was."

"*Unfit!*" Balless exclaimed with a nod. "But, that's it now. Can't fight much longer."

"Nor I," He-Dog admitted.

Beside them, Chop groaned something. They both ignored him.

Balless eyed the still unconscious Borus. "He's really out, eh?"

He-Dog nodded grimly. It was just like Borus to miss being massacred. He'd do it just for spite.

"Good thing we spent the coin before we came," Balless commented. The beastmen were coming again now, steadily. The awe of having their champion struck down was wearing off.

"I have the scroll right here," He-Dog breathed.

"On you?"

"Aye that."

Balless studied the man. "Can't see it."

"Under me armor."

"Ah. Urf."

"Safest place. Not that it matters now."

The tide surged forward, slinking toward them. These beastmen did not hurry, for they had seen the death the three man-things reaped. Beastmen of all tribes climbed over the barrier of their dead. They watched the battered and tired man-things backed against the wrecked koch. Evil looking axes, made for the splitting of flesh and armor, gleamed in the dusty light. The beastman ranks thickened. They were not taking any chances this time.

Balless watched them approach. "Hm," he grunted. "Time to go then?"

He-Dog sighed. It was just as well. He was starting to hate life, too. When that happened, he figured it was time to kiss it all good-bye. Beside him, Chop moaned. The man was another mess. He-Dog knew Balless was simply too stupid to die, but he didn't know what kept Chop alive.

He would never know.

"Right," He-Dog muttered and, grimacing, climbed to his feet. Balless got to his. Chop stayed right where he was, but his right hand kept a hold of his remaining blade. The beastmen would get the leather-masked man this time, He-Dog had no doubt, but if Chop was fortunate, he might be able to take a few with him before a war club finally bashed in his face.

The beastmen stalked them, hunched over with weapons ready. He-Dog could see the snarls and scowls becoming more pronounced. It would not be long now.

One beastman, a white, urged the others on. The creature looked directly into He-Dog's face, baring tusks and teeth in a hiss.

An arrow caught the beastman square in the chest. Another found an eye, snapping his head backward. Three more stuttered into his body and danced him back over the wall of unmoving flesh.

He-Dog's jaw dropped.

Arrows poured from the sky.

While all attention was on the koch, which had split the horde up the middle, and the man-things who refused to die, the gates of Foust opened and a line of heavy lancers had emerged and formed up. The horsemen wore dull suits of steel and carried long spears for the charge, with swords for more personal reaping. Behind them came a force of archers who quietly readied their bows and waited for the order. The lancers rode first, and when they were twenty paces away, the archers released.

The beastmen standing on corpses were the easiest to strike down. Arrows stabbed downward from the sky and struck several dead. The surviving beastmen stood and swore curses that He-Dog knew were filthy. More arrows fell and those beastmen standing and swearing were killed.

Then the lancers struck.

The line of horsemen punctured the beastmen ranks in one jagged thrust. With momentum on their side, the warhorses trampled the creatures and stomped out their lives, while grim riders dropped broken lances and went for their swords. Having no horses of their own and preferring to just eat the animals outright, the beastmen were caught unaware and unprepared and perished in the hundreds. It was the biggest counterattack since the siege of Foust began.

The riders made a line for the husk of the koch. Sweeping around it, the men of Foust drove the howling multitudes back. Several lancers stopped before the barricade of corpses and gestured frantically.

"Come on!" One lancer screamed at the three men and their still unconscious fourth. "All of you! Come *on!*"

They did not need any more encouragement. Reaching down into that place where will whips flesh into action, the three men pulled themselves to their feet. Balless grabbed a limping Chop and threw him across his shoulder. He-Dog cast aside his blade and pulled up Borus. With an oath and strength fuelled by desperation, he manhandled the senseless archer over his good shoulder. Borus' body brushed against He-Dog's broken jaw and the pain froze him in his tracks. Even unconscious, Borus pissed He-Dog off.

The rider who had called out to He-Dog was suddenly smashed from his mount with a metallic *whack*. He-Dog blinked to see the lancer speared through the middle by a huge, iron tipped spear. A spear from a ballista.

"*Hurry!*" One of the surviving lancers screamed.

He-Dog ran. Ahead of him, Balless loaded Chop onto the back of a lancer's horse. The rider immediately whisked him back toward Foust. Balless tried to mount a steed that already had a rider. The lancer pointed furiously at an animal whose rider had just been killed. Balless went for the beast. He'd never owned a horse, but knew they tasted great.

A barrage of spears ripped through the lancers and three of the men were cut down, spears puncturing their bodies like bolts through butter. Two of the horses toppled, but He-Dog reached for the third. He pulled a dead man from the stirrups and grabbed the reins. Out of sight but heard by all, the war drums intensified. He-Dog brought the horse about and mounted with little trouble. He thought briefly that the beast would not accept him, but the animal did not seem to care. He-Dog snapped the reins and the horse ran.

The beastmen saw the purpose behind the lancers' attack. They regrouped, rearmed, and pushed forward with long spears specifically built for gutting horsemen. The lancers were faster. Even though their first cut collapsed inward, a horn sounded for the retreat and they thundered back toward Foust. A last barrage of arrows stabbed at the horde and the archers retreated, running as if their arses were on fire. The gates began to close and for a moment, He-Dog wondered if they would be shut out. Screams flew past him and he knew the lancers in the rear were being cut to pieces.

The lancers hit the bare sand that marked the range of the battlement defenses and pounded toward the closing gates.

The beastmen, driven by madness and a lust for human flesh, charged after them and crossed the line onto the white earth.

With a frightening hum and snap of bow strings and catapults, the upper battlements unleashed a storm of missiles at their foes. The air sizzled. Hundreds were knocked back and skewered through the backbones by iron tipped arrows. Dozens were crushed into a fruity pulp by catapult shot. The beastman pursuers charged forward another twenty paces, brutally absorbing the sting of a thousand bows unleashing arrow after arrow into their unprotected mass. There was no possible way for Foust's defenders to miss, the horde was simply too thick.

After only seconds, the beastmen broke and ran back. Several hundred more died in the retreat.

As the last few beastmen struggled to get out of range of Foust's archers, the city's battlements sent up a roar of triumph. Foust had been under siege for a long time. It was extremely satisfying to cut out a piece of the enemy's arse.

With the last lancer within the safety of the walls, the gates creaked shut and were barricaded.

A hundred horsemen rode out to save the four fallen warriors.

Thirty-six made it back.

CHAPTER 9

After the slaughter, soldiers on the battlement heights peeked out at the pulsating mass of beastman warriors on the field. Beastman spears and bolts flew up into the air, misting it, to drop harmlessly out of range. After a few moments, the missile fire ceased, and the war drums played on.

Surrounded by surly looking men-at-arms, He-Dog and his companions simply sat on the ground, waited, and bled. Having reached the inner courtyard, lancers ordered He-Dog and Balless to dismount while Chop and Borus were rudely dumped in heaps. Borus remained mercifully unconscious.

He-Dog hated the man for that.

Sitting pleasantly, Balless drew a deep breath. The air was gritty, dusty, and not nice to taste. He let it go. As far as he was concerned the next moment could be utter shite, but at this precise instant… life was good.

The stink hit him.

Balless looked at He-Dog. The man did a quick study of himself and shook his head. A moment later, both of his hands found his face and he covered it, muttering curses.

Beastman blood.

"You men," a voice said. "You have anything for us?"

A battered and very much in pain He-Dog looked up into the face of a soldier. He was a bulky man, broad in shoulder as well as gut. A thick black moustache covered his mouth while a thin line of hair peeked out from beneath his helmet.

Not feeling much like speaking, He-Dog moved his wounded shoulder, grimaced, and proceeded to extract a flattened scroll from inside his armor. With a weary grunt, he handed it over. Blood beaded off his arm and fell to the sand. The soldier took the message, studied He-Dog's face, and exhaled heavily.

"We lost a lot of good men hauling your arse in," the soldier informed him in a resonant voice. "Men we can't spare."

He-Dog didn't reply. He was close to passing out. Recognizing the signs, he felt it coming.

Then he was gone.

Without a sound, He-Dog keeled over onto his side with a heavy thud. Balless and Chop watched him fall. Neither man made the attempt to stop him. It would have taken their remaining energy.

The soldier straightened, tapping the scroll on his chainmail vest. The pair who clung to consciousness weren't going to last much longer. Already the one with the shredded mask swayed dangerously to one side, his eyes fluttering. The biggest of the four, the one with the winning smile who was covered in beastman matter, watched the soldier.

Captain Krajin did not want to speak to him.

"Take these dogs to the infirmary," the captain finally said, his mouth hidden under the bush of his moustache.

He had a message to deliver to the Kratoe.

CHAPTER 10

His darkness buzzed.

He-Dog rose up from the depths of unconsciousness and opened his eyes. He waved a hand in front of his face, scattering black flies, and took a deep breath. He ached all over. Seddon and Lords above, what had done the dance on him this time? He looked down and saw his body wrapped in bandages as tightly as a newborn. They were clean, which was surprising. How long had he been out? He-Dog's brow flexed. At least he didn't wake up on the street. It was nice just to wake up.

He was splayed out on a straw pallet in a modest infirmary with bare stone walls and floor, and open windows showing nothing except another stone wall and daylight. Balless was on the pallet to the right of him, trussed up like a house about to collapse. Bandages covered just about everything except his face. He-Dog snorted. Someone ran out of bandages. Then there was Chop on the left, also in bandages and lying prone on his own bed. Borus was nowhere in sight. A dozen or so wounded men also waited for death to decide who to take first. Neatly lined up clay containers and what appeared to be flagons of water filled nearby tables. An assortment of knives, hooks, drills, saws, and other instruments hung from a nearby wall, placed just beyond three wooden tables—operating tables. Their surfaces looked old, stained, and scratched from heavy use. A brazier smoked in the corner, filling the room with a light odor. An open doorway lay to the left, dark and empty.

He-Dog lay back down and stared at the ceiling. He waved his good hand, dispelling the flies again. He drew breath and moved ever so slightly. He ached everywhere, but nothing serious. He would live.

Then he remembered where he was: in Foust surrounded by an army the likes of which he had never seen in all of his life. Whatever these people had done to stir the beastmen must have been bad. Quite bad. He-Dog bared his bad yellow teeth. Stupid people. He closed his eyes.

"You still on the mend?"

His eyes opened again.

Before He-Dog stood a man, bowed over and watching him. He was naked from the waist up, and grimy from the heat. A tuft of silver hair remained on his head, crowning an otherwise barren skull.

"Aye." He-Dog grimaced and touched his jaw. Heavy bandages kept it in place. He could barely open his mouth and when he tried, he remembered his broken jaw.

"Hurt to talk?" the man asked. His mouth hung open as if about to eat something it seemed, and He-Dog could see only half a set of teeth.

He-Dog nodded. "How long…"

"Were you unconscious?" The man frowned. "Two days. After a short fever. I'm the healer here. You weren't in bad shape, but bloody. Seddon above, two days ago, I thought you would all die in the morning. But you lived. I thought you would all die the *next* morning, yet you lived. You were a mess. Your friends were a *bigger* mess. Especially this one."

The healer moved closer and rapped knuckles against

the foot of Chop's pallet.

He-Dog tried to rise, but the healer quickly raised two hands and eased him back down. "Rest here, friend. You took a beating out there."

He-Dog scowled. This healer wasn't his friend. Two women entered dressed in loosely tied robes hanging off their shoulders. The sight distracted him.

The healer followed his gaze and smiled faintly. "You aren't all dead, I see."

He-Dog glared.

The healer chuckled. "Ferocious, aren't you? Well, that may be, but let me tell you this: my name is Sergius. Not bastard. Not pisshead. Not prick. Nor do I enjoy shagging animals. Or greasing up the bums of young boys. I am none of these nor do I enjoy any such activities. I'm a healer. And the one who saved your life."

He-Dog squinted. "Did I… say those things?" he managed through his clamped jaw.

Sergius nodded solemnly.

He-Dog grunted. He knew he owed the healer an apology, but found it simply too difficult to say the words.

Sergius waited with a benign expression on his face.

He-Dog simmered with growing anger. "Don't remember."

It was as close to an apology Sergius would get. "You raved a full day during the fever," the healer informed him. "Another assistant tried to get you out of your armor and you damn near crushed his balls."

A heavy sigh left He-Dog.

"You also punched and knocked out one of my female assistants, both of whom happen to be my daughters."

Punching a wench? He-Dog's brow crunched up. She must have deserved it.

"She," Sergius went on, "was bathing you at the time. Scrubbing you clean of the blood."

Beastman blood, He-Dog realized. Bathing. No wonder he smelled flowery. He bared his ugly teeth.

"I…" he struggled.

The healer looked down on his big patient. He-Dog was a warrior to the bone, and stubborn. Sergius could see that. "Just remember that when they bring your food. Your food will have to especially prepared because of your jaw. And they are the ones doing the cooking."

Grimacing, He-Dog wanted to be unconscious again. "Where's… Borus?"

Sergius' brow arched. "Borus? The one eyed one? He's here somewhere. He was the luckiest of you all, in fact. Minor cuts compared to the gashes you took."

Sergius gestured at Balless. "There is a lot of blood in that lad."

Balless was full of it, all right. He-Dog regarded the healer. "When… can we—"

"Leave?" Serguis finished for him.

"Mm."

A frown fell over the healer's face. "You can't leave. Oh, you mean the infirmary here. When you're ready. I give you a month or so. You were bruised quite badly, in addition to being damn near flayed to the bone. Your jaw for instance. The amount of blood—"

"Month?" He-Dog interrupted through clenched teeth.

"A month," the healer confirmed. "About that for all of you. But you can't leave Foust. No one is getting out of here. By the by, you were the messengers. What's the word from the outside?"

Sergius seemed anxious.

"Didn't… read," He-Dog answered.

"You didn't?"

"No. Private," He-Dog growled. He had, in fact, glanced at the message on the scroll, scrawled on a fine piece of traulh. But He-Dog couldn't read. He'd never learned.

The healer nodded, disappointed. "Ah, well."

From the next pallet, Balless stirred. His eyes opened. "Is I killed?"

"Not yet, but I daresay you'll be dead in the morning," the healer informed him.

Balless grunted at that. He met He-Dog's eyes. Slowly, purposefully, he extended a huge fist. He-Dog grudgingly extended his own. He pressed his knuckles to Balless' and kept them there for a moment. The two men held the pose for a moment, quietly giving thanks that they were still alive and, even though neither would admit it, in each other's company. Sergius watched them with interest.

"Smell like flowers." Balless snorted, dropping his fist.

"You were washed," Sergius told him.

Balless' bandaged head regarded him with disdain. "Shouldn't smell like flowers. Should smell like... *not* flowers."

Chop woke up. He raised his head and said something.

"That Chop?" Balless asked from the other side of him.

"Mm," He-Dog said as he and Chop pressed fists together.

"How's he?"

He-Dog studied Chop's terrible face, exposed for all to see. He-Dog knew he didn't like being without his mask when among people he didn't know. He also saw the bandages around Chop's forearm, chest, and head. His lower leg was also done up.

"Alive," He-Dog growled through clenched teeth. "Where's... his... mask?"

"The black one?" Sergius asked.

He-Dog grunted.

The healer looked at the foot of the bed and stooped. He rose with the tatters of Chop's leather face in his hand. He-Dog motioned for him to give it to its owner.

Stepping in close, Sergius did just that.

Taking his mask, Chop held it up to his eyes. A great sigh left him, and he visibly relaxed. He directed a sound of gratitude at the healer.

"Borus?" Balless asked, spittle running down his chin.

"The one-eyed man?" Sergius countered. "He was here

yesterday, but I don't know where he is today."

He-Dog scowled. Just like the half-blind topper to disappear. But then he realized something. "You… said… no one… can… leave?"

Sergius shook his head. "Not with that rabble outside."

Not with that rabble. He-Dog wanted to remind the man that the *rabble* probably was the most recent thing that had almost killed him. His jaw throbbed and his arm felt like a slab of dead meat. Borus was in the city. He wasn't going anywhere. He-Dog supposed that was a good thing. Then he thought about it.

"Did… he talk… to… anyone?"

"Some of the city soldiers," Sergius answered. "But they didn't talk long. They paid him and he was off."

Chop and Balless both looked at their leader.

"*Paid?*" He-Dog growled.

Sergius nodded. "Then he paid for you men. That's why you're still here. This is a private infirmary. You must pay for my services. Otherwise…" he trailed off.

The wounded men sat and stewed in the revelation that Borus was about, and with at least *some* of their money in his pocket. He-Dog didn't know why the soldiers paid him, but Borus would know. He-Dog looked forward to seeing Borus when he returned.

If he returned.

CHAPTER 11

The ale just didn't do it for him anymore.

Borus stared into the bottom of his wooden mug, deep into the remaining blackness that sloshed when he shook it. He blinked. He'd been on a drunken tour of Foust for the last four days and had forgotten every moment of it. Somewhere along the way, he came into more money which he believed he'd won at dice. It was either that or he robbed someone. Or he robbed someone while playing dice. But he was certain that he didn't kill anyone. He was positive.

He couldn't kill a conversation in his current state.

A great depressed sigh left him, and Borus felt his shoulders sag. He placed the mug on the counter and pushed it with the thumb and little finger of his right hand. They were the only fingers remaining there. He didn't even know how he'd lost the other three. It was cruel. If losing his eye wasn't bad enough, losing the string fingers was almost enough for him to take his own life. He-Dog knew that he wanted to die. Borus hated the man in a brotherly way. He was, after all, the only tit to give Borus something of a life after the massacre of his company. The bastard took him in when no one else would, and gave him something of a purpose. As much as a purpose as Borus could offer anyway, and that ate him even more. Who needs a half-blind, damn near fingerless archer poking around? Most of the world didn't. But for some reason, that bastard He-Dog did.

And Borus repaid him by leaving him and the others in a healer's care. It was the least he could do while he went about spending the rest of the gold cutaros the captain paid him. Damn fine of the man, too. A bonus, or something of the like. Borus couldn't remember. He was extremely drunk. He pushed his mug a little further until it tipped over. The last two swallows—when one drank as much as Borus did, one knew instinctively how much was left—spilled. Borus watched in drunken fascination as the beer flowed down the badly-built counter top and drip onto his right leg.

"Seddon's crack." Borus swore. All he needed. One eyed, seven fingered, and now looking as if he'd pissed himself. Simply great. He should be tickled by it all. But not too tickled. Borus did not want to risk shitting himself.

"*Dog balls!*" he roared.

The bar patrons left him alone. There was a siege on. Everyone was under stress as food and water supplies dwindled. The man wasn't hurting anyone yet and the barkeep believed he was harmless. The barkeep watched the half-blind man sway on his chair and knew that he was almost done.

As if on cue, Borus passed out and bonked his head off the surface of the counter.

The barkeep could see the man's nose smearing in the spilled beer as his body weight pulled him off his chair. There was a crash, and patrons around the bar looked toward the noise, but for only a moment.

With a sigh, the barkeep wiggled two fingers at some acquaintances. He couldn't have the bastard in here if he wasn't drinking. He certainly couldn't have the lout lying about unconscious.

He could piss all over his floor.

Being thrown into the street brought Borus back to consciousness. If he'd had a choice, he would have gladly remained *un*conscious, and gambled on being trampled by a passing cart or wagon or *something*. A hungry cat could have him, for Seddon's sake. He would at least serve a purpose then. Instead, Borus rolled over onto his back as if he had been riddled by a ballista. He then realized he was actually on his belly. He tasted dirt and he felt the urge to vomit. He didn't, however, and even that felt like a betrayal.

With seven fingers clawing the dirt and legs pumping from behind, Borus pulled himself out of the street and collapsed against the stone foundation of the bar. He hauled himself into a sitting position, gulping ominously for air. He felt his craw lurch and fought down the urge to vomit. Borus wanted to keep his beer where it was, at least until it was time to piss it away. He looked at passing shadows and breathed at them, his mouth hanging open like an ugly cut. Punces. All of them. He hated them for no reason. No, there was a reason. They all had a *purpose*. They all had a *life*.

He had shite.

Smacking his lips, Borus felt the urge to vomit come on again. He swallowed against it, cheeks puffing with the effort, but his stomach decided it no longer wanted its sloshing contents and sent them back from whence they came. Forcefully.

Borus bent over and emptied his guts into the street. When he thought he was done, he roared even more. His own stomach seemed to take a hold of his tail bone and shake the shite out of him. Even as he emptied his stomach, a part of him hated losing all of that merriment. He heaved three more times into the street— the last one being bile—marking his territory and causing passers-by to respect it with frowns of disgust.

After a while, Borus collapsed on his chest, barely

missing his own fragrant soup.

"Well… dog balls," he grumped, lips dripping. He puckered them for a moment, drunk and dazed, and admired the amount of beer on the ground before him. Borus decided that where he lay was as good a place as any to try and sleep.

"Better… better not… try…" He muttered a warning to anyone thinking of robbing him. Though drunk, he could still smash a thief or two. Or stick his war wounds into someone's face. Or…

Borus passed out.

Stepping out of the alehouse and watching the drunken man with interest, a dark figure lingered. Snores ripped from the shape sprawled out beside his own vomit. The figure's head slowly shook. He had heard the deep retching from inside the doorway. Mighty, indeed. He stepped forward and sized up the unconscious man still wearing his leather cuirass. The corpse had money. And the figure wanted it.

He eased himself around the pool and pulled Borus back by his ankles. The shadowy man hoisted the drunk to his feet and together, they made their way to a dark alleyway, always the best place for what was intended.

An easy mark. Or so the shady individual thought.

"Ooo are *you?*" Borus slurred with awakened indignity, smacking the man with the foulest of breath.

They stopped just at the threshold of darkness. Guardsmen, four of them patrolling the streets, moved toward the pair. The shadow paused, straining under Borus' bulk.

"I'm a friend." He winced. *Sweet Seddon above,* the drunkard's breath smelled like *shite.*

"If," Borus began, "you are truly me friend, you will brish me… *bring* me…"

The shadow listened, eyeing the ever closer guards. One of the bastards eyed him back.

"To a place when—*where*—I can drink… and piss. In

peace. Punce," he added as an alliterate afterthought.

The dark features split into a smile. "You have coin, do you?"

Borus waved his almost fingerless hand in the air, dismissing such a *stupid* question.

"Would you be interested in something more…"

"More *what?*"

The shadow flinched. "More interesting?"

"Wassh your name, asslicker?"

"Nuzzo." The figure hesitated. "At your service."

"Nuuuzo." Borus' body hitched, as if his stomach were about to send back more ale. Nuzzo cringed and tried to detach himself from the other man, but Borus held tight.

"Better not take me to some whore's shack. Can't pack anything tonight. Not fit for it."

"I understand."

"No *daisy's* shack, either—Not one of them. S'all I need this night issa be mistaken for a daisy."

"I see." Nuzzo's brow arched just a bit.

"And you better not… kill me. Either. You pisser. No need."

Nuzzo nodded his understanding.

Borus could see that he understood, which was excellent.

"Nuzzo," Borus finally flung out. "You seem a good man. I accept. Lead on."

With that, the once-archer released his new companion and indicated that he should start leading *immediately*.

Nuzzo took the lead and they wove through the alleyways and back streets of the mighty city of Foust. Borus became grateful for having someone else navigating. How this Nuzzo character found his way through such a stew of stone, brick, and mortar was beyond him. But he wasn't a bad lad, Borus admitted. The man paused several times for Borus to piss, and even once or twice for a dry heave, which, when one feels it coming, could very well be the real thing. False alarm or not, Nuzzo waited until

Borus signalled he was fine to travel again, before they were off.

Streets and alleyways. The alley became darker, less populated, and more isolated, if alleyways in a city could be called isolated. But Borus was drunk out of his skull and couldn't care piss in his condition. Nuzzo was his navigator. Nuzzo was the commander.

Nuzzo delivered him to a very dark place.

Smashed as he was, Borus still had enough sense to distantly realize, as if his consciousness peered out the portals of his eyes from deep within the vessel of his skull, that the part of Foust they were in did not inspire any feelings of safety. In fact, the more Borus' consciousness considered the situation, the more he realized that if he were sober, he probably would steer clear of such an area. The stench of sewage bloated the air. Drunkards or dead men littered the edges of the darkness. Sometimes Borus only saw their lower halves in the alley, sometimes he saw the upper. They all looked like corpses, and there were enough for him to try and formulate an opinion on the matter.

"Not the... liveliest... are they?" Borus muttered.

Nuzzo bounced him along like a boy with a heavy toy. "All satisfied customers."

"Izzat so?"

"It is." Nuzzo nodded. "But they failed to pay their rent, you see. Had to be thrown out into the street. The Hole is only for the paying."

The Hole?

"And here we are," Nuzzo announced.

They stopped in the blackest section of the alley, and Borus' eye squinted to see anything. There, in the center of the gloom, was a great heavy door made of thick wood.

Nuzzo rapped on its surface with his free hand.

"Your house?" Borus inquired.

Nuzzo shook his head. "*Your* house. If you have the coin."

"Oh."

There was a rattling, and a slot opened high in the door. Lantern light spilled forth, gloomy and sepia-toned. A shadow filled the slot, and eyes like light reflecting off of marbles regarded them. Borus' brow arched. If he were sober, he thought, he would probably be feeling an overwhelming sense of dread.

But since he was still blasted out of his mind…

He heard locks being undone from within, and the door swung inward a moment later on well-greased hinges. *Not a sound*, Borus thought, and decided that this just might be a place to steer clear of if one was in his right mind.

A big man filled the doorway. An impressive set of horns covered the top of his helm, while a smiling grill protected his lower face up to his nose. A long, narrow slit contained the eyes that had peered through the doorway only moments before. The man's upper body was unprotected and Borus could guess why, even in his drunken state. The knobs and knots of muscle lining the man's torso were enough to make even Borus keep his mouth shut. Scars ran over his exposed flesh. A half suit of studded ringmail started at the man's chest line and covered his abdomen, looking tight and uncomfortable and giving him the appearance of being squeezed around the middle. Borus knew the man must have had help getting into his armor. And the helm. The guardian of the doorway was a monster.

"Evening." Nuzzo greeted the monster. "Brought you a customer."

The helm's visor scoured Borus' face, and he felt a pang of unease.

"Can he pay?" came the voice within the helm, sounding deep and dangerous.

This was a question for Borus, and he was not about to let Nuzzo answer for him. "Certainly can, you horny git."

The insult flew past Borus' lips like a bird escaping a

thrown kitchen knife. He didn't see Nuzzo's sudden expression of fright.

The guardian didn't reply. He didn't move. He stood and stared.

"Well?" Borus asked again, and grabbed for his half-full purse. He jangled the leather like a cow bell. "What do you have in there, 'eh?"

The helmet moved ever so slightly, and its owner stepped back from the doorway, allowing the two men entry. Nuzzo bobbed his head in thanks and half-dragged Borus across the threshold. Borus wondered why his legs only half-listened to him.

The door closed behind the pair with a heavy sound and the air within no longer smelled of raw sewage. In fact, Borus though the air smelled of sweet spices, or something good to eat.

Then he saw the face of a silver boy and balked.

If the first guardian was intimidating, the second one was frightening. Another huge man, draped in a suit of scalemail, stood off to one side, blocking a room Borus could scarcely believe to be large enough to contain both of them. This one also wore a helm, but instead of horns and a fearsome grill, his was the silver face and head of a plump, curly haired boy with a benign smile. The eye holes contained those of a man, but the silver face disturbed Borus. The second guardian's heavy arms also disturbed Borus. They ended in spiked maces.

Borus whistled in awe at the twin weapons replacing the warrior's hands. Then his drunken sarcasm returned. "Must be a tickle to scrub your arse with those."

The smiling face did not reply, but the eyes followed Borus as Nuzzo dragged him away from the door. Borus looked over his shoulder at the pair of guardians receding as he moved forward. The passage stretched out magically, leaving the fearsome duo well behind.

"I thought you were dead back there," Nuzzo whispered in his ear. "Those two would bash in the skulls of newborns just to argue about the color of the brains. Don't ever speak to them again. I'm surprised that—"

"Did you see that one's hands though?" Borus interrupted. "I mean… dog balls!"

"Just don't talk to them again," Nuzzo insisted. "You have no idea how lucky you were. And that one with the hands? I've seen him sma—"

"Izzat real silver? His face?"

Nuzzo appeared to wonder about that himself.

Borus stopped talking, becoming interested in where he was going. The corridor stretched out before them, long and wrought with steps leading downward. He felt Nuzzo leading him deeper beneath the city of Foust. He had no idea how deep. Torches in nooks and crannies lit the passageway unevenly. They were in light one moment, then darkness, then light again. The tempting spice smell filled Borus' senses.

"Smells good down here," he muttered.

"It does," Nuzzo agreed.

They continued along a long stretch of corridor and Borus felt lost. On either side there were alcoves, some veiled with cheap cloth while others were open. Borus slowed Nuzzo down so he could peer into them. Bodies filled some, splayed on their backs and bellies, ripe and smelly of sweat and other foulness. When Nuzzo pulled him back into the main corridor, however, the stench disappeared. The shadowy light grew gauzy, and Borus wondered if he tasted the air, or still only smelled it.

Then he stood in a room, lit only a little more brightly than the corridor.

Two men occupied the chamber. One man was short and possessed a shaved head, smug features, and unevenly spaced teeth. He sat behind a stout table. His eyes gleamed when he saw Nuzzo and his companion.

"Nuzzo, my friend," the man said in a deep voice. Pretty eyes, but cruel if they needed to be, studied Nuzzo with interest. "What have you brought us this morning?"

Borus' senses swam. There was something more powerful at work than the alcohol in his system. He forced himself to sobriety, and only succeeded in presenting himself as even more intoxicated.

Movement at the edge of his vision caught Borus' attention.

Chop, or a bigger version of Chop, stepped out of the shadows. The warrior's black mask regarded Borus as if considering whether or not to squash an insect.

"Chop?" Borus whispered, not believing his eyes for a moment. It couldn't be Chop. Chop was in the care of the healers, but there was no mistaking the axe. This burlier manifestation of Chop possessed a huge doubled-bladed battle axe, the executioner sort, held across his pelvis with both fists.

Borus' vision spun. He was slipping into unconsciousness, no mistake. He only had seconds before succumbing.

Before he passed out, however, he distinctly heard the eager, bell-clear voice of Nuzzo at his side.

"I've brought you a customer."

CHAPTER 12

Morning sunlight shone through the infirmary's open windows, and Chop awoke only seconds after it touched his flesh. He shifted in his bed and slowly sat up, his ruined face contorting hideously with the effort. He noted that He-Dog and Balless both slept on. That was fine. He knew they would be up shortly. Quietly, Chop swung his legs over his pallet and studied his left leg. The bandages were clean, but the puncture wound underneath still ached.

Chop reached down and went about reliving himself in the piss-pan, which was the word He-Dog had barked out when he saw the receptacle. Chop sighed as he filled the clay pan and looked around the infirmary. He eyed the black leather mask, shredded in places, on the end of his pallet. His face. His precious face. Another sigh fled him. Once he'd tucked himself away and discarded the piss-pan, he struggled back onto his pallet and gathered up the mask. He spread the leather material across his bandaged hands and looked into the empty eye slits. It was too much for him to be without it. The mask had shielded him ever since he lost his true face. Chop gazed at the table across the room and saw the instruments. He cursed quietly at the assortment of blades, saws, and hooks. And in a place of healing! A scarier selection of weapons he did not think he'd ever spied.

He wanted two things.

Breathing hard and causing bright stabs of pain all over, Chop set his jaw and hobbled over to the implements of healing. He found some thread on a spool and a needle. He gathered both up and returned to his bed, breathing and sweating from exertion. Back on his cot, he spent another few moments threading the needle, cursing himself each time he missed. It wasn't his weapon of choice. He eventually got it right, and went to work stitching up his leather. He needed his face, now more than ever.

He-Dog woke to see the room darkening from the outside. Through the windows someone didn't think about closing the night before, darkness swallowed the sunlight and draped everything in gloom. He-Dog sniffed and smelled the change in the air. Rain was coming. He saw Chop sitting atop his pallet, with his bandaged back to him, hunched over and working at something. That was fine by He-Dog. With a grunt, he gently prodded his wounds and growled. He lived in a small world of hurt. Not the worst, but present nonetheless. He gathered up his own piss-pan and proceeded to void himself.

As if on cue, rain hissed outside.

He-Dog snorted, horked, and grimaced at the pain in his face. Once he finished pissing, he spat and drooled into the pan. He set it back to the floor and eased himself to a sitting position on his bed, facing the rain falling outside. A solid stone wall stood across the way. Whoever built this place did not consider a view for the patients. It seemed to be another boring day and He-Dog wished to be drunk.

"What are you doing?" He-Dog asked through his bandages.

Chop held up his mask by its leather scalp. It regarded He-Dog with eyeless evil, and he felt a twinge of unease.

"Alright." He-Dog grumped and looked to his left. The

mass of Balless slept. For such a big man, Balless slept as quietly as a dead baby. The only trouble was that the bastard would wake eventually. If only He-Dog could walk out of here and leave the horseshagger. He-Dog set his jaw and winced. He knew he shouldn't have done that, yet he couldn't resist. It was the same for Balless. He-Dog knew he should leave him, but he couldn't. So much for being the smart one.

The rain fell outside and occasional yells from passers-by punctuated the air. The day was cool, and He-Dog was grateful. He propped himself up on his pallet, and stared out.

A warrior stood outside the window, staring back at He-Dog.

He-Dog noted that the figure was armored and carried weapons. He took a deep breath and closed his eyes. As long as the brute remained outside in the wet, all was fine. He floated in his self-imposed darkness, smelling the rain outside. Rain. If only it could wash away his hurt.

He opened his eyes and found the man had disappeared. *Bright lad*, he thought. A sudden snore left the heap of Balless, loud and rattling, distracting He-Dog. The big man fell silent.

He-Dog saw that the armored man stood inside the infirmary.

Even worse, the bastard had brought friends.

Chop stopped sewing and turned his head only a little at the newcomers. Balless slept.

"Look at this, lads," spoke the man. "The bastards look right comfortable in here. All dry and out of the rain. Probably get wine as well." The speaker was an ugly man with half of his discolored teeth missing. Hair, like straw, stuck out here and there from under his open helm. A gleam filled his eyes, one He-Dog had seen before, but he didn't know this man, or why he hated him so. He-Dog had only just arrived in Foust. He hadn't had time to piss anyone off just yet.

The hilt of a broadsword swung over the warrior's shoulder, but He-Dog wasn't interested in that. The leader nodded at the other steel covered brutes. Four men grabbed and held He-Dog's arms and legs. He heard them subdue Chop. He heard a harsh clang and a grunt from Balless. There were only four on him, but He-Dog didn't have the strength to fight back. He felt worse than weak. When he tensed, he became aware of his many stitches close to bursting. He didn't need that, so he relaxed.

"Hold him steady, lads," came the voice of the leader. He-Dog just barely saw him wander over to the table full of operating instruments and take a moment to inspect them. "Saimon's blue pisspot. We've got an armory here." He sounded impressed. His hands glazed over hammers, picks, saws, and scalpels, but he didn't take any of them.

"I've been around torture chambers with just as many toys as this," the leader said, returning to He-Dog. "But there's something, something *special* about using the tools here. They're supposed to heal, but they can butcher just as quickly."

He-Dog snorted in disgust. Captors *always* picked him first.

One of the men drew back to get a better grip on his right leg, and He-Dog's eyes widened.

The speaker approached him with a long, skinny metal tube.

He-Dog knew about such devices. He knew that the instrument was inserted into the head of one's topper, right down the peehole, by a trained physician.

Not the animal at the foot of his pallet.

The speaker nodded, and the men holding onto He-Dog's legs pulled them wide. For the first time in a very long while, He-Dog felt what could have been called fear. He grimaced, eyeing the lengthy catheter.

"Who—"

"Am I?" The speaker finished for him and leered an unsanitary smile. "Doesn't matter. I think you have another problem at the moment." He felt the tip of the catheter with his fingers and frowned. "Razi, get a fire going. I don't think this sticker is warm enough for our friend here."

There was movement and He-Dog heard the strike of a flint. Moments later, a warrior stepped into his field of vision and held out a torch. Scowling now, the speaker held the metal catheter in its flame.

"I've seen this used before," the man said as he eyed the reddening metal. "On battle-fronts. Healers use them on old men usually. Not young pups like you. Looked easy to me. All one has to do is… have enough strong lads about to hold the patient down, and then just shove this up his pisser. Their eyes go wide even when senseless on herbs. Like you are now, I wager. But this…"

The leader withdrew the catheter from the flame and eyed its glowing tip which resembled a great proboscis. "This will wake you up."

He smiled and bared only half a mouthful of teeth.

The speaker came forward. He-Dog struggled as best as he could and failed to move anything. He felt his skin stretch, felt stitches rip, and pain enveloped him. His system had no sedatives in it. The leader's hand touched his thigh and ripped away He-Dog's undergarments. He felt the air kiss his kog and bells. Soldiers steadied his legs. The speaker drew closer and He-Dog looked down into his grinning features. The catheter glowed, poised and ready.

"Relax now," the speaker whispered with eagerness in his voice. "Won't be so bad. Your healer had hooks over there."

He gripped He-Dog's manhood like a length of rope. The glowering catheter came closer. His smile widened. He-Dog felt the extreme heat on the very tip of his topper, took three quick breaths, and readied a scream. Perhaps he could deafen them all.

"What are you men doing here?"

The catheter froze where it was, nearly touching He-Dog's sightless eye, and he almost screamed.

"What in Seddon's name…" Sergius trailed off. He stabbed a finger at He-Dog's would-be torturer. "I know your name. I know it. You're Bowlak. One of Krajin's lads. Aye, I know you."

"Get him out," Bowlak ordered the remaining warriors in the room.

"You'll do no such thing," Sergius' voice rose up like a storm wind. "I've stitched you and your lot up often enough times to call Krajin by his first name. You lay one finger on me and he'll know! You lay one finger on my patients and he'll know! By Seddon's balls he'll know!"

Bowlak scowled at the physician. "This one got our lads killed!"

"And how did he do that?" Sergius fired back.

He-Dog wanted to know that himself.

"Our lads pulled them from the beastmen and died doing so, without even a thank you. They lost their lives pulling these flies out from under that Beastman shite pile out there!"

"And he's responsible?" Sergius demanded.

"Aye!" retorted Bowlak. Several of his warriors voiced their agreement.

"What horseshite!" Sergius flung at them. "You're *soldiers*, you idiots. That's what soldiers do. They *die*! Shouldn't you be angry with Galt for ordering you out there in the first place?"

"It wasn't Galt," the one called Razi muttered.

Serguis eyes opened wider. "Oho, so it wasn't the butcher who cast your hell-pups out there, but it was the demi-god himself! Krajin! The one man who can do no wrong, eh? Well, it looks to me you men do indeed have a problem! You can't touch the one you like, so you decided to take out your frustrations on the messenger! Where's the wisdom in that?"

Bowlak simmered with chagrin. His smile disappeared

and his cheeks looked as if fires burned behind their flesh. His eyes darted murderously toward He-Dog, and the still-glowing catheter didn't waver.

"Let him go, and save your anger for the beastmen beyond the walls. They're the reason you're here this day." Sergius' voice was calm. Steady.

He-Dog squeezed his eyes shut. Easy for Sergius. It wasn't *his* kog Bowlak had a hold of.

What was worse, the man had a grip of iron.

"I'll dispatch my assistants to find Krajin," Sergius informed the men. "To ask him why his soldiers are here."

With a snarl, Bowlak released He-Dog. He rose from the pallet and flung the catheter across the room where it clattered off a wall.

"Now listen," Sergius went on. "You leave now, and I'll forget all. Stay, and I'll point fingers. If I'm dead, my assistants will point fingers, and you'll be wishing you'd never even considered this folly."

On the last word, Bowlak seemed to waver. He growled a length of impressive curses, and shot a look of hatred at He-Dog. That was fine by He-Dog. Hate, he welcomed. Being *topperless* was another matter.

Like a dark tide, the host of warriors withdrew from the infirmary, leaving the occupants and healer alone. Bowlak was the somewhere in the middle of the pack, and he didn't look at Sergius as he left.

When the room was empty, the healer stood with his hands on his hips, red faced and shaken. He looked at He-Dog. "You're welcome."

He-Dog didn't reply. A relieved sigh left him. He was happy to still have his prick. Not that he used it often, but it was better to have it and not need it than to have a burnt and shrivelled knuckle of flesh. The thought chilled him. He glanced over at Balless, who appeared to have just regained consciousness.

Balless rubbed at where the warriors had clubbed his head, and grinned his simple grin. Easy for him. It wasn't his topper.

"Who was that bastard?" He-Dog asked Sergius, still hurting from the image of the heated metal so close to his prized flesh.

"Bowlak?"

"Aye."

"He's one of Krajin's men. A Koor."

He-Dog scowled. "That was… an officer?"

"Aye it was," Sergius informed him. "A particularly brutal one. And I daresay one who will try and get back at you eventually. Not while you're here, not now anyway. Not while I'm around."

"That might get you dead," Balless grunted.

The healer waved a hand. "Not me. I'm too valuable to be strung up. There aren't that many healers in the city anymore, and I've done my share of work for the soldiers here."

"That was too close for me." He-Dog said in reflection, grimacing with pain as he forced his jaw to work. "Where's my… steel?"

"Gone," Sergius told him. "Along with your armor. We had to cut that all off you, you know. I certainly couldn't do it, and you aren't soldiers of Foust, so the cutter demanded to be paid. I told him to take what he wanted of your weapons."

"Took… everything?" He-Dog's jaw sizzled.

"He did." Sergius glanced over to where Chop held up his leather face. "The good news is, you're paid up for the month, which will be about the amount of time needed for you to be walking about. And I mean exactly that. A tussle in a whore's bed would probably do more harm than good right now, if you understand my meaning."

He-Dog lay back down on his bed, and stared at the ceiling. It wasn't the first time he had been caught napping, but it was the closest he had come to losing his topper. The thought did not sit well in his mind. He shifted and felt his remaining stitches tighten. He would have to get the healer to redo most of them. He sighed. Trapped in a city surrounded by beastmen, penniless, on the mend, without weapons, and now hated by the local soldiers. It was all bad.

He closed his eyes to think on it, and fell asleep instead.

CHAPTER 13

The most incredible feeling rushed through Borus' person—he was *flying*. He soared over valleys and across the brows of green mountains, through waterfalls of white, and forests bursting with color and life. He flew upright, as if walking, and did not have the energy or will to lift his arms. No matter that the sky was purple in this world, or that the colors of the forest were off, yet still vibrant in a way he felt blessed to see. Euphoria filled him. All manner of strange creatures and women, all laughing and obviously in fine spirits, waved to him as he soared past. He stopped for some of them and they welcomed him as if he was a lost son. They feasted. They drank. They partook in sexual pleasures Borus had only experienced when he was a champion, so long ago. He did not want to close his eyes, for fear of missing just a moment.

Don't take him. A voice crashed through his clouds, and Borus looked up from where naked maidens pleasured him.

Please don't take him, the voice cried out again, closer this time. Borus looked to the heavens and frowned. The maidens disappeared into vapor.

Oh PLEASE! The words came like a blast of thunder

right over his head.

Borus opened his eyes.

The larger, physically more impressive version of Chop was in the room. He had a man in his fist, held by his neck like a half-dead cat. Borus didn't recognize the man, but he seemed young. *Perhaps… young.* His drugged mind simply gave up thinking. He preferred things with his eyes closed, back in that wonderful world. Not here in this crabby reality.

"I beg you!" The cry came again.

Borus lay on his back, on a straw pallet. He slowly turned his head, as his disconnected muscles allowed him no speed, and spied the woman on her knees, holding onto both arms of the one Chop's bigger brother had in his clutches. Tears streamed down her red face.

"Don't take him!" she cried again. Dirty blonde hair, shoulder length, covered a narrow face.

The Black Mask shoved her back with a muscular arm. She fell on a straw pallet, kicking over a bucket in her fall. The stench of urine stabbed the air, causing Borus to make a face. This was reality, with all of its offensive stink. He didn't want to be here.

"I'll do whatever you want, Karast," the woman almost screamed.

The brute's captive looked unaware of his situation, and oblivious to the woman's pleading. A long line of drool stretched from his mouth to the floor. Borus grimaced. He didn't need to see that. Across from him, the woman drew breath to scream again. He didn't need to *hear* that.

"What's all this?" he croaked. Only then did he realize just how thirsty he was, and how dry his mouth felt.

How long had he been here?

The Black Mask—Karast—regarded him, and Borus felt a twinge of unease, even with the amount of White Tar coursing through his intoxicated system. White Tar, the name manifested itself in his head. It was better than the piss he drank earlier this evening.

What day was it? Borus thought.

Karast didn't speak.

"Well?" Borus repeated, hating to waste the effort. He remembered purchasing the drug on a whim, the best whim he ever had. An absurd amount, they had told him, but let him have it anyway. He remembered them saying he would be senseless from the amount of White Tar he bought and consumed. For a beginner, Borus thought he handled it quite well. Remembering the faces of Sabo and his men, he should have been in a drugged stupor for a week.

"They're going to take him away," the woman told him in a too-loud voice. Why couldn't the bitch whisper?

"That true?" Borus asked of the monster before him.

Karast didn't say a word.

"They'll kill him," the woman went on, laying out her troubles. "They'll kill him because he can't pay any more for the Tar."

"Oh." That didn't seem fair to Borus.

"How much then?" Borus fished at his waist. His purse was still there, as he distantly remembered Sabo promising him it would be. *No one steals from anyone this far under the earth*, came the words, and the glare of pretty eyes. *It's not good for business.*

"Neither is killing a lad," Borus said, not realizing he had just answered a voice in his head. "How much does he owe?"

The mountain Karast looked down. "You're offering to pay his debt?"

"Oh thank you kind sir!" squealed the woman.

Borus shushed her. "On condition *she* shuts up."

The Black Mask looked in the woman's direction, and she quieted with a hopeful expression.

"That's better," Borus said. "So, what is it then? Hurry lad, I'm losing my spell here."

Karast gave him the number owed, in gold cutaros.

Borus paid the man. "And here." He counted out several more coins. *Seddon above*, he could use some ale. "This is for him. And her. They're riding White Tar, right?"

"Oh, we are," the woman piped up.

"Then good," Borus struggled to look down at his leather purse. He had gold coins in there, not nearly as much as before. That didn't concern him. The faster he paid Karast off, the quicker he could fly back to paradise. "There, that's for her and him." Borus' head flopped back on his pallet. He held out the money. "And bring us more when we're low. Use this until it runs out."

"Are you certain?" Karast's voice was deep, as if coming from a mine.

Borus rattled the coins in his hand in reply. "And bring something to drink, too. Anything as long as it isn't piss."

He felt the gold being taken. He heard the young man being manhandled to his own straw pallet. And somewhere, in between flashes of reality and dream, he sensed or remembered, he couldn't tell which anymore, drinking something. He felt hands on him. And a body close by, pressing its warmth into his side. That was strange. He didn't think the pallets were that big.

"Thank you kind sir, thank you so much," he heard a voice. A woman's voice.

He asked her name.

Mage, she told him.

Hm, he thought. *Nice.*

Then he flew again.

And forgot the entire episode.

CHAPTER 14

He-Dog opened his eyes and stared at the ceiling, earth-brown and made of stone. Flies buzzed around his face and he sighed. *Smart flies*, he thought, knowing shite when they smelled it. He sniffed and felt the morning foulness of his mouth, and already the boredom of his situation tortured him. He crunched his stomach, pulling himself into a sitting position, and stared out at the morning. It was sunny, and the heat promised to be unbearable. He-Dog couldn't even swear right. He rubbed the side of his face, instantly regretting it as his jaw sang in agony. Teeth clenched, he leaned over and took the pain.

From where he'd sat for most of the night watching for vengeful guardsmen, Balless witnessed his companion struggle with the morning, and grinned.

"Need help?" Balless asked.

He-Dog growled obscenities, his words coming out as mashed sound.

"No trouble?" He-Dog got out a moment later, reaching behind his back and flipping his war braid over his bandaged shoulder and chest.

Balless shook his head, and scratched at his many cloth bandages.

After the incident the previous week, He-Dog had decided to place a nightly watch in the infirmary. They split the night into two shifts, with the third man getting at least one full night of rest. They did the same during the day, although during mid-afternoon, when the sun beat down on the roof, the infirmary felt more like a deep oven than anything else, and it was difficult to stay awake.

He-Dog breathed in and wrinkled his nose at the smell of dried sweat. He reeked. He swung his legs out over his pallet and almost put a foot into his piss-pan. Seething, He-Dog reached down and went through the morning ritual of relieving himself.

On his left, Chop stirred and struggled to sit.

Balless wandered over to his pallet carrying a broad axe, and sat heavily down while He-Dog continued to void. "Another day."

He-Dog didn't answer. Behind him, he could hear Chop kicking his own piss-pan. He smirked under his bandaged jaw at the sound of the fumbling. Unlike Chop, He-Dog had use of both arms.

"Think they'll come back?" Balless asked.

He-Dog shrugged.

A moaning began from near the south wall as the patient there woke up to find his medicine had worn off. The night before a different group of guards from the ones who had attacked He-Dog and his lads had brought in a soldier from the wall. The poor topper had fallen from the battlements and landed on both of his feet, shattering the bones in multiple places. Sergius had worked on the man as best he could, poking bones back into punctured flesh and trying to set and splint them. Among the healer's tools was a very sharp woodsman's axe, which Balless placed on his pallet. He kept the tool close during the nights, as it would serve in a fight. Saws hung from racks as well, but even He-Dog would take the chop of an axe over the grind of a saw if it came to losing a limb.

But that moaning was getting on his nerves. "Not

again," He-Dog muttered and tucked himself away.

Balless stretched his neck and peered over his shoulder. He made a face at what he saw. "Don't want to be smashed like that."

He-Dog agreed. They'd got off lucky compared to the poor bastard.

Another loud moan.

He-Dog rolled his eyes.

Balless started to rise—an abomination of bandages with a low tolerance for whiners—and made a fist. He-Dog made no move to stop his companion as he thought of doing the same. Sergius appeared in the doorway, however, and Balless froze in mid-rise. For whatever reason, he followed commands from the healer without question. It almost made He-Dog want to consider studying the healing arts. But not quite.

"Not thinking of giving any *medicine* to my patient are you?" Sergius warned Balless. The big man's grin faded and he sat back down.

As one, He-Dog, Balless, and Chop looked at Hesel and Samil, Sergius' daughters and assistants. Dressed in loose fitting, dark robes, the two women went about their duties in the infirmary. They were attractive wenches, dark haired and full figured. He-Dog thought the longer he stayed on the mend, the better looking they would become. Balless became quiet when the women entered the room, eyeing both of them with a happy gleam in his eye. He-Dog didn't want to think about Balless with a woman. The thought would turn his stomach. He listened to the moans coming from the lad with the broken legs and frowned. Saimon's hell, that's where he was.

"Everyone's awake, I see," Sergius said and moved to the moaner. "Excellent. Samil, bring me some of the new bandages and the jar of saywort. You there," Sergius called to Balless. "Come here."

Looking surprised to be called upon, Balless went to the healer. The patient's moans got louder.

"Now listen," Sergius said, scratching at the tuft of hair clinging to his head. "I want you to hold this man down, alright? Just *hold* him. *Don't* hit him like you did yesterday."

Balless frowned, obviously believing his way was best.

He-Dog listened for a bit while Sergius gave instructions to Balless. It would be a wonder if the brute remembered them all. Hesel stood in front of him, with a basin of water and a damp cloth.

"We have to change your bandages," she said warily and went to work taking the old cloth off of He-Dog. He kept his tongue, surly-looking and still somewhat embarrassed over punching her sister.

Sergius came over and inspected the healing cuts with a sigh. "Place more saywort on that, with a bit of cutwort to take the color out." He looked at He-Dog. "It's still raw-looking and I daresay you'll be dead in the morning, but we'll do what we can."

I daresay you'll be dead in the morning. The healer had a twisted sense of humour. The first time Sergius said that to the three men it had brought about tense looks from them all, but, as time wore on, He-Dog realized the old punce probably told all of his patients the same thing. He even told Broken Legs in the corner the same, which had led to Balless knocking the man out to quiet him. The more He-Dog thought about it, the more he believed it to be a smart thing to say. When one woke up, anything was better than death.

"Did you keep watch last night?" Sergius asked him.

He-Dog shook his head. "Balless."

"No trouble?"

Another head shake.

"I don't think they'll be back, to tell the truth."

He-Dog didn't share the opinion, and thought it prudent to expect the worst.

"If you do continue with these watches of yours, I ask one thing. One thing only, is that alright?"

A nod, a reluctant one, this time.

"Place the axe back in its place when you're finished. I know the location of every item in this place, and when one's missing it irritates me."

Sighing now, He-Dog called Balless back and gestured for him to return the axe to its proper place. With Sergius watching, Balless readied to throw the axe, drawing a breath of surprise from the healer.

Balless' brow furrowed. "No?"

Serguis shook his head. "Hang it from its nail, please. Don't embed the thing in the wall."

Balless did as he was told.

"Now then, Hesel here will take those bandages off, wash the cuts and such, and smear some more of the 'bad smelling shite' on you all. As always, Hesel and I will greatly appreciate your cooperation. No insults and no punching.   Understood?"

He-Dog shook his head, feeling both miserable and annoyed. Sergius had to keep reminding him of one mistake. He'd been *delirious* when he did all that, by Saimon's black hanging fruit.

Sergius looked directly at him, stern-faced.

He-Dog glanced away, nodding understanding. For some reason, he thought of Borus and wondered where the one-eyed dog blossom had holed up in the city. He-Dog hoped that, Seddon willing, wherever the once-archer was He-Dog would catch up with him. Becoming lost in his thoughts, he said not a word as Hesel worked on his healing wounds.

"I've been meaning to ask you," Sergius said, looking at He-Dog. "What was it that brought you to Foust in the first place?"

He-Dog's shoulders rose in a silent laugh and he pointed to Balless.

"Yes, that's probably best, isn't it?" Sergius agreed.

"What's best?" Balless asked.

"Your friend here directed me to you for an answer."

"Oh."

"Why did you come to Foust?"

"Oh. That. *Urf.*" Balless' grin returned. "Coin."

"Gold?" Sergius asked.

"Aye, that. Lots of it. We were asked to do it by a man—forget his name—to bring a message to Kratoe. He didn't want to do it. Knew there was a siege on. Knew it was bad. So he paid us to do it."

"And you took on this task without question? You didn't think about simply taking the gold and running off?"

Balless grinned as if the question was ridiculous. "Nooo. He gave us gold to do it. We…" the big man thought about it. "We do and done a lot of bad things. People ask us to do things, and we decide if we can do them or not. And if we say we'll do it, especially if we're paid to do it… we do it."

"Honorable lot, aren't you," Sergius said with respect.

"Nah," Balless waved his hand. "No honor to it. Or…" he thought about it and slowly nodded. "Aye. We are honorable. Honorable means keeping promises?"

Sergius' head tilted. "It does."

Balless beamed, again flashing a mouthful of missing teeth. "We're honorable. He-Dog usually calls us worthless pissers. Or shaggers. Or hell pups."

Sergius looked with disapproval at He-Dog, who kept quiet as Hesel worked on him. "I'm sure he didn't mean it."

Balless snorted a laugh. "Oh, he meant it. But if we're pressed to do something, we keep our promises. And if there's gold."

"You're mercenaries."

"Aye."

"Sellswords."

"*Urf.* Like mercenaries better. Or… what do you Zuthenians call them?"

Sergius straightened as if catching scent of something. "Sinders."

"Aye." Balless buzzed. "*Sinders*. Good name. I like that."

"That name is derived from Seddon you know, for the people that do evil against his will."

Balless nodded vigorously. "That's us."

Sergius smiled at this cut-up behemoth in his infirmary. "Well, I'll keep that in mind."

Balless nodded, as if it were a wise thing to do.

"Where abouts did you all come together, by the by?"

Balless appeared to think about it before answering. "He-Dog and I been together forever. Found Chop wandering the Paw forests with his face burned off. Found Borus way over in Mademia. He survived when his army got routed. Nasty business that one. Woke up in a pile of dead. Dezer horsemen did the lot of them. Right dangerous bastards, they are."

"They are, they are," Sergius agreed.

Balless lowered his voice. "He-Dog didn't want to leave either of 'em. So he took them on. Thought about forming his own band of ...sinders?" He almost squeaked, glancing at the healer to see if he got the word right.

"I see. And?"

"Didn't work. Not quite." Balless chuckled. "He-Dog's not pretty enough to attract the right crowd. Just us." He shrugged. "But we do fine."

"I'm sure that you do." Sergius said.

A day later, another soldier stumbled into the infirmary when the heat was at its peak and the patients sweltered in their bandages. He-Dog tried to sleep on his pallet, but the buzzing of flies around his head irritated him enough to keep him awake. Balless lay on his bed, like a great ogre simmering in his own sweat. Every now and again, he flicked his head to throw off the flies, as if to prove he still lived. Chop had his mask off again, and his melted features stared off toward the window, no doubt dreaming of times when he had a complete face. Sergius did what he could with Broken Legs, whose name was Anak. Great pain wracked the face of the soldier, and Sergius praised him for his tolerance. It had been a quiet afternoon.

Until the new arrival.

"Healer!" the soldier yelled and fixed on Sergius. "Get your boney frame to me this instant. Dog balls, man! I'm bleeding to death here, you ancient punce!" As he spoke, blood pattered down the length of his hand and dropped to the floor.

His armor marked him as a soldier of the wall. His chest strained against the chainmail protecting his chest and his bare arms were thick with muscle. He wore no helm, and his hair was cut almost to the scalp, like a dark shadow. The commands caught Sergius bent over Anak's legs. Sergius straightened slowly—too slowly for the newcomer.

"Seddon's ass, you old bastard," the soldier screamed. "Is this the speed Foust's soldiers can expect from the likes of you? Saimon's hell! I'm *bleeding* here!"

With that the soldier, his mouth in an open snarl, flicked his hand at the healer, dappling him with blood. He strode over to one of the bare operating tables and thumped his forearm down on it like a heavy steak.

"Get over here now, or by Seddon I'll clout you upside that bald crown of yours!"

Leaving a very much awake Anak, Sergius walked to the shouting man, mild amusement in his eyes.

"What do you find so amusing, maggot shite?" The soldier barked at him.

"Let me see," Sergius said patiently.

"See?" The eyes of the man widened in an already livid face. "See then." He flicked more blood at the healer. Sergius stopped in his tracks, eyeing the wounded soldier pensively.

"Seddon above, you old topper!" The soldier cursed, got up, and grabbed the healer by the back of his neck. "I'm *bleeding* here, old prick! I don't know what it takes to make you move your shrivelled ass faster, but I'll not wait on it. See *here!*"

Punctuating the word, the wounded man hurried Sergius back to the table. He slapped his forearm back on the table and manhandled the old healer to face the wound. He bent Sergius over by the neck, rubbing his nose into the broad cut. Sergius placed both hands flat on the table's surface and grimaced.

"See that now?" the soldier yelled. "Eh? See that? Put a bandage on that if you're able to, and do it fast, or by Seddon's balls I'll soak it up with your boney hide!"

"If you release me," Sergius offered, "I might be able to do something."

That got him yanked upright, and the soldier stared into his eyes with deadly intent.

"You telling me what to do maggot?" he hissed. "You telling me what to do? I'll tell you what to do, and you do it, ass licker, or I'll make damn certain you won't practice here again. Am I clear, pisser? Hm? Am I clear on that?"

A hand found the soldier's shoulder and his eyes sparked with rage. "What d—"

Balless' fist smashed into the man's jaw just as his head turned. It was a solid enough connection that the warrior released Sergius, but it wasn't enough to subdue him. He struck a second time. And a third. When the warrior's bloody arm came around, Balless grabbed him by his neck and slammed his face into the table, splitting it. The wall soldier's knees buckled and he would have slumped to the floor, except Balless caught him and heaved him onto the operating table. Grunting, he shifted the unconscious man until he was on his back.

"Alright?" Balless asked the healer.

"Just fine, lad," Sergius beamed back, rubbing his neck.

"He is bleeding," Balless noted, inspecting the wound. "Looks like a strange place for a cut."

"Probably did it to himself sharpening something."

"*Urf,*" Balless grunted, snarling at the body on the table.

"Thank you," Sergius said before he fetched his instruments and bandages.

"Noisy topper," Balless said.

Across the way, He-Dog muttered his agreement.

"Seddon above," Sergius exclaimed as he inspected the man's face. "You knocked out three of his teeth."

Balless shrugged. He lurched in the direction of his pallet, but Sergius held up a hand.

"Just a moment," he said and called to Hesel. The woman appeared moments later, and both of them got to work on closing and bandaging the bloody wound. Balless lingered in the background, eyeing the patient in case he should awake. He did not.

"Well then," Sergius said. "I'll just say it. I think you're a handful, the lot of you." He included them all with a nod. "But I'm a practical man. With his senses fully intact. If you weren't here this day, this lout would've probably brained me before Samil returned with a patrol. In a case like this, one of them always runs for help. This lad was blood crazed, plain to see, but with his own blood. It happens sometimes."

He-Dog grimaced. That *lad* was an idiot. He'd seen it many times. A big man-boy used to throwing his weight around to get what he wanted. Might've even raped one of the healer's daughters if she had shown her pretty face.

"Regardless," Sergius went on, "thank you for coming to my aid. I've come to realize one such as you is useful around here."

Balless straightened and bared a mouth half full of teeth.

"Your lad paid me for the month, but to be honest, it might well take longer for you to be fully healed. If you'd give me a hand with some of the more difficult patients here like this one, I'll gladly see to it that you're taken care of while you're here. It isn't gold I'm offering, but an exchange of services. What do you think?"

Balless looked at He-Dog. And after a moment, He-

Dog nodded. "Done," he pushed through his broken jaw.

"Excellent," Sergius said and gestured at Balless. "Then keep an eye on this bastard, would you? And if he wakes up saucy, you have my permission to sedate him."

Sergius fixed him with a look Balless clearly understood.

Hesel moved about the healer, and gave a little smile to the warrior. Balless covered up his missing teeth with his lips and winked back.

Sergius did nothing to impede the exchange.

CHAPTER 15

Borus flew again. He flew across purple and orange skies, and dipped into valleys bursting with green and so real, so beautiful, that it brought tears to his eyes. Beauty like this, he thought and opened his mouth to say the words, but he choked on them. He tried speaking again, drew breath to try, but choked even more. He tried closing his mouth, but whatever choked him filled it…

The once-archer woke up spitting and pulling at his mouth. Hair! He opened his eyes and saw a dark blonde head before his eyes. He leaned back and the hair slid out from between his jaws. He had breathed that stuff in while he was under the White Tar's spell. His tongue lashed about like a headless snake, and he spat twice more. Drawing a breath, he settled back to his pallet. His one eye opened wide.

Who was this woman?

And why was she in his bed?

He realized he had his arm draped around her, which raised an eyebrow, and that his forearm pressed up against what Borus distinctly knew to be a set of exceptionally soft breasts. The thought made him blink in confusion, and he struggled to think—while keeping his arm where it was.

No sense being foolish, he thought. He moved the rest of his limbs and felt relief when all signalled where they lay or were pinned, like his other arm, which was under him. He moved his hand and felt the softness of a rump. A sigh escaped him. What man didn't consider himself fortunate to wake up alive with his limbs feeling the pillowy comfort of a woman's body? He knew others would be envious of him. No sooner did he think the thought than it was gone, chased from his head by another. He couldn't see her face—what if she was hideous, and missing most of her teeth? *Oh… sweet Seddon above.* He could be feeling up an old woman for all he—

She moaned. Stirred. Her movements like those of a sleepy cat, and they stopped Borus as if he were encased in bronze. She let out another moan, and the scent of unwashed flesh made him wrinkle his nose. She moved against him, her round bottom wiggling its way into his lap. Borus felt something *stiffen* down there.

He jerked away from his pallet mate and tumbled to the floor. He bounced to his feet, and the sudden elevation struck him dizzy. He staggered forward, back over the woman, and placed both hands against solid brickwork. Breathing rapidly, he looked around the small room, saw that it was dark but there was torchlight from the outside, beyond a thin curtain. Three straw pallets occupied the room, two of which were full. The one opposite him had a man in it. He gulped air, and looked down at the woman again. His eyes were well adapted to the poor light. Blonde head.

She rolled languidly onto her back and stared at him.

His first feeling was one of relief. She wasn't an old crow. *Thank Seddon for that.* In fact, from what Borus could see, her looks were quite nice. A thin upper lip complimented by a full one underneath, and dark blue eyes.

"You aren't a beauty by any means," Borus whispered.

In the gloom, he saw her frown.

"Um, what I mean is, you're still easy to look at."

The frown remained, and she kept staring.

Borus sighed. "I mean, look at me, half blind and cut up like a whipped ham."

The woman blinked, slowly. She studied him and sighed deeply, perhaps wishing for sleep.

The once-archer scoffed, his old self returning. The hate swelled within him. "What do I care what you think anyway. I don't even know you. Who're you anyway?"

Silence. She blinked again.

"What's your name?" Borus asked gruffly.

"You don't remember?" she answered in a peculiar voice.

"You never told me, bitch."

The frown returned. "You smell."

"What?"

"I said you smell."

"We all smell in here."

"But you smell bad, like you pissed yourself."

Borus blinked this time and took a few testing sniffs about his person, not caring if the wench saw him.

"There's a spring in the corridor. You can wash there. And drink," she informed him, drawing out her words in her strange, quirky voice. It wasn't high like a woman's should be, but rather off key somehow, like an instrument needing tuning.

Borus ignored her and went into the corridor, shoving aside the curtain. He looked left and right, seeing numerous entrances much like the one to his own little room. Hate flashed through him like a wave of fire on a prairie, but he didn't know exactly why. Not that he needed a reason. For Borus, simply existing was reason enough to hate. He found the water, and screwed up his nose. There was indeed a trickle of water, smelling faintly of earth, trickling from a crusty fountain set into an alcove. The water flowed from a simple spout, down over wet brick, and exited by way of a wide drain. Rust and green algae covered half of the drain. He exhaled in disgust. He palmed a few handfuls of water over his head and face. He felt an ache from the inside of his thigh and, after a quick glance in both directions, dropped his leggings to see what the problem was.

Borus cringed. In his White Tar spell, he had pissed himself. Several times. Enough that the urine had soaked his clothes and burned the flesh about his fruit red and raw. He prodded the burns with his fingers and hissed. Without a care he stripped off his leggings and smelled the garment's crotch. *Seddon's grace!* He shook his head in disbelief at the stench. He splashed water over the garment, wetting it, and rubbed it between his fists. Every now and again, Borus sniffed again experimentally. The water had diluted the smell, but he knew the leggings weren't completely clean. He would have to buy new clothes. And he felt his stomach ache for food. What time of day was it? How long had he been under the spell of the Tar? He didn't know, but just thinking of the weed gave him a shiver. It was better than anything bought at an alehouse, and just thinking of it made his teeth and gums ache with longing.

Taking a breath, Borus gripped his wet pants and walked down one of the corridors. He didn't know where he was going, only that he had the chance of being half-right. He passed room upon room. Some were empty, most were occupied. Some occupants moaned under the spell of the White Tar, and other talked gibberish. The smell of unwashed flesh and urine rankled his nose again, but there was also a scent of the Tar.

Mage popped into his mind. The woman's name was Mage. Nice name.

Ahead, the torchlight flickered indistinctly, as if smoke filled the corridor, but it didn't as far as Borus could tell. He kept going, noting that the smell was getting better. Up ahead he saw figures move, passing the mouth of the corridor. Borus could see a door.

A figure stood in front of him.

The face of a boy with curls, all in silver, loomed and blocked any further passage. The figure stooped over somewhat, just to fit in the corridor, and both hands that weren't really hands but spiked balls hung by his sides. A scalemail vest gleamed in the torchlight, and Borus realized that he was staring at this monster... while he was half naked.

"Ah... hello," Borus said. "I, uh, seem to have a problem."

The silver face with the plump cheeks of a baby did not move.

"I soiled myself, see." Borus held up his leggings for inspection, but the face didn't seem to care. Behind the silent brute, the second guardian, the one with the horns, moved into view.

"I need to..." What was it that he needed? He knew he stood at the entrance. "I need to go a buy some new clothes."

The silver face did not move.

"I'll come back again," Borus told them. He had every intention of returning.

Perhaps the two guardians of the Hole's entrance knew this, for the silver baby-faced one stepped aside. Just behind him, the guard with the horns threw back locks and opened the door. Fresh air smacked Borus in the face, and he smelled sewer once more.

"I'll be back," he promised and walked out, edging his way between the pair. They remained silent, watching the man as he exited the chamber, into the evening.

Standing in the street, Borus glimpsed the door closing quietly behind him. He realized he was bare below the waist, and with a curse, tried to get back into his wet leggings. His foot went through the crotch, and rage coursed through him.

Cursing he set off bare-assed in search of a clothing merchant.

Borus found his clothing merchant in a public square in the heat of the day. People watched him stomp around. Some children even pointed and giggled. Borus glared and moved on until he found what he wanted. He bought a pair of black trousers, noting that he still had about thirty gold coins in his purse. He bought a second white shirt, and practically thrust the money at the merchant. Now fully clothed, Borus searched for food. Trade and foodstuffs had been choked off by the siege, but Borus still managed to buy a loaf of bread and a half-cooked roast. Four apples also went into a cloth sack, as did a skin of water and one of wine. It all cost him three expensive gold coins. He bought two legs of lamb, grossly overpriced at a gold cutaro, and sat down to eat it on a set of steps between two houses. People watched him as he ate, some eyeing him with venom for whatever reason, others lingering on the food he devoured. He ate it all, amazed at how good it tasted and how hungry he was. He ate an apple after the lamb, marveling at its sweetness.

He finished some time later and, feeling much better, he thought of what he would do for the evening. Being trapped in Foust presented him with limited options. He could stay here, find an alehouse and drink himself into oblivion, or… he could fly again.

Borus wasn't a stupid man. He knew he liked the White Tar. Perhaps even too much.

He thought about it all the way back to the Hole.

The two frightening, ever-quiet warriors let him in through the heavy door and closed it behind him. Borus walked down the long corridor once more, smelling the Tar in the air and the stench of buckets full of excrement needing to be dumped. He knew the Hole was just that, but the urge hooked him by his ribs and drew him forward.

"You actually left us?" Sabo exclaimed when he set his pretty eyes on Borus. He barked laughter, humourless and louder than it should have been.

"I had to," Borus said. "Pissed my clothes. I needed to buy new ones, and some food."

"Ah," Sabo said from behind his table. "I see. Well, what is it I can do for you?" He smiled. In the torchlight, Borus thought it was interesting the White Tar man didn't burst into flames. Karast stood to one side, silent as the previous two guards and still wearing the black mask.

"The Tar, if you please," Borus said, fishing out five gold cutaros.

The smile stretching across Sabo's fleshy face was greasy, reptilian.

"That's quite the amount."

"I might share."

"Very generous of you." Sabo got up from his seat.

"You don't mind?"

The smiling man frowned, as if it made no difference to him.

Borus handled over the gold and Sabo produced enough of the reedy weed that would enable the once archer to travel to places in dreams, and stay there. He wrapped it in some cloth and handed it to his customer.

"Here," Borus tossed two more coins onto the table. "That's to keep the shite bucket in my room empty, and clean straw in the pallets."

Sabo made the gold disappear with one swipe. "Anything else?"

Borus thought about it. "Who is that woman in my room?"

"A long-time customer. You were more than generous with them. I'll have Karast remove her and her brother. "

"No," Borus said, remembering how the woman felt. "No. But…"

Sabo leaned ever so slightly forward, wearing an expression of both puzzlement and concern.

"No," the once-archer said. "Nothing. They're fine."

"As you wish." With that, Sabo indicated that their customer be escorted to his room, and the man called

Karast obeyed. Sabo watched with his pretty eyes and knowingly smiled as Chop's bulky cousin led Borus away. Borus noticed the leader didn't ask how long he would be staying, and remembered Sabo's first words to him.

No one steals from anyone this far under the earth.

Now he understood why. There was no need for Sabo and his men to steal from him. They would take it all eventually. They had what he wanted.

The White Tar.

Karast led him back to his room, and stopped just beyond the entrance so that Borus could enter.

"Here." Borus tossed a gold coin to the Black Mask, feeling like he was tossing roast of fresh meat to a dangerous dog. Karast caught it easily.

"Make sure what I asked is done."

The black leather face slowly nodded, and Borus nodded back. "When I woke up, the place smelled terrible."

With that, he left the big man in flickering torchlight and entered his room. *His cell,* he thought, for he knew it to be just that. The most fiendish kind.

Shadows cloaked the room, but he could see Mage on the pallet with her back to him. He sat on the third pallet, and sniffed the straw. It was clean, but the shite bucket reeked. Not looking at the contents, Borus placed it outside in the corridor. He held onto his cloth bag of food, and sat back down on the pallet.

"You're back," came that strange, off-note voice. Borus wondered if Mage had been teased as a child for that voice. He probably would have done it.

His eyes had adjusted to the gloom and he regarded her, just the length of his leg away, spread out on the straw. She watched him with eyes that might have been mesmerizing in the dark, but now seemed glassy and only semi-conscious.

"I did."

"Why did you come back?"

Borus held up the handful of White Tar. That got her attention. Mage licked her lips and pulled herself up, dragging her legs over the edge of the bed. She wore a loose, white shirt with black leggings. The shirt, Borus noted, was open at the throat, and he could see the curve and swell of her breasts. She stared at him, and Borus recognized the look.

"I can smell it from here."

Borus sniffed the White Tar and sighed. It did smell wonderful. Mage studied him like an animal waiting to be fed, and ready to perform any trick to get it.

The once archer ignored her. He took one of the strands in his hand and placed it slowly, deliberately in his mouth. He chewed theatrically, giving a show of how good it tasted. He sat back on his pallet and regarded Mage.

Licking her lips, she got to her bare feet, greyish in the half-light. She stepped to him, seeming to glow, and her hands came up to his shoulders.

"What are you doing?" Borus asked her.

"What?"

"You stink. Get back over there."

Silence. She stood before him a moment more, and Borus wondered if he would have to push her away. He didn't have to. She stepped back, her shoulders sagging, and sat back down on her pallet. Her hair fell forward to cover her face as she looked at her feet, and he heard her sigh.

Taking a breath and smelling Mage and the other man— *her brother*, he remembered Sabo saying— Borus stayed quiet as he regarded the space on his straw bed. He pushed the cloth bag to the inside, against the wall. He knew where the water was. It wasn't ale, but who needed that when one had the Tar?

"What's that?"

Borus regarded Mage. "What?"

"The bag." Her face was dark.

"That's my breakfast. And lunch. Maybe dinner."

She said nothing for a moment, and Borus thought he would have to throw her out, suddenly not trusting her.

"May I have some?"

"What?"

She didn't ask again.

Borus blinked in the shadows and studied the woman. He believed he knew why her shirt was so large on her. Mage had been much bigger at one point in her life. She'd lost weight. He thought about how he'd eaten the lamb outside and how famished he was, and he wondered once again what day it was.

"For him," Mage said, breaking his thoughts.

"Who?"

"My brother."

"Why doesn't he ask me then?"

Mage didn't answer. "He's not well."

"What's wrong with him?"

She waited a moment before replying. "He's dying."

"What?"

"He's dying."

Borus wasn't bothered in the least by her admission. "So why don't you help him?"

Another moment. "I'm dying, too."

"What?"

"And, if you stay here," Mage continued on in her odd voice, "You'll die as well. You're as good as dead. You were away, but you came back. Why? You were *out*."

"I can leave any time I please."

Mage smiled weakly in the shadows, obviously having heard the lie before. "That's what I said, when I came in here. Trying to save him."

"From Sabo?"

She shook her head. "The White Tar. My brother couldn't stop eating it. They let me in here, knowing I wouldn't leave. I thought they would… rape me, but they didn't. My brother wouldn't leave. I begged him, but still he wouldn't leave. We had to get out of the city. The beastmen were coming."

She drew a deep breath. "But… the only way he would go, was if I tried it. He would leave if I tried it *once*."

Her face turned in the direction of her brother, lying on the far pallet with his back to them both.

"Now, I can't leave." A resigned expulsion of breath. "And now neither can you."

"I can leave whenever I want," Borus repeated and rubbed the side of his face. He felt it start to go numb. The Tar worked quickly.

She didn't say anything to that.

"Anytime." He lay back down on his bed, nudging the wall.

The Tar slowly took him away.

*

He woke some time later, seeing torchlight glowing through a thin curtain. He smacked his mouth and felt the dryness there. Water. He wanted a drink. The spell had been especially magical this time, and he suspected the only reason he woke up was because he had ingested only a small amount. How long could he remain under the spell if he took more? He wondered. He would ask Sabo.

He rested there in the dark, listening to the low drone of silence in his ears. He heard something *plink* outside, and sometimes a creak of wood from nearby. There was nothing quieter than stone, he thought, and wondered for a moment if the dead could hear the earth in their graves.

He noticed the smell. It wasn't so bad in here anymore. They'd cleaned the straw, and emptied the shite bucket. He took a breath of the straw beneath him. It occurred to him that they had to move him to change it. The Tar had been strong enough to take him away from all of that, and the notion amazed him. He felt the bag of food at his leg and sat up. In the shadows, he felt for the bucket, and located it. Fishing his manhood from his trousers, *dry* trousers he noted, he went about relieving himself.

Across from him, Mage was missing.

Curiosity got the better of him and he leaned forward, still emptying his bladder, attempting to see where she might have gotten off to. Her brother slept on, his back still to Borus. What was his name? Did Mage tell him? He couldn't remember.

When he finished with the bucket, he tucked his topper away and considered the sleeping man. Mage said he was dying. He certainly looked *unmoving* to Borus. Maybe he already passed on and Mage left? Becoming increasingly curious, the once archer got to his feet and felt the dizziness give him a spin. He steadied himself and walked to the still man's bed, eyeing the white shirt the man wore. The man before him remained motionless, as if in a deep sleep. Borus stood above him, watching for any signs of breathing. He could detect none, which reinforced the idea the sleeping man really had passed on. The brother had curled up on the pallet with his hands close to his chest, like a child with a favorite toy. Borus cocked his head to the side and gazed down at him. The smell of sour sweat and urine was strong here, causing the one-eyed man to catch his breath. Shadow hid the profile of Mage's brother, which irritated him. He wanted to see his face, and reached down to roll him on his back.

"What are you doing?"

Borus stopped with his hands almost on the shoulders of the sleeping man. The voice with its off tone belonged to Mage, and he turned to face her. She stood in the doorway, and let the curtain fall behind her.

"I wanted to see his face."

Without a word, she walked over and stood beside him. She reached down and pulled her brother onto his back.

"Klos," she said. "Wake up, Klos."

Borus leaned in to see, stepping to the side to allow some of the glow from the doorway to reach the sleeping man. What he saw make him pull back in dismay.

Klos was skeletal.

His eyes were shut and appeared like sunken caves, dark and dead in the meager light. His skin was stretched taut over his face, marking the hollows of his cheeks, and the bloodless cut of his mouth. His hair, also affected by the lack of food, looked thin and had same texture as a straw broom. When Mage flipped him over, his eyes opened just a crack, and Borus felt he wasn't looking at a man, but a skull. Klos' hands—still clutched to his chest—flexed once like the legs of a spider, and were still.

He opened his mouth, and Mage held a wooden cup to his lips.

"This man needs food," Borus said. Mage helped her brother to drink. When she didn't answer, he looked at her profile and caught himself. Klos' sister, while not as far gone as her brother, could also do with a meal. The flesh of her face appeared tight and her cheek bones flared out. The lines her throat stretched like a collection of strings, attached to a too-prominent collar bone. When she swallowed, Borus felt something inside him break. There was a siege on, but he still managed to find something to eat. Anger flickered.

"You're just as bad as he is!"

Her head tilted to the side. "Not quite. Maybe soon."

"Why don't you get something to eat?"

She smiled, and Borus saw her teeth, white in the shadows.

"I have no money."

Borus' face twisted. "What? How do you buy the Tar?"

Mage sighed, gazing down at her brother while he drank from the cup.

"Well?"

"I give them what they want," she said quietly.

"You're a whore?" Borus asked pointedly.

"No," Mage replied and took a breath. She took the cup from her brother's face, placed a hand on his forehead, and looked Borus in the eye. "Far from it, but I let them have me, and they give me Tar. It's only them. And soon, they won't want me anyway. When that happens…" She shrugged.

Borus kept silent for a moment. He had been a champion in his time, a warrior and just about everything a man of privilege could be. Hunger was something he could not abide. Even as he thought it, he went to his cloth sack and pulled forth the loaf of bread he kept there as well as the roast.

"Here," Borus said.

Mage looked up at him. "What's this?"

"What does it look like? You both need something to eat, so here."

She took a breath and he could see how just the smell affected her. "We'll share it."

Borus didn't care. "Just eat it."

She tore the loaf in two and pinched off a piece. She seemed to think of something, and left Borus with her brother while she left the room. Borus couldn't help staring at the poor, starving bastard on the pallet. Mage returned shortly, her cup full of water. She returned to his side while Borus backed up and sat on the corner of Klos' bed. He gnawed on the cooked roast, noting that it was a little dry and off. How long had it been in the bag? He'd thought he only went on a short White Tar spell.

Mage dipped the bread in the water and forced it into her brother's mouth. Borus shared the meat with them until only a thin bone remained. They ate quietly. Mage stopped and said she could eat no more. She fed Klos what Borus saw to be White Tar, and he felt his gums ache for it.

Mage turned to him. "We'll share." She held out half a weed.

"Keep it. I have my own."

"We'll *share.*"

"I don't want to share."

Mage's dark face trembled in the shade, and she

seemed uncertain about something. She got up and sat down next to Borus. He noticed that she didn't smell so badly.

"I don't want that either," he informed her quietly.

"What can I do then?"

"Just…" Borus trailed off and didn't know how to answer. He felt her closeness, but knowing that Sabo had probably taken her to his bed chamber repelled him. "Lie down on your bed. And save that for yourself." He indicated the weed. He reached into a belt pouch and brought out the wrapped cloth. He unfolded it, and noted how Mage's head drew back at the sight of so much White Tar.

"Here's more. For him as well, so you don't have to…" Borus waved his hand at the curtained door.

With fingers that were close to boney sticks, she took some.

"There. Now then," Borus said, trying to force humour into his voice. After such a long time, it was difficult, and he failed. "We've eaten, and have food for later. So, let's enjoy ourselves."

With that he ate a full strip of the weed, and indicated that Mage return to her bed. She did, and after a while, consumed her own portion of the Tar.

"We can leave anytime we chose," Borus said as the spell crept over his senses and the warm sun brightened the stone above his pallet. "Anytime…" He spoke, his consciousness leaving.

*

Mage watched him in the dark and heard him leave with the Tar. He was flying now, she knew, in places where she had travelled and longed to travel again. Her brother flew in the same place. Part of her willed her to leave this place, struggled to gain control and just go, but the greater part squashed the idea, and *promised* that this time would be the last.

She felt her cheeks warm, and she knew the spell was descending over her, but the last thing she did, the last thing she wanted to do, was to be with someone when she left this time. Taking a breath, Mage got up from her pallet and crossed the floor. She lay down beside the one-eyed man, breathing in his staleness, but feeling safer as she snuggled closer. She molded herself to his person, one leg even draping over his, and her last clear thought before the spell of the Tar overcame her, was how soft he felt.

She didn't even know his name.

CHAPTER 16

"Soup." He-Dog breathed in disgust. It was all he could eat for two weeks, and as long as it took for his jaw to heal. He looked sadly at the broth in a wooden bowl. Piss. S'all it was. And they fed it to him daily. He had to slurp it up like a dog, and it constantly soaked the bandages on his face. If he had to eat any more of it, he believed his guts would send it back with force. That would not be a pretty sight.

"You have—" Samil began when He-Dog grabbed the bowl and plunged his face into it. He sucked the soup up as loud as he could, and handed the empty bowl back when he was finished. Samil looked at him and frowned.

He-Dog glared at the woman as she took the bowl away. He thought it best to eat what they gave him as fast as he could. With a snort that stung his face, he leaned back down on his bed. Across the way, Balless ate his soup quietly, with a piece of hard bread.

The second week of being on the mend was more monotonous than the first, and it was only going to get worse. Saimon's hell, He-Dog called it, and several times the warrior sat and sulked by the window, watching the citizens of Foust walk past. His wounds slowly healed, as did Balless' and Chop's, but the broken bones would take longer. Weeks, in fact. Sergius told them all of this, and kept informing them they would probably be dead by the morning. He-Dog thought the joke growing stale, but whenever he tried to tell this to the healer, the half-naked old topper would only smile at him with the tuft of hair on the apple that was his head swaying as if possessing a life of its own.

He-Dog had stared at the ceiling and huffed again.

"You're lucky, you know." The healer's voice reached him. "Not everyone gets a meal in Foust. I'm dedicated to the profession. Can't have my patients starving while under my care."

"I think he just wants to be out there," Balless muttered, dabbing his roll carefully in his soup and nibbling its end. Of the three, he was the only one who could speak sensibly, though He-Dog knew it was rare he showed any sense.

"He'll be released soon enough," the healer informed him. "You all will, and I'll miss you once you're gone."

"Really?" Balless asked.

"No, not really."

Balless chuckled.

Sergius moved between the beds, studied the bandages covering the great bulk of Balless, and nodded. "You're coming along, it seems."

Balless beamed. "Will I be dead in the morning?"

He-Dog rolled his eyes.

Sergius shook his head. "Doubtful. I can't say the same for your companions. They could go any time."

Chop sat still on his pallet and gazed out the window, showing no indication that he had heard.

He-Dog watched the healer survey his infirmary. Aside from the one fellow with the broken legs, the place was nearly empty of patients.

"Are you the only healer?" Balless asked.

"Lords above, no." Sergius scratched at the little bit of

hair on his head. "But I think I'm the most capable."

Balless flexed his brow at that and finished his meal. Hesel took his bowl away.

"Interested in word from the walls?"

"Aye. Let's hear it."

"The beastmen seemed to have lost interest in attacking," Sergius said. "On some of my trips to the market, I've run into some lower officers who tell me that since you've arrived, no one has as much as raised a spear in our direction. Something of a blessing, wouldn't you say?"

Balless nodded.

"Could be something happening out there, however. Who really knows what goes on in a beastman's mind? But as long as they aren't attacking, no one is dying. A brief respite. Too bad there's no respite from the siege, however. And while we rest up, they are resting as well. Keep that in mind."

"Not safe," He-Dog slurred, drawing the healer's attention.

"You don't think so?"

He-Dog exhaled mightily. "They're… beastmen," he struggled to say, each word slowed by the bandages keeping his jaw in place.

"Well, our walls have held firm for some time now," Sergius countered. "And in this heat," he emphasized by drawing his forearm across his head, wiping away the sweat there. "I think they'll withdraw before we give in."

He-Dog snorted.

"No?" The healer sounded unsure himself.

The warriors in his care didn't bother replying.

Standing in the open window, inspecting them all, stood the man called Bowlak with several of his soldiers. Dressed in armor and carrying swords in scabbards, Bowlak nodded at the wounded men, and eventually grinned, exposing horrible teeth.

Sergius turned to face Bowlak, his mouth puckering in

anger. "Didn't I tell you not to come here?"

"You said *in* your infirmary," Bowlak clarified. "We're plainly outside."

"Leave this instant, or I'll notify Krajin."

"For walking along a side street?" Bowlak looked incredulous. "We were on patrol, set by Captain Krajin himself. We're protecting the peace down here."

"Patrol someplace else."

"We cannot," Bowlak replied with a smirk. "Talk to Captain Krajin if you must. Meanwhile, answer this before you go…"

Sergius' brow tensed.

"Is all well here?" Bowlak asked mockingly, suddenly appearing quite concerned. Some of the guards with him smiled.

"Be gone!"

Bowlak's missing teeth gleamed and he met He-Dog's eyes. "For a little man, he certainly is a brave one. If I were you, I'd thank him this day."

He-Dog only stared back, and did not bother with a reply. Next to him, Balless eyed the soldiers, his own smile gone. No one bothered to glance at the mess that was Chop.

"We'll be back, good healer," Bowlak announced. "At least twice this day, and the days to come. Just to keep an eye on the peace, of course."

"Off with you," Sergius said sternly, walking toward the window and shooing the soldiers.

It didn't work. Bowlak's smile disappeared for a moment, and he gave the healer such a reproachful look that He-Dog selected the blade he was going to go for on the rack of surgical tools. The soldier considered the healer before him for several moments. If he wanted to, he could have reached across the low wall and grabbed Sergius by the neck.

Not that He-Dog or Balless would have allowed it.

As if coming to the conclusion that throttling a healer

wasn't worth the effort, Bowlak turned and marched out of sight. He took his time, making it clear that he left because he chose to, and the small mob of soldiers followed him.

Sergius craned his neck to see where they had gone, and after a moment, he drew back and placed his hands on his hips. "Well, they're gone. Wise, I'd say."

Balless looked at He-Dog.

But his leader kept silent.

CHAPTER 17

It had been almost a month since the death of the beastman king, Blood Skull. One month since the man-thing crushed the beastman beneath its wheels. In that time, the horde surrounding Foust froze. Leaderless, the tribes who had gathered and united under the War Skull could not proceed with their plans for one critical reason: Blood Skull was the only one who *knew* what those plans were.

Mired into inaction on a plain of war, the chieftains felt that it was too late to disband. To gather so many of their kind in one place to crush the man-things was a momentous feat, and not one that should be thrown to the wind with the death of War Skull. They remembered the effort it took to mobilize such a monstrous army, and the success they'd had up until Blood Skull's death. The chieftains sensed they were close to breaking the jewel that was Foust. To disband now would mean defeat, and perhaps even losing the opportunity to drive the race of man from the Lands of the South.

On this, they could agree.

Yet, they could not proceed until a new king was chosen, a new War Skull. They took the next logical step:

honor the fallen Blood Skull with the traditional period of mourning befitting a king. For almost a month, not one beastman raised an axe in the direction of Foust. The horde remained beyond the range of the arrows and catapults of the city, while the united tribes repaired their war machines. They waited. They healed. Within the mass of beastman hides, ambitious chieftains made their play for power. Beastman politics were a straightforward affair. If one wanted to rule, one had to fight and defeat the current ruler. In this sad situation, the chieftains decided it was only fair that the leaders wanting the mantle of king should fight for it.

All at once.

Deep within the throng of tents and siege machines, the massive war pavilion housed the gathered chieftains of the twenty-nine tribes. In truth, twenty-nine tribes had been pressed into serving under the War Skull, but there were a hundred more on the continent. Destroying fabled Foust would only add to the momentum of the beastman war against man, and word of the victory would bring tribes flocking to the War Skull's unifying scream. For now, the forces of twenty-nine tribes were assembled, and their chieftains sat, waiting for a new War Skull.

In an arena whose walls were the watching chieftains and their guards, five chieftains eyed each other with fierce contempt over a burning fire pit. A scattering of human bones littered the edges of the blaze, while the skulls of fallen beastman chieftains rose on spears behind the gathered spectators. Gauzy smoke lingered in the air, smelling of wood and burned meat.

A red shaman detached himself from the wall of flesh and entered the ring, adorned with decorations befitting a holy figure. Bones, assorted blades, iron flasks half-filled with sloshing contents, and the yellow jawbones of men hung from his mottled form. In his fist, he carried a long pole with the white skull of Blood Skull affixed to one end. Part of the shaman's lips had been sheared away, exposing teeth worn down to almost nubs in a permanent snarl.

The shaman flung a handful of powder into the fire. Flames rose, snapping and devouring the dust and sending a plume of grey smoke heavenward, toward a hole in the pavilion's vast canopy. The shaman stalked about the sand, thrusting the grinning skull of the dead king into the faces of the five contenders for the throne. The holy figure spoke in harsh tones, heaping curses upon curses in the beastman tongue, and telling of a day when the whole of the lands would drive the man-things back into the Big Water. The shaman swore and seethed, depicting the rise of Blood Skull and the unification of many tribes.

Blood Skull had united the tribes, but he wasn't the one who would take Foust.

The shaman drew a deep rattle of a breath, as though his ribs were about to burst through his chest. He told the chieftains he knew Blood Skull was only the first, and that the real king of the beastmen would emerge from the five warriors present. The new king would lead the way, finish killing the man-things, and shove all their enemies into the Big Water.

All that was left, the shaman told the watchers, was to see who the new king would be.

As the shaman's roar faded into stillness, the gathered beastmen roared their approval, and called for the heirs to show themselves.

Thrusting the skull of the former king into the smoky air, the shaman invoked silence and exited the ring.

The five who wished to be king stepped forward. Since the death of Blood Skull, the five had bullied, battered, and killed their own to reach this point. None of them wore armor of any sort. Two black beastmen stood arm's length apart. One carried a large war club while the other held a single-bladed war axe. Both were covered in scars and cuts. Both looked eager to break open the bones of their adversaries.

The third beastman, a dark melon green, stood

grinning, snarling, and brandishing a long shafted mace. The creature's biceps bulged and his massive chest heaved with eager breath. His right eye socket stared darkly, the orb having been ripped from his head years before. A spiked mace replaced his left hand, which had been chopped away by a man-thing's axe. The chieftain had fixed and nailed the weapon there himself.

Next was a large red holding an axe. Great oversized jaws marked the creature, and his burning eyes took in the other contenders over the curve of a double-bladed battle axe.

The last beastman stood tall and quiet, eyeing them all. The gangly white stomped the sand and held out a hand. Behind him, other whites filled their leader's hand with a chipped greatsword that had lost its edge so long ago that it was presently more of a maul than a blade. The white held the steel in front of him, studying the weapon's length and nodding in approval.

The five took their places around the fire pit, like the tips of a crude pentagram

Surrounding them, the spectators began a low chant, the sound barely audible over the snapping of the fire.

No sooner had the chant begun when the black with the war club pivoted on his foot and crushed the unprotected knee of the other black. With a grunt, the wounded beastman crashed to the ground, grimacing and clutching the ruined pulp of the joint. In agony, he looked up and his face became a mask of surprise when a double bladed battle axe split it from muzzle to forehead.

The remaining black lashed out at the red, who quickly jumped back while wrenching his axe out of the first dead chieftain. The black body of the beastman landed heavily on the sand.

Across the way, the green squared off against the white. The white beastman brought his greatsword to high guard, waiting for the other to move on him. The white snarled and urged the green on with a stream of insults. The green took a step to attack and the white brought his greatsword slicing down, seeking the green's head. The chieftain sidestepped the blow and the long blade plunged into the ground with a sandy crash. With a roar, the green brought his long shafted mace down on the greatsword while snapping the spiked ball of his left arm forward. It smashed into the jaw of the white—bone and flesh breaking under the connection and the force whipping the head back. The green finished the combination by driving his mace into the open stomach of his victim like a maul smashing a block of butter. Without a sound, the white toppled onto the sand, landing on the remains of his stomach.

The one-eyed green placed a foot on the exposed back of the fallen white, saw that the spikes had gone deep enough, and yanked his weapon free in a glitter of gore.

The chant continued.

The black swung at the red's head. The beastman ducked and countered with a cut aimed at the other's legs. The black saw the flash of the steel though the smoky air and nimbly jumped back.

To have his head caved in by the long-shafted mace.

The red stepped back and brought his axe to bear as the monstrous green drove the spiked ball of his left arm into the dead black's body, pushing it away and letting it drop into the fire pit. The flames licked the flesh of the corpse, and the snapping and hiss of beastman fat filled the air.

Grinning savagely, the green peered at the red over maces speckled with fleshly matter. The red snarled back, snapping his oversized jaws and urging his foe on with his axe. From where spears spiked them, the empty skulls of the fallen chieftains watched with shadowy eye sockets, and the beastman chant droned on.

The green feinted with his stump mace. The red bared his tusks and did not fall for the trick. The green swore at the red, spewing forth a stream of curses that made several of the beastman chanters smile with evil mirth.

The red charged, swinging his axe in a flat cut. The green backed up. The red jabbed his weapon toward his adversary's face. The green deflected it with his mace and sparks lit the smoke. The two beastman chieftains circled the fire pit, mindful of the two corpses littering the sand. A puff of steam rose into the air from the cooking carcass of the dead black.

The green edged closer, and swung with his stump mace. The red's axe parried with a clang and stopped the swing of the second mace. The red backed away, holding his axe in front of him and studying the stalking one-eyed green. The mace-wielding beastman spoke to the red, taunting him for retreating.

The red pressed forward, swinging his axe with the power of both arms. The green moved to the side, evading the blow. He countered, thrusting one mace at the red's stomach. The axe stopped it. The green stepped in close, and smashed his stump mace downward for an exposed thigh.

The red twisted out of the way, bringing his axe to chest height.

The green howled. He swung his mace and crushed the last two fingers on the red's left hand. The red stiffened in pain, grimacing as much in anger as in agony. He backed up again, placing the fire pit between him and his foe, and held up his hand to inspect the damage. Both digits hung by shreds of flesh.

From across the pit, through the thickening smoke, the one-eyed green barked laughter and pointed with his stump mace.

The red brought his hand closer to his face and bared teeth. A growl scratched his throat.

The green paused, recognizing the chieftain with the oversized jaws. He'd heard of the red's reputation. His laughter suddenly choked off. He remembered this beastman's name.

Two-Bite.

Baring tusks and fangs, Two-Bite bit off both his ruined fingers with one snap of his mighty jaws. Blood fountained weakly from the stumps. With a huff, Two-Bite spat both fingers into the flames. Pain meant nothing to him.

For what was pain… to a *king?*

With that thought, the red surged forward *through* the fire pit, using the sizzling bulk of the cooking black as a bridge. His axe came up in a flash, splitting smoke like a bolt of lightning. Two-Bite roared as he brought the weapon up and then down, smashing through the upraised maces of the green and embedding half its edge into his face. The force of the blow put the beastman on his back, stunned but far from dead, with a horrible axe wound through his good eye.

Two-Bite stood over the fallen green. He stomped on his foe's chest, freeing his axe with both hands while blood from his missing fingers ran down the length of the shaft. The battle axe's edge kissed the neck of the green. The now-blind beastman sputtered in pain and shock, still very much alive.

Two-Bite declared himself king and drew back the axe. The chanting rose.

And the new king and War Skull of the beastmen shattered his foe's skull.

The spectators roared approval.

Brought back to his senses by the shouting beastmen, the fallen white propped himself up on his elbows in a pool of his own blood and viscera. Before him was his greatsword, the old metal dull against the sand. The white raised his head.

The dead coming back to life quieted those who saw him, and the lull in the beastmen's adorations drew the attention of Two-Bite. The big red walked over to the white and, without a word or curse, smashed in the beastman's head with one blow of his battle axe.

His first order of business completed, Two-Bite left his axe in the dead and gazed upon the living. Teeth gleamed through the smoke. Two-Bite raised his muscular arms and took a deep breath of smoldering flesh.

*

From the heights of Foust's battlements, two soldiers on watch stopped and listened. The beastman army below them was unusually quiet. For weeks they had pounded drums and howled at the walls of Foust, and the soldiers keeping watch were simply glad to be above and away from them. This night, however, was different.

They stood and listened, faintly hearing the periodic sound of metal on metal, but the wind carried it away before either of them could be certain.

Then nothing could be heard at all.

Until one voice pierced the quiet, from somewhere deep inside the beastman army.

And the whole night shouted with it.

CHAPTER 18

Captain Galt strode through the inner chambers of the Kratoe's palatial keep. He wasn't a tall man, but broad in the shoulders and thick in the arms. He kept his blond hair cut close to his skull, and it hadn't escaped his attention that spikes of grey were appearing more often. Not that growing old bothered him. He had no doubt that something would kill him sooner or later, and he welcomed its arrival. He wanted to meet his death quickly, so he could get to work on whatever business had to be done on the other side of existence. The only question truly concerning him was the state in which he would arrive in Saimon's hell, and if he would be able to wreak as much terror there as he did on this plane. On nights when he drank too much, Galt believed that death didn't want any part of him, simply because it would be too much of a struggle to take him. That notion set him to giggling madly.

He walked down a stone corridor with an arched ceiling. Four of his handpicked guards walked behind him. Galt recognized and appreciated their callous attributes; they reminded him of his younger self. They wore leather cuirasses, much more comfortable in these temperate zones than full mail suits, and carried swords and round shields.

They stopped before a pair of dark-robed servants standing in front of a set of ceiling-height bronze double doors. Galt eyed his thin reflection in the polished bronze panels. He appeared as if he had been stretched out on a rack. He looked back at the four men behind him with a critical eye. Satisfied that his personal guard was presentable, he turned back to the doors and twirled an impatient finger at the servants. The men bowed; each gripped a door handle and pulled. The doors opened slowly, and Galt took a steadying breath to control his irritation. If these men were under him, he would kick both to death for such sluggishness. Perhaps he just might, anyway. The Kratoe seemed uninterested in much of what he did these days. Maybe he would test just how far he could go before the old man reined him in.

Galt could wait no longer and pressed forward when the men had the door open wide enough to allow him through. His guards followed at his heels. As he passed, Galt glared at both servants, letting both know what he thought of them.

Inside, Galt ignored the sparse beauty of the throne room. He ignored the size of the chamber and the high, arched ceiling. He didn't spare a glance at the mosaics on the walls, the open windows, or the unlit braziers. The stone floor was fitted with a single walkway of black veined marble that led to a crystal fountain in the shape of a fish weakly spitting water. The marble path curved around the fountain, and Galt cursed the builders for placing such an opulent eyesore in the middle of the floor. He had no time for any of it. Perhaps he would if any of it was his, but it wasn't.

It wasn't the Kratoe's either, but since King Narijo of Zuthenia hadn't set foot in Foust in over fifteen years, or so it was said, the old man treated it as if it were his alone. As long as the copper found in the hills and mountains of

Foust flowed east to the homeland, Narijo had no reason to visit.

The Kratoe could do as he pleased.

Galt chewed on the inside of his mouth, screwing up a middle-aged face shaved every morning. Grey eyes, the color of thick ice he was told, sized up the empty throne. Fashioned from white marble, it squatted against a wall depicting what Galt once thought to be a blazing brass sun framed in expensive and very hard to come by black wood. The Kratoe had once dourly informed him that it was, in fact, a moon with the beams falling to earth. Galt's eyes lingered on the red cushions that adorned the otherwise hard seat. Soft cushions for a hard, yet pampered ass, Galt mentally scoffed, snorting air that reeked of flowery incense. He stared ahead and exhaled again, keeping his eyes on the throne and not the hidden peepholes to the left. He hoped that whoever announced his arrival to the old man would do him the simple courtesy of announcing his arrival formally. Galt pursed his lips. Every passing day he grew increasingly tired of living while surrounded by stone, and soon, very soon, he would start killing people. He could feel it building inside. He wanted out of Foust. He wanted to leave soon and beastman rabble be damned.

A black-robed servant, delicate looking and utterly stomach-turning, came into view. He bowed in Galt's direction, as well he should. This personal servant to the Kratoe had had the annoying habit of not giving Galt a display of respect, that was until Galt cornered the sweet-smelling topper in a secluded corridor, and threatened to scoop both his eyes out with a dull dagger if he continued to be so defiantly blind. Since then, the righteous prick bowed at the very mention of Galt's name. The captain also observed that all other servants of the inner keep now did the same. Interesting how a few words and a gnashing of teeth obtained the best results, but that was the way of the land in Foust.

The Kratoe appeared, tall and thin with his features

covered from head to toe in the thin black robes of his office. The man's white, age-mottled hands were visible, in addition to the slits in the material for his eyes. Galt wondered if the old man actually thought that wearing those robes fooled anyone. The ruler of Foust moved slowly, and appeared slightly buckled over at the head and shoulders, as if he were constantly ducking under something. Galt knew the man rarely, if ever, ventured outside in such colors. The Kratoe had once informed him that he despised the heat, and that much of his time was spent lounging in cool baths beyond that brass moon.

Galt thought it sounded nice.

The Kratoe walked to the throne he clearly thought of as his own and sat down heavily. He placed both hands on the arm rests, leaned forward, and sighed. For moments he didn't speak at all, and Galt wondered if the old man was ever going to break the silence.

"What is it?" the Kratoe finally said.

Galt gave a short bow. "Last night, those dogs outside our walls sounded as if they were ready to fight. If I was to place a wager, it would be on something happening very soon. After a month of nothing, I believe they are of a mind to come at us again."

"What does Krajin think?"

Galt straightened before answering. "I didn't speak with him. I trust my own instincts in this matter."

"I see."

"Well?"

The Kratoe didn't respond. He leaned back on the throne and took a deep breath. Galt knew that he was thinking, and he had to admit that the old man did think deeply. Sometimes, the shagger decided to reveal his master plans to him. More often than not, Galt was left guessing, but he did know *some* of the Kratoe's plans, perhaps even the more important ones. Any plan that included him was important to Galt.

"We will..." The Kratoe spoke, taking a long pause.

Galt didn't mind the gaps of silence so much. Despite what he might think of the ancient pisser, he had to acknowledge the fact that the man was intelligent.

"Send a messenger to the dogs," the Kratoe continued. "That will tell us what they are thinking. Whether or not… they are readying themselves for another stab."

He appeared to think again, and Galt kept his tongue.

"Have there been any reinforcements?"

Galt knew he didn't mean Foust's. The message delivered a month ago by the four mercenaries made that perfectly clear. There would be no troops to aid in the defence of the fabled city. They were on their own. "None, Kratoe. But they could be arriving under the cover of darkness."

"Do you believe that?"

"No, but it is a possibility."

"How go our own preparations?"

"As well as expected."

"Hmm." The Kratoe arched his head back, as if taking in the ceiling. Galt couldn't see the man's eyes well enough to know if he was actually looking or not. "Perhaps I should bring in another officer. Perhaps Krajin."

Galt frowned. "Captain Krajin would probably try to stop you. He's very much for the people, despite his harshness. I believe we have enough. If anything, we can later send word for mercenaries at any port city. Some will be louts, and raw. Some will be cutthroats. But there will be those with training and loyalty, who will be the core of your officers. Anyone without training can be trained or killed. Really, that part is simple."

Silence.

"Very well," the Kratoe said. "Keep at it. You will bring my eyes and ears to the dog army outside."

"I, Kratoe?" Galt would do no such thing. "I'll assign some men to escort your messenger to the pack outside. I see no reason to risk my own head by going out there."

"Very well. Assign someone. Anyone you can risk

losing. It's not important."

"When do you wish this done?"

"Right away. You," the Kratoe turned his head toward the aide at his side, the same asslicker Galt had threatened in the hallway. "You will go with Captain Galt. I will prepare a message for you to deliver to the dogs. A delaying tactic, if anything, but it will give us time. Speak directly with their king. Ask them plainly if peace is possible. Tell them that I desire it, and will give gifts to ensure it. And speak slowly, as I'm not certain the curs can speak the tongue."

"Nor I," Galt admitted.

The Kratoe's black veil fixed on the captain. "Then our meeting is over."

Galt agreed.

CHAPTER 19

In the pavilion of Two-Bite, the new ruler and War Skull of the gathered tribes, things were happening. Two-Bite sat upon a charred stump—exceptionally rare in this mountainous land—fashioned into the shape of a small throne, and thought. Reds from his tribe were in attendance, the strongest and most loyal to Two-Bite, either guarding the slit entrance to his war tent or standing at various points around the dark, hide walls. He'd sent the other chieftains away, wanting peace for a moment. The new War Skull's hand throbbed from where he'd bitten off his fingers and then burned the stumps in the fire pit, but the rush of assuming complete command over so many beastmen took much of the sting out his wounds. Unlike Blood Skull, Two-Bite knew that sitting and actually thinking brought just as good results as bashing away at something. Sometimes even better. It had been easy to claim the title of chieftain among his tribe. He already possessed a reputation large and fierce enough to deter all others. Once he announced his desire to be king, few questioned him. Two-Bite was well aware of the ferocious and unpredictable nature of red beastmen, and it gladdened him that he didn't have to kill any more than necessary to bring the rest in line.

It took less time to dispatch the other would-be heirs to Blood Skull's throne.

But now, it was time to sit and think, much as it irked Two-Bite. He much preferred smashing brains to using his own, or twisting bones in their sockets and listening to their music to deep thought. He sat on the stump and mulled about Foust's walls, forgoing any celebration of his new station. The other twenty-eight tribes welcomed his leadership, but Two-Bite was no mindless cur. He knew his power lay in his ability to bring down Foust and kill as many man-things as possible. If he did not do that, the tribes would turn on him, although that didn't worry Two-Bite in the least. He would do the same.

Foust's walls were tall and well-guarded. *Tall and well-guarded.* Two-Bite knew an answer to the puzzle was close… he simply had to mull more thoroughly.

A flurry of sound came from outside and two of the brutal red beastmen standing guard there turned and crowded the entrance, their hands on spiked mauls. One guard glanced out, allowing a ray of sunshine to penetrate the gloom, and then looked back at Two-Bite. He asked in a gruff, to-the-point tone if the War Skull wanted to speak with man-things.

This caused Two-Bite to hitch up the lips on his prominent jaws in puzzlement. He looked to his left, and eyed Turn-Bone, one of his longtime companions. Turn-Bone stood at the same height as the War Skull, but much thicker in body and limbs. Turn-Bone's bare, mottled-berry flesh bore innumerable burns, bruises, and scars. More than a few beastmen joked that the murderous red wore his innards on the outside, daring anyone to touch them. A man-thing had once struck Turn-Bone's skull with a mace, cracking it open, but Turn-Bone did not die. Instead, onlookers spoke of Turn-Bone yanking the man-thing off his feet by the neck and crotch and splitting his back over his knee. The beastman went on to kill half a dozen more man-things before finally wrenching the embedded mace from his cracked skull. In time, the bone healed, but the dent left there was perhaps Turn-Bone's proudest badge of honor.

However, Two-Bite admitted, Turn-Bone had been much more talkative before having his skull smashed in.

Now, the fearsome red gazed back at the War Skull and kept silent. His hooded eyes squeezed shut and then opened, Turn-Bone's way of offering no counsel.

Two-Bite *whuffed.* He thought of Turn-Bone as irreplaceable, but he realized he needed thinkers around him, as well as man-killers.

The War Skull told the reds at the entrance to allow the man-things in. If nothing else, Two-Bite had not eaten that morning.

A river of blacks and greens entered the tent, collecting in the center, but mindful of the fire pit. They stepped on the blackened bones and scorched gristle of man-things killed long ago, but stored and dried for food. Within the folds of the beastman rush, were seven man-things. Six wore armor that gleamed in the dim light, while the seventh wore only black robes.

Two-Bite leaned forward. This interested him. Clearly, the man-things in metal protected the little one, but none of them drew the swords at their waists. They carried shields bearing the mark of Foust, and presently they shoved the rounded pieces of metal and wood against the beastmen crowding them.

With a wave of his hand and a snarl, Two-Bite ordered his subjects to stand back. They did, but leered and growled at their armored guests.

The man-thing covered from head to toe in black robes stepped forward with his chin held high.

"The Kratoe of Foust sends his regards to you, King of Beastmen, and wishes to make his thoughts known to you, so that perhaps a… solution to this fight can be found."

Two-Bite's Brow knotted up. He looked at Axe-Jaw,

another trusted red who had killed as many man-things as any three beastman warriors and informed him of his wish. Axe-Jaw's sensitive muzzle had been split by a man-thing axe years ago, and it was a wonder that he even survived. His wound uneased more beastmen—as well as man-things—than Turn-Bone. Without a sound, the large henchman took two steps to the robed man and ripped the robes from his front in one savage swipe, revealing the hairless chest of a boy. The man-thing even shrieked like a child. Axe-Jaw's arms rippled with power as he gripped the throat of the man-thing, choking the voice from him. The blacks and greens surrounding the armored warriors surged in with an eager rumble, overwhelming the protectors and wrestling them to the ground. Axes, mauls, and spears used for prying open metal shells came into view.

Raising his voice, Two-Bite called them off.

The command made Axe-Jaw lift his head in confusion. Two-Bite told his followers his wishes, and the poised weapons relaxed. The mass parted, revealing the six man things pinned to the ground, their limbs held down by several beastmen. He commanded Axe-Jaw to release the man-thing in his clutches, which the red did immediately. Two-Bite liked that.

The man-thing in shredded robes looked back at his six guardians. Two-Bite could see his scrawny chest go in and out with fright. That pleased him. He concentrated. He had to use words, and it had been a long time since Two-Bite spoke in the man-thing tongue.

"I... king," Two-Bite growled, baring his teeth in a snarl. "I not... *stupid*. You *bow* to I."

Sobbing and blithering in fright, the man-thing looked at Two-Bite with red rimmed eyes and sniffed hard.

Two-Bite snarled a second time.

To punctuate the direness of the situation, Axe-Jaw produced a knife that had been sharpened almost to breaking. Once a thick piece of steel, it now appeared as a surgical tool, as menacing as a skinner's blade. Axe-Jaw placed the curve of the weapon under the man-thing's chin. This brought on another bout of terrified bawling, but the man-thing, puffing cheeks and clenching jaw, mindful of the blade tucked under his chin, slowly bent over at the waist and bowed as low as he could without toppling. When he rose, streams of snot bubbled from his nose.

Two-Bite nodded curtly, before scowling at the trapped man-thing.

"You *urf* tell Kratoe-man. Tell he, *I* Two-Bite. I king. He not w*uff*. Tell he, come here. Speak with Two-Bite. Face face. Then. Talk. Yes?"

The man-thing nodded.

"Kratoe-man come here," Two-Bite's brow knotted. "Bring man who… kill beastman king. Bring man who kill many beastman. Foust gate. Yes?"

Again, the man-thing nodded, but not too enthusiastically as Axe-Jaw still held his blade close.

Two-Bite stopped to think. He could not remember the man-word for good. In the end, he motioned to Axe-Jaw to release the man-thing. That gesture alone conveyed *good*.

"Go," Two-Bite commanded. "Come here… again. *Urf*. Kratoe-man. Together. Man who kill Beastman king. Come here… again. No stupid."

The man-thing bobbed his head frantically. With wide eyes, he glanced at the men still held on the floor.

"They… stay." Two-Bite growled, and snapped his teeth. The War Skull waved his arm and barked a command. The wall of beastmen parted all the way to the tent wall. Two-Bite barked again, and Axe-Jaw went ahead, fully aware that he was responsible for escorting the man-thing back to Foust. He marched through the folds of the opening and disappeared outside. Sunlight briefly stabbed the gloom.

The man-thing ran off after Axe-Jaw. The man-things

trapped on the ground struggled and cried out, speaking too fast for Two-Bite to follow, but he guessed at the meaning. He stood up, regal in posture, and stepped away from his charred stump of a throne. Two-Bite leaned over the trapped man-things. Their limbs stretched over the sand like animals about to be butchered.

Their armor fascinated him. He squatted, and tapped a claw off the shiny hardness. The prisoner held his breath. Such armor was not the way of the beastmen, but with the recent slaughter by the arrows of Foust, Two-Bite mulled over the idea that such a way could change. He tapped the chest of one man thing again, and then traced a derisive line down toward the waist, where he finally lifted the claw and stood. The reds, blacks, and greens all watched the new king with eyes full of curious, but deadly, intent.

Two-Bite made a decision. He would have his own force of armored beastmen. A force who carried shields much like the trapped enemies on the ground. He possessed weapon makers who could fashion armor to suit a beastman frame.

Two-Bite smirked. It was a good idea.

And suddenly, he knew how to overcome the walls of Foust. It would take time and strength, but those were two things he had. Foust had neither.

Two-Bite gestured to Turn-Bone, who had a hungry light in his eyes and held a great battle axe to his chest. The War Skull turned his attention back to the struggling man-things on the ground, spreadbefore him like a banquet.

"You." Two-Bite indicated his prisoners. "You… stupid."

Two-Bite chose a man-thing and pointed.

The bulk of Turn-Bone moved in, raising his axe.

CHAPTER 20

Borus woke with half a smile on his face. The spell was over, but only for as long as it took to drink something, wash his clothes, and eat more White Tar. He lounged on his belly, and felt one of Mage's arms around his waist. He no longer shooed her away when he was awake. He gently moved her arm and sat up, taking a breath. The straw needed to be changed again, and he scratched at bites from insects he never saw.

Borus moved around Mage, not wanting to break her spell, and went to the shite bucket. He relieved himself, the half-smile still on his features, no longer bothered by the smell from the receptacle. Finishing that, he went into the corridor, and caught a glimpse of a dark figure shuffling into one of the many rooms. He didn't see the face, didn't want to, but was instead pulled by the smell of the water. He drank his fill, and thought he should get the cup for Mage. There wasn't any food left, they had eaten it all long ago, and really, Borus wasn't hungry anyway. The less he spent on food, the more he had for White Tar. And there was plenty of water in the Hole, so that was fine.

He returned to the room, found the cup, and went to fill it. He didn't disturb Mage. She had been quite upset a week ago when she went to wake Klos from his spell to administer the next dosage, and discovered that her brother had died. Borus had seen a lot of death in his time, but other than Klos' weight loss and his eroded gums, he thought the man went peacefully. That was the way of the Tar. Peaceful. An extra piece of the weed took away any sadness Mage might have had for her brother's passing. Borus remembered what she said, when they both had lain down after Karast had taken the almost childlike frame of Klos away. She held on to him tightly, sniffing in the nape of his neck, her nose nudging through the scraggly beard growing there, and whispered, "Just us, now," and let the spell take her away. Borus knew what this place was now. He had searched for the Hole ever since his debilitating wounds had robbed him of his life.

He was going to die here.

But *his* way, while under the spell of the Tar. He could think of no way as peaceful. Perhaps passing away in one's sleep would suffice, but even then, sleep only sometimes held the ever-steady dream world brought on by the Tar. A dream where one could do whatever one pleased, as long as the Tar lasted. Borus thought of it as a wondrous place with the grim surface constraints of the Hole as a mere veiled gateway.

He contemplated when he wanted to cross over. He returned to the room with his cup, listening to Mage's breathing. Sometimes, if he woke before her, he could hear the rattle in her chest. It didn't last long, but it was there, and he wondered how long it would be before she left him. Borus sat down beside her, and reached out with his good hand, noticing the new trembling in his fingers. He ignored it. His hands didn't tremble while under the spell of the Tar. He brushed the brittle hair from the woman's face, and quietly gazed at her. He traced a finger from her thin eyebrow, down the side of her face, to her lips, caressing her flesh with the barest of touches. Her cheekbones were more pronounced now, and the valleys in her face were deeper, darker. His hand drifted down, to the cords in her neck, and he turned his palm over to run the back of his hand across her skin.

Mage's eyes twitched and opened. Her eyes had once been a deep, hypnotizing blue, Borus remembered, but now they were faded. She focused on him, dreamily, and Borus gazed back.

"Good morning," he said.

"Is it morning?"

"I don't know. Maybe."

"It feels later."

To this, Borus smiled.

"You're getting thin," Mage informed him.

"Am I?" He rubbed at his beard.

"Yes."

"Well, then, shall we eat?"

With that, Borus reached to his purse and made it jingle. It didn't make as much noise as a month ago, and Borus pursed his lips at the diminished rasp of metal on metal. With shaking fingers, he opened the drawstrings of the purse, and looked inside. A smile stretched across his face again.

"Is there any left?"

"Yes," he pulled out two gold coins. "Enough for a very good meal."

Mage blinked lazily and took a deep breath. "Will you get it?"

"If you like. Oh, here." Borus remembered the water in the cup, and brought to her face.

"Thank you." She struggled to get up. Her shirt fell away from her neck and Borus saw her protruding collarbone, and the deep valley around her neck. He glimpsed her ribs and breasts that were no longer full and inviting.

Mage pulled the loose cloth of her shirt, now much too big for her, up and around her chin. She didn't say a word, but one of her frail hands rose and closed around Borus' right hand with its missing fingers. He watched her drink, and she watched him over the rim of the cup. When she finished, she gasped, and looked content. Borus wondered who ever looked so content after a drink of water.

"Forgot how good it tastes."

"Me, too."

She leaned back on the pallet, keeping her eyes on the man taking care of her.

"Are you alright everywhere else?"

"You mean, if I need the shite bucket."

Borus cringed. He didn't mind using the term, but for some reason, he didn't like women using it, as if he refused to even consider that they voided like anyone else.

"I like that face you make," Mage said.

"What face?"

"That one. The one you made just now. When you hear something you don't like."

"I make a face?"

"You do."

"I do not." But Borus was smiling. Smiling came quicker to him these days. "I'll have you know that at one point in time, if I indeed 'made a face,' there were some very nervous people about."

"Ohhhhh," Her face softened into a little smirk. It occurred to Borus it was the first time he'd seen her smile.

"It's true."

"I don't believe you," she said in that odd off-key voice.

"Well, I can tell you…"

"Shhh."

"What?"

"It just occurred to me." She looked oddly uncomfortable. "I don't know your name."

"I think I told you."

"No… you didn't."

"After all this time? You've forgotten."

"No, my mind is fine. The rest of me…" She trailed

off. "But my mind is fine. You never told me. I told you mine."

"I'm sure you told me."

"You forgot my name?" she chided him, but didn't really seem to mean it.

"I didn't. You're teasing."

"You did."

"I…" Borus exhaled. She *was* teasing him—he knew she *liked* teasing him. "I have some things to buy."

"Bring me back a cooked chicken." Mage's voice took on a whiney tone.

"I'll bring you back something better."

"Something better than a cooked chicken?"

"Yes."

And he left her, before she could guess what it was and before she teased him further about his name. He was certain he'd introduced himself. Positive.

He left the little room, and made his way toward the back of the Hole, to the place where the hellion lurked. Borus remembered that he had disliked Sabo from the very beginning and over time, the dislike remained. The trouble was he could do very little about it.

When he approached the open door—he believed the door was always open—the mountain that was Karast blocked passage from inside. The black mask looked down on Borus and for a moment, he thought that Sabo's henchman wasn't about to move for him, but Karast stepped aside like some large, fleshy door.

Sabo lurked in a previously unseen alcove, and emerged from its shadows to stand alongside his table. He glanced at Karast and then gave his full attention to Borus.

"Welcome, my good man, welcome," he said in a deep mocking voice the one-eyed archer had come to detest. "What shall it be today?"

"This," Borus answered and placed his last two coins on the table.

Sabo pursed his lips, scooped up the money, and made

it disappear. He rubbed his shaven head. "It looks like your stay with us will be at an end soon."

"Maybe."

"Allow me to express my regret about the death in your room," Sabo spread his hands. "These things happen sometimes. The Tar is a strong weed to handle, and I'm afraid that all too often we get the lesser people coming here who stay, and simply don't wake up after a while."

"What did you do with Klos?"

"Hm?"

"The death in my room," Borus clarified. "What did you do with him?"

"Oh, Karast took him."

"Where?"

Sabo fixed him with laughing eyes. "Where all of the dead go, dear man."

A memory returned to Borus, one that he had pressed under his consciousness by force of will. It was of being mistaken for dead and cast into a pit full of corpses. Borus remembered waking with a dead man's fingers in his mouth, and limbs piled on top of him. He remembered moments of insanity, as he squirmed, clawed, and kicked his way through a rotting tunnel of flesh, to air. He remembered the soldiers assigned to burying the dead, and what they must have thought upon seeing a bloody carcass rise from the mass grave. Shortly thereafter, he met up with He-Dog and Balless.

Sabo appeared to be on the verge of laughing in his face. Seeing that Borus did not share the joke, he quieted, shrugged, and brought the one-eyed customer his White Tar: two long weeds, dark and resembling bamboo stalks. They caught Borus' attention. Having bought what he came for, Borus turned to go.

"By the by," Sabo said. "Karast tells me that the woman you're with isn't sounding too healthy. She has the death rattle."

Borus stopped on the threshold.

"When she passes on, Karast will be there to remove her."

"Don't touch her," Borus quietly warned.

Sabo hesitated and looked at his guard with an amused expression.

But then Borus, the champion of old who once had not cared if he lived or died or what crumbled around him, surfaced in a flash of wickedness, daring either of them to say anything more. The appearance of such a specter silenced the merchants of White Tar, and sent a wave of tension through the chamber, thick enough to make Karast ready himself to grab his axe.

It passed, and Borus left them to wonder who exactly the one-eyed man was.

He returned to his room in the Hole, and swept aside the curtain. He sat on the pallet of old straw and gazed down at Mage.

"I don't see any chicken," she said, making him smile. "Did you get me anything?"

"I did."

"Good."

"Here." With that, he fed her the weed, holding her gaze with his own as she chewed and swallowed. He did the same.

"It's the last."

"Is it?"

"Yes," he informed her.

Mage slowly blinked. "Good."

Borus reached down and adjusted her hair, pushing it back from her eyes. Her brow furrowed.

He lay down beside her, snuggled in a little closer than he might have, and waited for his spell to begin.

CHAPTER 21

One month and five days.

From the time they woke up in Sergius' infirmary, to when Bowlak and his louts periodically visited and threatened them with leers and jokes, to the many days afterward, He-Dog and his companions woke staring at the same ceiling, eating the same bread and broth, and eying the same women folk Sergius had warned them from the beginning not to touch. They woke up, voided when necessary, had their dressings changed, and listened to the usually half-naked healer inform them that "you'll be dead in the morning." Until this day, when He-Dog's bandages came off and stayed off, when the stitches were removed and only pink remained. He flexed and rotated his shoulder and nodded at the feel. It was stiff, but he saw the wound in his shoulder had healed. He-Dog's jaw felt much better than it had a month ago, but Sergius still cautioned him to eat only soft food for a while. His bruises and cuts had healed completely, and he found new and interesting scars decorating his person.

Sitting on his straw pallet, the place he had spent most of his time for the last month, he looked at Sergius with a question on his rough face.

"I think you're fine to leave," the healer informed him. "Just heed what you are doing. That's all I ask."

He-Dog rolled his eyes. That wasn't going to happen and they both knew it. He-Dog's mind had bordered close on insanity in the first week alone, and it was only the short trips to the window to peer out that staved off outbursts of violence. That and the ringing in his ears which had caused him to black out at times. The ringing had also disappeared in the last week or so.

He looked over at Balless. His companion's little piggish eyes looked back at him: black balls set deep in a thick skull. His wounds had healed up even faster, but for the last few weeks, Balless had taken up the role of sole guardian, especially during the night, in case Bowlak and his friends decided to visit unannounced. The guardsman hadn't returned in more than a week, however, which disappointed He-Dog. He supposed he would just have to go find the man.

Chop studied He-Dog from his pallet as well, his leather mask on his leg. The melted features of the man stared at He-Dog for a long time, and he didn't know if Chop grinned at him or grimaced. His wounds were the worst of all, but his broken arm and eye socket had mended, his chest and leg wound healed, as were the numerous other nicks and scratches. Chop's head angled to one side in a question.

He-Dog guessed he knew it. "Aye that," he breathed. "We leave today."

Standing in front of He-Dog, Sergius regarded them all with a little smile. "Stay away from trouble. The siege is still on, I'll have you know. And there was some news yesterday."

"What?"

"Ah," Sergius said. "They sent a messenger to speak with the beastman king. No one knows what it was about, but no doubt they talked about ending the siege peacefully. The beastmen sent the Kratoe's man back, frightened to the edge of sanity from what I heard. No one knows for sure what was discussed, but later on, the beastmen pushed a catapult to the front and bounced the bodies of the messenger's guards off the battlements. Not something to wake up to, I tell you."

Sergius eyed them all fondly. "Wait for a moment." He went to the dark doorway of the chamber. He called out to his daughters, Hesel and Samil, and looked back at his patients. Moments later, the women appeared carrying clothing. They went to each of them, handing out shirts and trousers.

"They aren't new, but they're clean. They should fit you. And I'll burn those rags you've been wearing."

He-Dog held up the dark shirt, and nodded approval at Sergius. He stripped off his old clothes, not caring if the two daughters saw him naked or not, and quickly got into the fresh ones. He noted that the daily meals of soup had left him just a little trimmer. The clothes fit, and he pulled out his war braid from the back.

"Is that a thank-you?" Sergius asked.

He-Dog frowned and grunted an affirmative. He looked at the others. Balless squeezed into a white shirt that bulged about his arms, but the trousers fit well enough. Chop looked almost civil, except for his ruined face. He covered that with his black mask.

"I only wish I could give you weapons of some kind," Sergius said. "Once you leave here, Bowlak and his lads will eventually find you. I don't want to think what will happen then."

"Neither do I," He-Dog said under his breath. "Where might we find them?"

"You mean to find them?"

He-Dog reached back and adjusted the long braid at the back of his skull. He didn't answer.

"Go to the main gates, I would imagine. They'll be there sooner or later."

He-Dog made a fist and shrugged his shoulder. Loud

cracks popped the air as his joints loosened. He had battle rust, of that he had no doubt. They all had it, but he knew how to remedy it.

"Good fortune to you," He-Dog said to Sergius. It was as much gratitude he was capable of displaying. He eased himself over the wall.

Chop walked by the healer, and gave a solemn dip of his masked head. Then he too was out the window.

"There is a door, by the bye," Sergius muttered.

Balless stood eying and smiling mischievously at the sisters, neither of whom shied away from him. It was always the same for him, cold and fearful in the beginning, and more than willing in the end. Even He-Dog knew that. He bowed to the two daughters, making them giggle.

Sergius frowned at the big man, who nodded at him and left each of the daughters with a wink.

"Thank you," Balless said when he reached the window. His limbs groaned as he fitted his way through, but he stood on the other side.

Sergius and his daughters watched the three men leave.

They had just turned the corner, when the scowl deepened on He-Dog's face. He could only stomach so much tender care when he had to think about smashing something. Free once again, his first thoughts were about finding the men who threatened them. Then something to eat. And drink.

"What now?" Balless scratched his arm.

"We go to the walls."

"The walls," Balless repeated and nodded. "What then?"

"Find this one called Bowlak."

That brightened Balless' face. "He has weapons. Armor."

He-Dog looked over his shoulder at the larger man, and Balless grinned back. They were alive, healed, and hungry.

Weapons and armor made no difference.

They moved through streets full of people appearing at their wits' end. Desperation filled many faces, and those who didn't look desperate were either too sick or drunk to care. People lay in the gutters, baked by the sun and dead-looking. Here and there, He-Dog smelled meat cooking. It heartened him to think there was something still left to cook and drink in the city of Foust. None of them had any money or valuables other than the clothing on their back and their boots. He-Dog and Balless had been in similar situations before and survived the best way they could.

By gambling.

Fortune, He-Dog knew, only waited to be grabbed by those who sought it.

He paused in wide roads only long enough to get his bearings. The walls of the city were high and easy to see through the building rooftops. Once he spied them, He-Dog headed in their direction, leaving Balless and Chop to follow.

It was time to take stock of the situation.

Foust's soldiers became increasingly numerous as they got closer to the gates, and on the final street, wagons filled with spears, arrows, and barrels of oil came into view. Men fussed over the supplies, and the newly released trio could see that the battlements were still impressively ready for war. In the courtyard, large catapults stood ready at a moment's chop to release a load of rock. Ballistae dotted the walls' heights, as did a fence of archers and spearmen. At points on the ramparts, crews struggled with barrels and bushels of supplies, moving toward the higher towers. Below, under rough planked roofs, the clanging and beat of an armorer's hammer rang out. Weaponsmiths repaired and fashioned new tools for killing. A scent of horseshite wafted across the noses of the three men, and they knew stables were nearby. Groups of soldiers marched here and there carrying out orders, and other groups lounged and relaxed under shelters with wide black roofs to keep the murderous sun off their heads. Some drank water from deep barrels, and others ate what appeared to be dried meat.

"They're ready for whatever, eh?" Balless asked, craning his neck.

"Hm," He-Dog grunted, squinting when he took in the height of the walls. He looked at a set of steps and saw a post of warriors at the base as well as at the top. He spotted two more sets of stairs guarded in the same fashion. The number of guards told him that the commanders took their task seriously, which relieved He-Dog. There was no worse feeling than that of leaving one's life in the hands of idiots, and he had served under his share.

The smithy attracted He-Dog's attention. He walked toward the low building with its wide doors thrown open, taking in a round and heavy looking man with his face covered in a sheen of sweat, and wearing the black apron of his profession. The smithy hammered a red sword on a venerable anvil, and sparks jumped with each connection. Behind him, three other men and a boy on the cusp of manhood moved about at various tasks. He-Dog eyed a long rack with blades of various sizes, and a longing made his chest ache.

"Bit expensive right now," Balless said from his side.

That didn't bother He-Dog. "If we're here long enough and there's a fight, they'll be quick to give us arms."

"That might mean being pressed into service." Balless scratched at the grooves and scars of his chin. "I don't want that."

"Nor I," He-Dog admitted.

They stood for a long while, gazing at the men working in the shade but sweating as if exposed to Saimon's fires. Across the way, a wagon full of kindling stopped in front of a stall. The driver got down from his seat and patted both horses that had labored with the load. He disappeared around a corner, and He-Dog noticed Chop sizing up the wood in the wagon. The masked man left his companions and made his way to the rear of the wagon. He stooped, and selected a long piece of kindling, roughly the length of a short sword. Holding it at arm's length, Chop rooted through the rest of the load, searching for something more.

"You there," the driver called as he emerged from the stall. "What you got there? Eh? That's not for the grabbing."

Chop stepped back from the wagon, holding two lengths of wood. The driver stopped before him and waited for an answer. When one didn't come, the man waved a dismissive hand and shrugged. "Keep it. Things aren't that bad yet."

With that, he climbed back into the driver's seat and urged his horses forward.

Chop watched him go before turning his attention back to his wooden swords. He clacked them together, and approved of the solid sound. He stood in the middle of the yard with the sun beating down on his black mask. Soldiers and workers moved around him until he was a rock in a stream.

He stretched out his arms, and held both lengths of wood.

"You! Swordsman!" a voice called, causing Chop to pause, his weapons before him. "Swordsman! Show us something!"

Both He-Dog and Balless turned at the voice, and saw a group of soldiers lounging in the shade of one of the open shelters around a water barrel. Some of the men sat hunched on benches, some drank from wooden cups. All wore what appeared to be the standard armor of soldiers of Foust, a chainmail coat with steel plates attached, and wide shoulder pauldrons. The heavy protection made them look formidable.

He-Dog knew looks weren't everything. He sensed a wager on the wind.

"Come on lad, swing those sticks!" a soldier bawled.

"Perhaps he'll beat out a tune for us?" called another.

"Do something else I spear those pieces up your hole!"

Chop faced the soldiers, crossing his weapons in front of him.

He-Dog approached the group, slowly as to not frighten them. He glanced at Chop and wondered if the man had spotted him yet or not. He scratched at his war braid and hoped the masked man wouldn't start anything until after the wagers.

"I know that man," He-Dog declared when he was close enough. "And I tell you, with those sticks he's three men to anyone here."

The gathering of soldiers regarded He-Dog.

"He's three men eh?" one man shouted back.

"He looks like a punce to me."

"Why does he wear the mask?"

"Gurry! The lad's a piece of rot, is what he is!"

He-Dog frowned as he felt the sweat stain his shirt. Heat. How he hated it.

"Who cares to make a wager?" he pressed.

"A what?"

"A wager, you stupid shagger, a wager." These men were not the sharpest. All the better. He had their attention now.

"How much?" one man shouted.

"I'll bet five gold cutaros my man can take any challenger," He-Dog dared, gambling with coin he did not have. "Five."

That quieted the lot of them.

"S'lot of money," one soldier muttered.

"Three cutaros then," He-Dog offered.

"Still a lot."

"Two then." He-Dog hadn't expected to get the *cheapest* lot. "For any man to take my lad."

One soldier brayed a laugh and stepped forward. He drew his broadsword and took a few practice swings, splitting the air. "I'll take that wager." He slapped an open face helm on his head.

He-Dog nodded back. A bite. The fish were game after all. He looked at Chop, standing as he was in the harsh sun, still striking a pose as if someone were about to paint him. Irritation made He-Dog scowl.

"Done."

Balless edged close to Chop, and spoke. The black mask dipped in agreement.

"Flat of the blade is it?" the man with the sword asked, gathering a round shield.

He-Dog thought about it. "As you will."

"Doubt it'll stay that way," one soldier chuckled to his friends.

"First blood," another said loudly. He-Dog agreed.

"Prepare to have your balls paddled my little git!" another soldier shouted gleefully, as if addressing a child.

The challenger walked out to meet Chop, and Balless backed away a few steps.

"Come on then, you black leather topper," the soldier urged Chop to attack. "It's too hot—"

Chop flew at the man like a rabid dog breaking free of a strained leash. A series of loud crashes, the wooded clubs connecting with armor, and the Foust soldier was on his back, dazzled and dazed.

The seated soldiers laughed and cried out in glee. They pointed and insulted their downed companion. Some even doubled over in laughter, placing hands to knees.

Chop stood over the fallen man, poised to thrust one or both of his weapons into the soldier. The defeated soldier raised a hand in surrender.

"Fast he is," someone cried.

"Aye that! A proper hell pup!"

The laugher subsided, and another soldier prepared himself and walked forward, his shield and sword ready. He shook his head and grinned broadly.

"Wait a moment," He-Dog said to him.

"Two gold on my head, you ugly cow kiss," the warrior

shot back.

He-Dog scowled. He wanted Chop to take his time with this one.

The new opponent inched forward, his sword held at low guard. Chop backed a step with both lengths of wood pointed at his larger foe. The Foust soldier rushed him. Chop blurred forward, side-stepping at the last second and clanging one club into the front of the warrior's helm. The blow stunned the man for the split second it took to smash him from behind, sending him into the dirt.

Victorious once more, Chop pounced on the man. He made a show of it and slowly tapped the tip of one club off the base of the fallen soldier's skull.

Behind him, the first warrior got to his feet and adjusted his helm. Anger clouded his face, and without warning, he raised his blade overhead and ran at Chop from behind. But the smaller man ducked, spun, and brought both clubs across the knees of his oncoming attacker, sending him crashing to the ground.

He-Dog looked at Balless, who covered his cringing face with a hand.

"Alright," He-Dog grumped. "I won—"

But three other warriors, no longer joking, detached themselves from the lounging pack. The watching soldiers were no longer laughing. Seriousness had spoiled their fun, as surely as the sun overhead would rot meat. Faces once red with laughter were now drawn and tense.

He-Dog saw them approach and shook his head. "Wait a moment—"

"Stand aside else we paddle your balls." One of the men warned him, drawing his sword and pointing it at He-Dog. "The fight's with that one, and that one alone. For now…"

He-Dog stood down, shaking his head in exasperation.

Chop left the fallen soldiers in the dirt. He backed up two steps, black mask unmoving as he sized up the new challengers. He rolled his shoulders, his head, and shook out his arms. Pops and cracks echoed through the air.

He attacked.

Two men crashed to the ground within heartbeats. The third hesitated long enough that Chop inserted one club between the lad's legs, tripping him, while batting his helm soundly with the other and laying him out flat.

The black masked man stood among five soldiers of Foust and whirled about, clubs at the ready.

A crowd began to form.

An uncertain Balless appeared at He-Dog's side and whispered. "We won, right?"

Even as the five soldiers groaned and struggled to get to their feet, the last of their group, seven fresh men with scowls of murderous determination entered the fray. They spread out in a circle, mindful of their companions on the ground and wary of the black masked hub at the center. One onlooker jeered at the Foust soldiers and the obvious unfairness of the match. Two more swore at the men, and the air scorched with insults.

"He's only *one* man, you stupid asslickers!"

"Are these the tits we've guarding our wall?"

"Why don't you call down the other fifty, you motherless, ungodly punce?"

One of the Foust soldiers screamed and charged the man in the black mask. That one scream prompted the pack to attack from all sides and the ring surrounding Chop collapsed inward with a roar.

What happened next would be the talk of many dinner tables later that same evening.

Chop knocked out the first man within range, snapping the point of his club flush into the charging soldier's nose, smashing it like a hard grape.

The second and third men had their ankles shattered, and went down in a stunned huff.

The fourth man, only a second behind the pair, froze in shock at how quickly his companions had fallen and had two clubs jammed up under his chin with enough force to take him off his feet. Before the fourth man hit the ground, Chop whirled under a blade and pushed his attacker off balance. He parried another sword with his club and a chunk of wood spun off into the air. Chop threw the ruined piece into the eyes of a fifth man, and stabbed the tip of his remaining club into the gut of the sixth. The man doubled over in pain and Chop brought his weapon down across the back of his helm, slamming his foe to the ground in a cloud of dust. He cracked the fifth man square across the jaw, shattering it and dropping him like a stone.

The seventh man rushed in and stabbed, but Chop nimbly stepped to the outside of the thrust and smashed the outstretched arm, breaking it in one blow.

Three of the original attackers struggled to their feet too slowly as the black masked man turned on all three in succession, battering each of them about the head and driving them back to the ground. Off-key notes pierced the air.

Another warrior stood, screaming his rage, and Chop stalked him. The Foust guard cast aside his shield and brought his sword up two-handed to high guard. "I'll kill you," he breathed, white froth coating his lips. "I'll kill you, I'll kill you, I'll—" He charged.

Chop gracefully ducked under the falling sword, released his club, and rammed both fists into his attacker's throat. With a horrible choked cry, the last Foust man dropped his weapon, dropped to his knees, and clutched his throat as he toppled over.

Retrieving his club once more, Chop slipped into guard and surveyed the mass of bodies about his feet. Some writhed, grasping their legs and arms, others remained still. Yet another man tried to rise to his knees and fell over again, dragging his face across the ground as one hand reached out for help.

The ring around the contest roared, startling both He-Dog and Balless.

A human tide enveloped the black masked man, and not even the magnetism of Chop could hold them at bay. Cheers went up, and the mob hoisted the club-wielding man and heaved him into the air.

Balless and He-Dog exchanged looks. The corners of He-Dog's mouth cranked upward in a bad grin, and Balless matched him. It was the story of their lives. When their fortune was bad, it was terrible.

But when it was good…

"Enough!" A voice cried from above and all heads turned. The mob still held Chop aloft, and even he struggled to see who spoke. Coming down from the battlements with a line of soldiers behind him was an officer, one who didn't appear particularly happy.

"Here come the other fifty!" A voice from the crowd shouted, and the people roared with laughter.

Faces raised and squinting against the sun, He-Dog and Balless; elation wilted. Neither of them wanted to spend time in a dungeon so soon after being released from one. He-Dog even had the inclination to point fingers at Chop.

"Put that man down," the approaching officer bellowed. He-Dog remembered the man's face. A captain, he was certain. Soldiers fanned out behind the man.

He heard the name Krajin rippling through the gathered crowd. *A fat captain*, flashed through He-Dog's mind, sizing up the man's girth and the thick moustache hiding his mouth. Krajin wore the same armor as the twelve men lying senseless on the ground, and his dark eyes pushed the mass of people back with one glare. The crowd deposited Chop before the captain, offering him up like a chunk of meat.

He-Dog and Balless stood their ground, as did Chop, whose black mask shone in the sun.

"I know you men." Krajin branded them with ferocious eyes. "You came here weeks ago. Been on the mend, have you?"

"Aye, that," He-Dog answered, wary of the captain.

Krajin walked to him, stepping over the soldiers only starting to regain consciousness. The captain faced He-Dog and glared at him. Not impressed, He-Dog glared back.

"You're a hard one," Krajin said, not relenting in the least. "It takes a dangerous kind of fool to do what you did to get into Foust. I should expect no less. What are you doing here?"

"Hoping to see what's over those walls," He-Dog said.

"Those walls," Balless repeated by his side.

Krajin turned his glare on the larger man, who merely grinned.

"Beastmen," Krajin told them. "I'm not holding any secrets. I should be asking you about what you saw when you came here a month ago, but I expect the answer would be the same. Beastmen. There's an army out there. The only thing that's changed is that they haven't come at us since you arrived. Interesting, that."

"Why, do you think?"

"I don't share my ideas with mercenaries." Krajin scowled. "I might make a bargain of some sort, but I don't think you have anything of worth."

He-Dog smirked, exposing his own winning smile. "Take a look around you, Captain. Or did you just miss the fight? Want to see it again?"

"Aye, again?" Balless repeated.

Krajin did not answer right away. He stood and simmered, no doubt wondering if he should imprison the three men. He-Dog waited for the command. It wouldn't be the first time he and his boys were tossed into a dungeon on someone's whim.

"No," Krajin answered, surprising He-Dog. "But why did you fight my men?"

"A wager, Captain *sar.*"

Krajin's soldiers aided one of the fallen to his feet. The captain spotted him. "You there, is this true? The fight was a wager?"

"Aye, sar," the man groaned. "Two gold cutaros if we could best that one there." He indicated Chop with a slow nod.

"Two gold *each*," He-Dog added. "Someone forgot the rules of the contest and made the match a little more. A little rough your lads are, Captain."

Behind He-Dog's shoulder, Balless shook his head in exaggerated disgust.

"A wager," Krajin breathed, the air coming out of him like steam from a kettle. He broke away from the three mercenaries and regarded his beaten men. "One man did this to twelve of mine."

He-Dog said nothing, but Balless loomed over his shoulder, nodding *he did.*

"You worthless lot of gurry," Krajin hissed, color erupting in his cheeks. He took deep breaths and He-Dog knew the man wanted nothing more than to curse his men as long and loud as possible, just as a prelude to the real punishment.

Krajin turned to Chop, who stood silently. "Well fought. I didn't hear the wager from above, but I saw the fight. If you ever wish to earn some coin, come see me. I'd have you train the rest of my lads."

Chop voiced a mangled reply and Krajin looked at He-Dog.

"What he said was," He-Dog took up, but in truth he didn't know what Chop was trying to say either, "he already made some coin here this day. Will your boys honor their wagers?"

"Saimon's blue pisspot, they will," Krajin muttered, visibly controlling his anger. He placed his fists on his hips and ordered the twelve to pay their lost wager, and right away. One by one, those who were able to walk faced Chop and delivered the coin owed to him. "All of you," Krajin declared when he saw some of the men hesitate.

"And a coin more for blackening the city's name," the captain commanded. Some of the defeated men's jaws dropped, as they looked at Chop.

He-Dog wondered why they did that. It wasn't his problem.

In embarrassed silence, the men paid the victor his winnings. When finished, He-Dog motioned to his companions that it was time to leave.

"Don't try this again," Krajin warned them. "I might not be so forgiving."

He-Dog didn't bother answering the captain. He knew better than to tempt a fuming officer with a sizeable force at his back. Chop did well against twelve louts, but He-Dog had no doubts what their chances would be against so many, and he didn't want to spend another month in some infirmary.

"Spend it wisely," Krajin told them.

When the three companions were out of sight of the captain, Balless asked, "What are we going to spend it on?"

He-Dog looked at Balless and Chop, the shock clear on his battered face. "You have to ask? After a month of soup?"

CHAPTER 22

In a walled city whose troops were next to worthless, weaponless and without armor, hated by at least two factions of guardsmen, and surrounded by an army of beastmen, He-Dog, Balless, and Chop did the only thing they thought might lift their spirits.

Drink.

And eat, at least a little.

For when one thinks one is about to perish, one will throw coin at just about anything.

They had found the alehouse in the early afternoon. The keeper told them he had precious little in the way of food, as there was a siege on and all, and much of his pantry had been taken by the soldiers and distributed to Foust's populace. He did have roasts left, and few vegetables, but they would be costly. As for drink, have no worries, he informed the three, for he had casks of ale still untouched under his house, and he would rather sell them to paying customers than leave it for the beastmen. If it came to that.

He-Dog didn't care. He would've paid in *mothers* for one roast and called it a bargain. As it was, the three of them feasted on two large chunks of cooked beef and a portion of potatoes and carrots as well. They took a table away from the main floor of the alehouse, ate like it was their first real food in weeks (which it was), and drank like it would be their last opportunity. They figured they only had enough gold for food, as the price to be outfitted with weapons and armor was still beyond their means. For that, He-Dog figured Chop would have to fight a lot more than just twelve men, and now that people knew about him, he doubted Chop would ever get such odds again.

Balless, however…

He-Dog gave up on the notion. One look at Balless, he figured, would be enough to scare off any sizeable wager. Into early evening they drank, and for a while, paid little heed to what transpired beyond the walls of the alehouse. Chop had rolled up his black mask to his upper lip, and both He-Dog and Balless had become drunk enough to include the man in direct conversation.

Gathered around a table filled with empty platters and pitchers, they continued to drink until the blue sky outside turned orange with gashes of red and purple, and night chased it all from sight.

"What well… wesh do… tomarra?" Balless drooled, his face down on the table, lapping up the ale spilled from his wooden mug.

His eyes hooded and glassy, He-Dog looked across the room and said, "Wha?"

But Balless had gone back to lapping at the spill. He came to a large portion on the wooden table, and decided it was best to place both lips to it, which he did in an unsteady fashion, and *slurped*, loud enough to startle a nearby Chop.

Balless leaned back and would have fallen onto the floor if Chop hadn't reached out and stopped him.

"Thank you." The big man winked fondly at the masked one.

"What did you say?" He-Dog wanted an answer.

"I said… I forgot."

Chop moaned loudly, and slapped his hand against the thick wood of the table. He-Dog frowned at him for rattling the table and gathered his mug closer to his chest. It was like gold now.

"Like gold," he slurred, glaring at Chop. "Slap another table if you wan…" He exhaled, puffing out his cheeks and took a deep breath. "Woo," he said afterwards. He believed he'd drowned his brain this time.

"Time to dance!" Balless exclaimed and drained his mug.

He-Dog made a face and slowly shook his head. "Why… must you… do that evra time we drink? Evra time."

Balless suddenly appeared quite concerned with this. "Dunno." He looked around the alehouse, and belched like thunder. "I don't see any women in here."

"They would only… turn you away."

Balless grinned. "Not so bad… in my state."

He-Dog agreed with that.

"Need more… of this," Balless pointed to the empty pitcher. "Gimme some gold."

He-Dog reached to his trouser pocket and brought forth a small mountain, roughly a third the size of when they'd started. He separated three coins and pushed them to his companion.

"Don't get the black," He-Dog warned him. "Get the gold."

Balless' brow scrunched up.

"The gold ale. Get… get that." He-Dog took another deep breath. "Don't—not the black … ale. Can't stomach… that shite."

Balless nodded. "Gooooold," he stressed. He stood up and swayed to the right, almost landing on Chop who sat next to him, but caught himself at the last moment. He stood up straight, and nodded confidently at the others.

Chop moaned and muttered something through his mangled lips, and He-Dog believed he understood the man perfectly. "I know. .. but I can't stomach… the thought. Of *wasting* it coming back here."

The masked man nodded.

Balless made his way to the bar like a mountain on two very unsteady legs. He ordered two pitchers of golden ale, and stood teetering at the bar until the barkeep brought them. Returning to the table was a trick unto itself, but Balless performed it with little spillage. He placed both pitchers on the table and then headed for the door. He-Dog eyed him with an expression of drunken puzzlement.

"Need to piss." Balless chuckled.

He-Dog pointed to the doorway that led out back to the latrines.

"Need fresh air, too."

He-Dog gave a rare chuckle at that. "Watch yourself then. Bowlak. And stay out of the alleyways."

Balless would be careful. His mind giggled. *Careful taking a piss*. He passed the few patrons in the place and stepped into the street. Not so fresh air buffeted his senses, and he suddenly longed to be free of the city and all of its stone. His shoulder brushed the brick and wood of the alehouse, and he walked along it until it was no longer there, whereupon he turned a corner. *Alleyway*, Balless thought, and peered into the darkness ahead, like a narrow cave. Seeing nothing and feeling the urge to relieve himself intensify, Balless entered the shadows. He faced a wall and fumbled with the front of his trousers. He freed himself, and rumbled in relief as he released the ale his bladder had collected. He leaned forward and placed a heavy forearm against the building and his forehead against that. *Piss*. Even the of the word sounded nice to Balless. Just relax and *piss*. After a few moments, he finished, tucked himself away, and turned to leave.

And stopped in his tracks. A dwarf watched and waited for him at the mouth of the alley. Balless blinked and focused. Not a small dwarf. A boy. He approached the figure, shadow covering much of the lad's face, and saw the long hair.

"I'm hungry," a small voice said.

A girl, Balless' mind corrected him. The warrior blinked and stooped over, inspecting the face of the little one. She was tiny, dirty looking, and wearing filthy clothes. Dark eyes looked into his as her little mouth moved in fear. At least, it looked like fear to Balless.

"Are you scared?" Balless asked.

She nodded.

"Why?"

She didn't answer right away and Balless thought she might be unfit in the head. He stared and looked away once to belch.

"I'm… I'm hungry," the little one said again.

"Issat all you can say?"

"No."

"Well then, how old are you?"

She held up a hand, fingers spread wide

"And you're here?" Balless' face opened in wonder. He gestured at the streets. "It's dangerous!"

The little one looked at her feet, and Balless could see the straight part in her long, dark hair.

"I know, but I told my mother I would—I would look for something to eat."

"You're hungry." Balless clarified.

She nodded emphatically.

"Well, I can do something for that," Balless said, and gave her a little smile. "You wait here, alright?"

"Alright," she said, twisting uncertainly this way and that.

"Hungry," Balless said to himself as he staggered back to the alehouse. When was the last time he'd been hungry? He couldn't remember. Even in the infirmary he'd had meals, eating his share of the soup and bread. Before that, there were times in the field when he had nothing in his gullet, but he couldn't remember exactly why he'd had nothing to eat. Regardless, that a five year old didn't have anything and roamed the streets asking strangers for hand-outs did not sit well with his drunken consciousness.

He walked into to his companions' table and stood there for a moment, politely waiting for He-Dog to finish a tale. He didn't wait long.

"Whass wrong?" He-Dog inquired.

"I need some gold."

He-Dog appeared to think about it before handing over three gold coins from the dwindling pile on the table. "This alright?" he asked without argument.

"I think."

"Where you going now?"

"Buy some food," Balless answered and didn't wait for another question. If anything, Balless thought himself to be a man of action. *Simple* actions, as he left the more difficult things to He-Dog, but action nonetheless. He stopped at the bar and got the barkeep's attention.

"What do you have left to eat?"

"Not much, I sold it to you men," the barkeep answered, confusion knotting his face.

"You have anything back there?"

The barkeep looked at him. "How much do you have?"

Balless showed him his gold. The barkeep took two coins, and exhaled through his nose. "Wait here."

"Put it in a cloth bag," Balless said to the man's back as he disappeared into the kitchen. He looked around the bar, seeing a few hard men eying him over their mugs. Balless smiled at them all, sending most of the men to look at something else.

The barkeep returned a moment later with a small cloth sack. He thrust it at Balless. "That's all I can spare."

Balless peeked into the bag. There were two apples in there. A small chunk of cheese, half a loaf of bread, and a small cut of what appeared to be ham. He grunted with approval and left the bar, the bag held in his scarred hand. He found the little one lurking around the corner. Balless wrinkled his nose in distaste. The alley reeked of piss.

He squatted before her and held out the bag. "Here." Her eyes sparkled as she peered inside the bag. When she looked up, her mouth opened but no sound came forth. She looked thankful to Balless, and that was enough for him.

"Take that…" He nodded at the bag, "back to your mother. And here." He handed her the last coin. "Take this to your mother. Buy what you can with it. Alright?"

"Alright," the little girl replied.

"Good. Off you go then."

She hesitated for a moment, and realizing their business was done, she bolted off down the street. People watched her as she ran past. Balless stood up as she disappeared among the few people still out, and felt glad that he was able to help. He hoped they made that little bit of food last a long time. He didn't know where *his* next meal would be coming from. He did know where his next drink was coming from, and that knowledge brightened his mood considerably, for what was tomorrow if not today? That thought made him feel even better. It wasn't often he had good thoughts and he told himself to remember that bit of wisdom so he could tell the others.

He turned to go and found a group of soldiers watching him.

Balless straightened and did a quick count. There were only four of them, which was fine by him, but he didn't see the one called Bowlak. Unfortunate. He hoped that was a problem they would solve soon.

"You there," the lead man said. "You're presence is requested by the Kratoe of Foust. You will come with me."

"The Kratoe?"

"The Kratoe."

"Oh."

"Where are the others?"

Balless peered closely at the man. "Who're you?"

"My name's Galt, *Captain* Galt."

"Oh."

Galt glared at him, and Balless knew what he wanted. "Ah, they're inside, drinking. We're all drinking. Heeee."

The captain kept silent, and Balless got the distinct impression that the officer wasn't particularly impressed with him. That was fine with Balless. He was used to it.

One of the guards behind the captain turned and savagely pushed a passerby away from him. The soldier made to strike the passer-by, who stumbled away raising a hand to his face. Balless saw it. He didn't like men who heaved their weight around for no reason.

"I'll get them," he said, no longer thinking about hungry little five-year olds. His feeling of well-being faded.

"Yes, do that," he heard the captain's voice from behind him.

CHAPTER 23

As Galt escorted He-Dog, Balless, and Chop to Foust's inner keep, two others woke from their last spell bought with their final coin. Within moments of each other, they opened their eyes to darkness, forehead pressed against forehead, and gazed upward at a dark ceiling. Moans could be heard from beyond the curtained entrance to their room. Someone wasn't pleased about something. Borus discovered that, during their Tar-induced dream, he had become entwined with Mage. He made no immediate move to untangle his limbs from hers. Neither did she.

"Good morning," Mage whispered in her squeaky voice.

Borus smiled at the sound. He had come to like it. "Well… morning, anyway."

"What's there to eat?"

"Nothing."

She exhaled through her nose and Borus felt it on his face.

"Just a moment." He felt for his purse. He found it and confirmed what he suspected. Empty. Probably for some time now. The sad thing was he couldn't recall when he'd spent it all. His hand rose to rub one side of his face and he felt the beard growing there.

"Anything?" Mage asked, sounding only half conscious.

"No. Nothing. I spent it already."

"What did you spend it on?"

"You."

He turned his face to see her smile at that, and she nuzzled her forehead into the nape of his neck and held him a little closer.

"What should we do today?"

"We can't buy any more Tar."

"I can get some."

Borus' brow clenched. "How?"

"You know..." she trailed off.

Sweet Seddon above, she was proposing she'd offer herself to Sabo and his men. He didn't like the idea or the vision in his head. She'd done it before, when Klos was alive. But now, after waking up with her so many times, he felt she was more his than anything else, even though nothing had ever been said. They'd shared a lifetime of emotion in their mutual spells. He felt she even trusted him, and Borus couldn't remember the last time that had happened. He-Dog came into his mind. Even Balless. For all their faults, they still took him in when no one else wanted him. And for that, Borus had abandoned them with a healer, and took whatever money was left over. He'd felt it the thing to do at the time. Now, he regretted it.

But the Tar. The Tar had no conscience, only the most vivid of dreams, bursting with color, sound and touch. The Tar had become the single thing he wanted most: to return to that inside place, and simply marvel at it.

Tar. He swallowed. Would it be so bad, letting her do as she said she would? She'd done it before, given herself up to Sabo and his men in return for Tar. She could do it once more, before she lost any more weight. There would be a time when they would not want her at all and then where would they be? With one word, she would be off, and he thought that in the Tar's spell, he wouldn't even think about the deeds she had to do. The thought caught on something in his mind. The champion archer allowing a woman to sell herself on his behalf? If he did it once, he would do it again, as often as he could wring Tar out of Sabo. Sabo. Smiling Sabo who knew they would come back as often as possible.

"You stay." Mage pulled away.

He stopped her. "Borus."

"What?"

"My name's Borus."

"Oh."

"Remember it this time." He smiled at her.

She returned it. "I will."

"Don't go."

Her shirt, the extra one he'd bought, hung off her thin frame and he could see the tight cage of her ribs.

"No?" she asked.

"No." His mouth became a thin line. "Today will be very hard. For both of us."

She blinked at him.

"We're leaving."

"I can't leave," Mage told him. "I can't."

"I'm leaving. Today."

"Don't go."

"I am," Borus stated. Hate for his growing dependence on the Tar and the likes of Sabo swelled in him. Hot and thick and energizing. He and He-Dog were alike in that respect. It was very easy to draw strength from hatred. The trick was, Borus now realized in a moment's clarity, to channel it. Like the strength of a river, hate could kill you if you let it sweep you away.

"And you are as well," he informed her.

"No, I can't," she moaned, and in that instant Borus pitied her. He reached down and pulled her up. Then he thought better of it and got off the pallet himself. He went to the spring with their cup, as he now thought of it, and filled it for her. He brought it back, and let her drink.

"We can't leave."

"They won't let us?"

"The Tar won't let us. You were out… and came back. I thought you understood."

"I can do it again," he said and pulled her up. He hauled her to the water, and washed as much of her as she would allow. All the while, she moaned, *"no, no no."*

Borus refused to listen. He'd eaten his share of the Tar, and he concluded that Mage'd had more than enough. He scooped her up in both arms, and almost fell. His strength was practically gone. *The Tar*, he thought and snarled, realizing how it had earned its name. He concentrated, confronting the many chains of need trying to keep him in the little room, the death room, where Mage's brother and countless others had perished, and would continue to perish after they were gone. Borus only knew he was finished, and his mind plunged into the tentacles of addiction in his core, facing them and trying to hold them down. The Tar was a sinister thing now, as lethal as poison, and it fought him.

With Mage in his arms, he pressed toward the exit. He leaned against the walls when he could, taking deep breaths, but didn't put her down. He was too frightened that if he did put her down, she would try to go back, and if she tried, he didn't know if he had the strength or willpower to go after her.

He stumbled toward the light ahead, trying to keep Mage from harm, and walked directly into a chamber with a solitary figure sitting behind a table loudly eating an apple, cutting its flesh with a dagger, lips smacking. Sabo didn't pause when Borus and Mage entered, but kept right on eating.

"What is it?" Sabo asked.

Borus blinked and looked around. Mage pressed her face into his chest. They weren't in the entry room. In his foggy state of mind, he had turned the wrong way and walked toward Sabo's lair. The mistake made him smile at the irony.

"Well?" Sabo dropped the apple and dagger to the table.

Borus looked at the man. "We're leaving."

Sabo worked something from between his teeth before answering. "Oh. Well. Off with you then."

This took Borus aback. His arms ached and he placed Mage on the stone floor, almost falling himself.

"Be careful," Sabo purred.

"Did you hear me?"

"What? About leaving?" Sabo's brow arched in question. "Of course I heard you. And I believe you. I also *know* you'll be back. With coin," he eyed Mage, "or without."

"No, we're finished with this place."

Sabo chuckled. "My son, no one is ever *finished* with this place. Half of my customers were once finished. Oh they left, time and time again, but returned. They always returned. Or didn't you notice the trail of bodies coming into this place from the alleyway? Poor, poor souls. All begging to be allowed back in. Can't, however. They have nothing to pay for the Tar, you see. All have to pay in either cutaros... or flesh," he ended with another look at Mage. "And some don't even have that, anymore."

Sabo looked at Borus and smirked. "But you'll be back."

The former champion didn't like the smug tone of the weed merchant, and he certainly didn't like the way he sized up Mage. "You're wrong."

Sabo scoffed. "Believe what you will." He smiled. "But, I'm telling you, the sting won't be so bad if you just... allow both of us the benefit of the doubt."

"You're shite."

That made Sabo bark a laugh. "Am I? What does that make you then? Do you have any idea of how long you've been here? Hm? Buying Tar from me? You've been existing *beneath* this shite. *Feeding* from it. Pah. Go. Leave. You'll be begging to come back in soon enough."

The confidence Sabo exuded annoyed Borus. He turned to pick up Mage.

"She'll be back as well. Pleading. Promising. Would you like to know what she promised us last time? *All* of us. And how she fulfilled her promises?"

Borus stood slowly, his one eye, narrowing to a dangerous slit.

Sabo went on, watching him. "The pleasures she bestowed upon all four of us. At once I might add, was the stuff of talk for—urk."

Sabo stopped talking at that moment, for with unimaginable speed, Borus scooped up the dagger on the table and stabbed the weed merchant up under the jaw, through his throat and into his brain. The man's eyes fluttered for a moment, his back stiffened, and his fingers tapped a spasmodic beat on the table. Borus twisted the blade before releasing it, and Sabo relaxed. The dead man hissed for a moment, like a pot being removed from heat.

He fell off his chair with a clatter.

Borus looked at his left hand. There hadn't been any thought in the action, simply the stabbing itself. He felt no wrongdoing in killing Sabo, having killed plenty of times before.

Beside him, Mage let loose a hoarse whimper, her eyes wide with horror. "What have you done?"

"We're leaving."

"They'll…" Mage couldn't finish. Borus pulled her up and swept her off her feet. She buried her face against his chest. "Oh sweet Seddon above. They'll…"

Borus carried her back out into the long corridor, knowing he headed in the right direction this time. He focused on the darkness and torchlight ahead. He pressed her head closer, stifling Mage's terrified whimpers. Fear powered him now. He knew full well who *they* were, and what would be in store for them if Sabo's brutes discovered him dead. He marched on, past the torches and the patches of light, smelling the residual aroma of consumed Tar. They had to leave now. There was no going back.

The corridor came to an end. Mage kept her face close to his chest and her eyes clenched tight as if not wanting to see the monsters guarding the entrance.

Borus held her tight.

"Let us out," he said to the two men guarding the heavy door. The silver faced boy looked at the man with the horned helm. There was no sign of the one called Karast.

"We're done here," Borus said, "let us go."

The two monsters did not move. Either one of them could have easily picked both of them up and carried them back inside. That image alone made Borus uncomfortable. What if they brought them all the way back to Sabo's corpse? Dying Seddon, that was an image Borus didn't need. He lifted his chin, hoping it looked defiant. Why the hesitation? They *knew* that Borus and Mage would return eventually. Borus hoped beyond hope that these killers thought the same way as their dead leader.

After a long, considering moment, the horned man undid the many locks on the door and hauled it back. The many scents of the city rode an air current through the opening and smacked Borus in the face. It galvanized him. He pushed on, and entered Foust. He looked down and saw the shadow he cast on the sand, framed in an arch of torchlight. The door behind him closed and the night consumed him.

Borus didn't look back. He knew if he did, he might relent and beg to be let back in. Mage clawed at his shirt, and buried her face in the cloth. He had to distance both of them from the Hole. He didn't know the city well, and if he went into the many side streets, perhaps they could lose themselves in its maze. Believing it was the wisest course of action, he walked. Feeling the chains to the Hole stretch but not break. Amazement filled his brain. He'd only just woken it seemed, and already the need for Tar had doubled, demanding that he return.

For what? a voice said coldly from within. Borus recognized it. It was the hateful side of him, the part of him that at one time hadn't cared if he lived or died. The part of him that wanted to burn the world for forsaking him after his wounds. Now it was different, though. Now he had Mage.

Baring teeth, Borus took all of that inner hate and threw it at the need for Tar.

He turned to his right and walked. He passed the addicts in his path, people wanting the Tar but not able to buy it. He ignored the eyes glittering at him from the shadows. Struggling with Mage's weight, he stumbled away from that dark place, back into civilization.

He walked past guard patrols who ignored him. He walked past streets filled with miserable, hungry people. He went deeper into the city of Foust, wondering now if what he had done to both of them was such a good idea, and stepped onto a street of cut and fitted stone that led up to an important looking set of bronze and wooden doors. There were more soldiers on this street, and Borus went down the first alley he found. He placed his back against a brick building, and if he leaned out, he could see the gates and the copper towers beyond the wall. He was somewhere important, but wasn't sure where.

But he was out of the Hole.

"Where are we?" Mage asked him, without opening her eyes.

"We're away from it."

"I want to go back."

He shook his head, knowing she didn't see him.

"I need to go back," she moaned, her voice breaking.

He held her tighter.

"You—*we* can't."

*

They discovered Sabo long moments later, after Karast had returned from the city with food. The black masked man found the weed merchant on the floor, face pale, his clothes soaked with blood. Jun-Jun—the man with the boyish silver face—entered the chamber of dead Sabo and stared. Jawbone, the warrior with the horns and smiling grill, gaped in horror. The three of them stood that way for a long time.

"Find them," Karast finally whispered.

CHAPTER 24

Somewhere in He-Dog's drunken dream, he saw himself, Balless, and Chop being herded through the city. He remembered a long road of fitted stone, leading to a gate of bronze and wood. He heard the words "inner keep", but upon entering the place, thought that it was more of a palace. He remembered Chop vomiting somewhere along the way, and how both he and Balless giggled at it. Captain Galt, as he came to know the man, did not think much of Chop for dumping a load of ale by way of his throat onto the pretty stones. Galt said something about letting them sober up before something, and He-Dog found himself on his back, staring up at a dark ceiling, where he and his boys currently lay, breathing, belching, and trying to sleep. Sleep came slowly to He-Dog. Every time he closed his eyes, he felt the room begin to spin. If it wasn't for the amount of drink in him, he would have better enjoyed the ride.

He had nightmares.

He-Dog woke to pounding on the chamber door. It opened and servants brought trays filled with pitchers and fresh baked bread. They placed the food and drink on a table at the center of the floor, and departed under the red rimmed eyes of He-Dog. When they were gone, he sat up on his pallet and smacked his lips. He noted that a snoring Balless and Chop were on pallets of their own, and He-Dog thought it strange that he had slept on a straw bed in such fine guest quarters. He remembered who he was, and scowled. Hate bubbled from his core, and slowly dried his senses.

He-Dog got to his feet and inspected himself, still in the clothes the healer Sergius gave him. He picked up one of the pitchers, found it filled with water, and downed a third of it before stopping for breath. The sound woke Balless.

"Where are we?" he muttered sleepily.

He-Dog shook his head and nodded to the food. Balless made a face at the bread, but gladly took a pitcher and drank. He-Dog went to a shuttered window and threw it open. Sunlight blazed in and almost scorched the eyes from his head. Outside, evening ripened the skies.

The door behind him opened. Chop jolted awake and the three of them looked upon a frowning Captain Galt and a handful of warriors.

"Excellent," he said. "You slept the whole day away, but no matter. Finish up quickly if you can, and I'll take you all to see the Kratoe. He's very interested in speaking with you."

He-Dog exchanged wary looks with Balless. "What about?"

Amusement filled Galt's leather features. "A task I believe the Kratoe wants done. A task he's willing to pay well for."

Coin? Again, He-Dog and Balless exchanged looks.

"Now hurry," Galt commanded. "Time's a wasting."

*

Galt and his soldiers led them to through the inner keep, down rich stone and marble corridors. Servants pulled open a pair of bronze doors and bade them enter.

He-Dog kept an eye on the back of Galt's head, but the captain did not seem to notice. They entered a throne room bright and big enough to cause Balless to arch his neck and mutter an expletive. He-Dog agreed with his companion. The Kratoe possessed more wealth than they could ever hope to in their lifetimes.

Galt and his men led the three around a large crystal fish spitting water. Chop traced a finger along the rim of the fountain, as if testing to see if it was real. They walked on paths of black-veined marble, and He-Dog wondered if he could chip a chunk of it away from the floor, if it would be worth anything. At the far end of the room and sitting on a throne filled with red cushions was the Kratoe. Black robes of office covered the man from head to toe, and He-Dog wasn't certain if the man wasn't, in fact, a woman. Until he spoke.

"Welcome," the Kratoe spoke in a masculine voice filled with breaking high notes. "On behalf of the people of Foust, I thank you for accepting my invitation."

Invitation? He-Dog's mind hooked on the word. That wasn't the way he remembered it. But he was drunk at the time.

Galt stepped aside and clasped his hands in front of him, studying the newcomers with a critical eye.

"I've heard you did quite a bit of drinking last night. What was the occasion?" "Being alive," He-Dog said, raising his chin and flexing the hand that had once been crushed. He scratched at his nose, feeling where the bone had healed. He didn't like being unable to see the man's face.

"Ah yes," the Kratoe replied. "Considering these times, any reason to drink is a good one. Very hard times we've come upon in Foust. Not since the beginning of the city and the opening of the mines have we experienced the hardships brought on by the army surrounding us. The beastmen are like a great hairy fist about our throats, choking us. From early times we co-existed on the continent, that is, until recently. Why, my father himself told me of times when beastman actually worked alongside men mining the hills and mountains, in an age that was prosperous for all—"

Galt cleared his throat. He-Dog noticed the impatient look on the captain's face. The Kratoe also seemed to catch the officer's meaning.

"I'm sorry," the Kratoe said with a nod. "I waste time when there is none to waste. To the heart of the summons then. I was told there were four of you that delivered the message from the coast to us?"

He-Dog saw Galt swing his gaze upon him, and he didn't like the predatory malice lurking there. "Aye that, Kratoe. But we don't know what happened to the fourth man."

"He left us in the city, while we were on the mend," Balless said and got a scolding look from He-Dog.

"You don't know where he is?"

"No, Kratoe."

"No matter." The Kratoe shrugged. "We have the three of you. I need to converse with the beastman king and convince him that further fighting here does not serve either of our purposes. Being under siege, we cannot mine the ore in our hills. Time is wasting and profits are being lost. It's only a matter of time before the king of Zuthenia mobilizes a force to put down the beastman threat. Costly, but he will do it, and then he'll wage war on a scale these dogs can't imagine."

He-Dog doubted that. He knew those *dogs* could imagine quite a bit.

"I want you to escort me to the beastman king." The Kratoe's fingers rapped on the armrest of his throne.

He-Dog straightened. It wasn't often he got to speak with men of position like the Kratoe. He wanted to be selective in his choice of words. Keeping that in mind, he cleared his throat.

"You want us to escort you out there? To the dogs

trying to get in here?"

The Kratoe nodded.

"You're not fit in the head." He-Dog watched how the ruler froze in his seat as if he'd been goosed by a lance. Even Galt seemed to regard He-Dog in a new light.

After a moment's reflection, the Kratoe spoke. "I'm sorry?"

"You heard me," He-Dog said with Balless nodding agreement at his side. "To go out there now, with them in the mood they're in, isn't the wisest thing to do. If I were you, I'd drop a bucket with a message scratched on a piece of whatever and hope that one of them can read it. Then, *maybe*, the message might reach their king. But to go out there... just the four of us."

"You'll be paid, of course."

He-Dog made a disgusted face. "There isn't enough coin in Foust to pay—"

"You'll be paid handsomely."

He-Dog stopped to think about that. "How much gold is *handsomely*?"

"As much as you three can carry."

Balless' familiar grin seeped into his repeatedly beaten face.

"We can carry a lot," He-Dog informed the ruler.

"I have no doubt you can," the Kratoe went on, "but these are desperate times. In the mining around Foust, not only copper was taken, but gold as well. And other valuable metals. My point is this, whatever gold you can carry, you can have it. On condition you escort me there and back."

He-Dog mulled it over. Something bothered him. "Why not have your own men do it? You have enough." He indicated Galt and his warriors with a thumb.

"You men came through an army to get here. *That's* who I need as my protectors. Not the uncut ones manning our walls. I know their feelings, I'm afraid, and those men don't instill confidence. No, you lot are the warriors I want around my person."

"I heard you sent someone already, and the beastmen sent the guards back in pieces."

For a moment, the Kratoe became quiet, as if remembering something. He held his peace long enough that Galt gave him a questioning glance.

"That was… before," he heaved out. "At that time… only a messenger was sent to speak with their king, who requested that he be addressed as a king, by the king of Foust. There is no king here, so I go in his stead as I rule here, in King Narijo's name."

The Kratoe fell silent again, and once more He-Dog's instincts rumbled. He knew he had nothing better to do, however, and the idea of hauling away as much coin as he could carry appealed to his mercenary side.

"We'll need to be outfitted."

"This very moment."

"And we'll need weapons."

"You'll be brought to the keep's armory. I can assure you, you'll find what you need there."

"We'll do it, then," He-Dog said, warming to the idea of having access to an armory. All manner of delights might possibly await him there. "For all the gold we can carry, and weapons and armor from the keep's armory."

"Done. We'll leave tomorrow."

He-Dog flexed his jaw, feeling the stiffness there. "We leave when we're ready. Balless here has difficulty finding armor that fits him. If your armorer can get him into something quickly, we'll leave that much faster, but we go during the day, agreed? Unless you really want to go at night."

"Day is fine. I'll be waiting for you. Galt, take these men to the armory."

He-Dog saw the captain give the Kratoe a withering look.

"Captain Galt," Kratoe said in a sterner voice.

That broke the officer's thoughts, and he nodded

without a word. He faced the three mercenaries. "Seems you struck a bargain there," he said, with a hint of contempt. "Well done."

He-Dog ignored the man.

"This way," Galt informed them. "My men will take you there. I'll be present shortly."

To this, He-Dog saw the Kratoe visibly tense, but he didn't care for either man. Turning, Galt's four warriors led the three from the throne room.

They were led through the halls of the keep and down stairs. The corridors were more dungeon-like, and He-Dog actually felt more comfortable here than in the throne room. The lead guard stopped at one stout door and opened it with a low grunt. Another went in, lighting torches inside, and setting the contents of the room agleam.

The three men gazed in from the threshold as the shine from the weapons grew, impressed with what they saw. Balless entered first. Chop followed. He-Dog stayed a moment longer, his hands slowly hitching to his hips, and simply stared.

A hint of a smile glossed his hard features.

He liked what he saw.

Racks upon racks of stored arms filled a wide chamber that stretched back into the darkness where one soldier walked, lighting torches in their sconces and throwing the dark back like a heavy blanket. Broadswords gleamed with a sleepy, but deadly, air. The tips of spears, some cruelly barbed, winked in the torchlight. Quivers filled with feathered shafts hung from walls. Pole arms and battle axes, the curves of their blades smiling blindly, were on display and a feast for the eyes. Thick daggers, almost shortswords, lined a rack like barbarous teeth ready to be bared and used. Bows lay on tables, curved and carved with intricate symbols, eager to be played like angry harps. Two-handed swords, monstrous double-edged blades dangerous to even gaze upon, rose up like crowns and almost begged to be taken away and used to full, bloody potential. Exotic blades, straight and curved like the arc of the sun, twinkled and left the three hardened men of war wondering just how to use them.

Then came the display of armor.

He-Dog knew he'd gotten the better part of the bargain.

"What in Seddon's name do you people do here?" He-Dog commented in awe, rubbing his jaw. He tore his gaze away from racks of armor and peered up the particularly fearsome length of a trident fashioned with spikes.

The guards did not answer.

Balless walked among the axes, enraptured. He stopped in his tracks when he found the maces and war hammers. Across the way, Chop pulled up short sword after sword, pulling some from scabbards and thumbing the blades before taking practice swings. He-Dog stopped before a blade still in its scabbard, its pommel fashioned in the likeness of a dog skull, teeth bared, with its lower jaw missing.

"The weapons here are of the highest quality, as Foust's weapon smiths and sword makers aren't capable of anything less," Galt announced from the doorway. "They're a diligent hardworking lot, I'll say that. They even travelled far to trade designs with weapon makers from places unheard of…"

"Anything in here is ours?" He-Dog asked in a half statement.

Galt exhaled, sounding irritated. "It is."

He-Dog took the scabbard up in both hands and slowly withdrew the dog sword, seeing his distorted face in the steel. It was a thick broadsword and very well weighted, with a slightly serrated edge to the cutting tip. A sword as fine as this would cost a ransom in any market.

"Good," He-Dog muttered and slammed the sword back into its scabbard. In one motion, he strapped it across his waist.

Chop whirled two short blades, curved and as bright as silver. In the torchlight, it looked like both of his hands held spinning shields, or the faces of furious moons.

Balless lifted a massive mace, its iron head shaped like a diamond and topped with a single steel spike powerful enough to pierce the thickest plate. The big man grinned evilly as he studied the length of the weapon and hefted it.

From the threshold, Galt watched these barbarians choose their weapons, and felt a twinge of wariness within his breast.

Seeing how it was all theirs for the taking, the three took other weapons—short swords, daggers, and throwing knives. Even if they didn't use them, they knew the quality would fetch a high price in any market. He-Dog found a leather curiass shaped for a lord's physique, and perhaps the best piece of armor he would ever lay eyes upon, let alone own. The hardened leather was braced with narrow plates riveted underneath. He stripped off his shirt and strapped himself in. Even better, it fit.

Chop selected a leather cuirass made in much the same fashion. He experienced more difficulty in finding one that fit him, but settled on a corselet with wide shoulderguards and fitted with leather sleeves.

As they settled on armor, more men arrived, escorted by Foust guards.

"These men are armorers," Galt informed the three. "If there is something that won't fit you properly, let them know. They'll make it fit."

Hearing the captain, He-Dog shook his head. It was all almost too good to be true.

"Now?" Balless asked, holding up a chain mail shirt and hood.

"Yes, now," Galt snapped. "You have work to do and if we can get you outfitted tonight, you'll be delivered to the beastmen tomorrow. Enough time has been wasted. So plug your eyes back into your skulls and get to work, or by Saimon's balls I'll cast you out as you are and laugh at the beastmen's reception."

He-Dog met the captain's eyes and neither man broke the stare, which lasted seconds until an armorer began talking. He-Dog looked away for only a moment to answer questions asked of him, and when he turned back, Galt was gone, along with one of his henchmen. He-Dog simmered, not liking the man's tone in the least, and let his thoughts wander over possible replies to the man.

"Pay attention now," demanded the man going over the leather cuirass. He-Dog glowered at him.

The armorer cleared his throat and took a more even-mannered tone. "Good sar," he added hastily.

*

As the night dragged on, in another part of the city, a single man plainly dressed but carrying a sword rapped on the heavy door leading to the underground dungeon known as the Hole. His name was Brakuss, one of Galt's four hand-picked killers, and he frowned in the dark. He didn't want to be here in the dark among the dog shite of Foust, out of armor and alone. Galt had given him a task to do, however, and Brakuss prided himself on getting things done.

Someone from the other side pulled back the cover on the door slot and peered out at the visitor.

"I wish to make a purchase," Brakuss informed the eyes.

The cover slapped back into place and a moment later, the door groaned open from the inside. A monster of a man wearing a horned helm bade him enter. Taking a breath, Brakuss did so.

He emerged from the Hole a short time later, breathing deeply of the night air and thankful that the job was done. Shaking his head, he blinked, and left for the inner keep, the door to the Hole echoing its closure in his wake. When he arrived at the inner keep and was allowed to pass through the gates, it was almost midnight.

*

From the shadows of an alley, Borus sat with his back against the wall and Mage's head in his lap. When the late arrival entered the keep, Borus stopped stroking Mage's unmoving head and stared. Then the man was gone, and the one-eyed former archer resumed combing Mage's hair with his fingers. She sighed softly in her sleep, and despite the heat in the night air, shivered as though with fever. The day had been difficult for her, and he dared not let her out of his sight for fear of seeing her sickly frame wander back to the Hole. He did leave her in the same alley at midday, just to find water for them both. The relief he'd experienced at finding her where he left her frightened him. He recognized the sign, and inwardly admitted that he cared for the sick woman.

Mage muttered something in her sleep, and Borus leaned over her, shushing and adjusting her head as gently as possible. Weak, he felt weak to his core, but his hate kept the need for the White Tar at bay. The only worrying thought was that his hate was burning itself out.

He closed his eyes, fearing the need for Tar, the minions of the Hole, and the ghostly smirk of the dead Sabo.

CHAPTER 25

Morning.

Two days later.

He-Dog and his lads stood at the gates of the inner keep, waiting with a group of Galt's men. He felt relaxed at the moment, but knew that would change once he stood in the middle of the beastmen. He glanced about and snarled a yawn. The last couple of days and nights had been comfortable for him and the boys. They'd holed up in the Kratoe's keep, ate food He-Dog knew the general populace didn't know about or have access to, and waited for Balless' armor to be fitted. Balless was a big man, and not many chain mail shirts would cover him. They'd found one, and had to adjust the shirt around the arms so that it would reach around him. In the end, leather sleeves, much like the ones Chop now wore, covered Balless' upper biceps. They couldn't find bracers big enough for his forearms, and had difficulty fitting a set of greaves to his shins. In the end, he was ready. They all were.

Seddon's rosy ass, how they *shined.*

Chop had found a set of bronze bracers and greaves for his forearms that would flash in the sun once its rays found him. Greaves were plentiful in the armory, so He-

Dog had taken a set as well to wear below his crenulated skirt of leather strips. Balless didn't partake, as his chain mail stopped just above his knees. Bits and pieces of leather and plates were strapped or seemingly nailed to Balless' person, and even He-Dog wondered how the armorers had gotten the big man into the metal. They'd removed the mail hood that came with the shirt, as Balless' new open-face helm, complete with a nose guard, wouldn't fit otherwise. He-Dog had wanted him to simply leave the helm behind, but Balless had fallen in love with it. The brute also found a pair of spiked gloves, which he immediately claimed. Along with the new long-shafted mace he acquired from Foust's armory, Balless almost unnerved He-Dog himself.

Almost.

They stood admiring each other when Galt appeared with his soldiers. Walking at the center and draped from head to toe in his customary black robes was the Kratoe. The man looked unsteady on his feet, and several times he leaned against a nearby soldier for support.

"All set are we?" Galt inquired with a predatory smile. He-Dog met the man's grey eyes again, projecting evil thoughts into the captain's head. Galt stared back, his teeth wet and shiny in the rising sun. Over the past two days, the captain had quipped barb after snide barb at the three men, almost daring any of them to do something. It was a good thing Galt was on their side, He-Dog thought; else they would've killed him long ago. He kept his icy gaze directed at the captain, who seemed amused for all the wrong reasons. He-Dog began wishing for things that he knew would only end badly.

"We can stand here gazing into each other's eyes." Galt smirked. "Or we can get you through the gate. Which will it be?"

"The gate," He-Dog replied coolly, but he didn't break his gaze. "What's wrong with him?"

"Him?" Galt's eyes narrowed. "He took a little

something to help ease his nerves. Benefits of being a Kratoe. Pay no mind. But help him should he fall."

"Ease his nerves?" He-Dog repeated, squinting.

Galt ignored him and broke away first, sneering. Fine with He-Dog—in his mind he won that round.

"Follow us then, and don't speak to the Kratoe. He's… *concentrating* on the meeting to come."

He-Dog exchanged questioning glances with Balless. Shrugging, he placed his open face helm on his head, hefted the only shield any of them carried, a simple round one at that, and followed Galt's lead. The gates to the inner keep opened, sunlight splashed over them, and the procession pushed onward.

*

From the shadows of an alley, Borus looked up as he heard the gates open. He opened his mouth, dry as desert bone, and stared on in dumb fascination at the armored column emerging. He raised a shaking hand, and scratched at a dusty beard. A dark man walked at the center of the column, and from among the soldiers three men caught his attention.Withdrawal from the Tar warped his senses and the figures were stretched impossibly taller or squatted as if bashed on their heads with a maul. They looked familiar, but he couldn't place their names. He spied the man in the black mask, and his eyes bulged.

Karast!

Borus pressed himself up against the wall in fear.

*

He-Dog felt eyes on him, but only glimpsed a one-eyed corpse in the alley. The last thing he saw was how the man's head wilted over a second figure with its head in his lap.

Then they were gone.

Paying them no further mind, He-Dog walked on within the column, feeling like he was marching to his own execution. Not that it mattered. He had walked into several of his own executions and lived to tell of it. This day would be no different. As long as the Kratoe stayed on his feet. Was the man drunk? The thought didn't comfort He-Dog.

They followed a number of back alleyways, which struck both He-Dog and Chop as rather odd, while Balless simply enjoyed the morning walk. The people appeared even more stricken by hunger and the siege, and He-Dog wondered if, in fact, food was at a lower level than he had been led to believe. It certainly wasn't the case inside the keep, and Galt and his lads certainly appeared well-fed and watered. One thing continued to bother him, however, and that was the Kratoe as he walked and stumbled as if in a dream. He-Dog looked at Balless, who cocked an eyebrow but said nothing.

Galt marched on, fixated on his objective and heedless of the suffering around him.

They finally arrived at the main gates of Foust, and He-Dog smiled in spite of himself. He never thought he would be leaving Foust in the shape he was leaving, and he looked at the dark mask of Chop, the white stitches of battles past clear in the leather. The eyes behind the mask seemed to read He-Dog's thoughts, and slowly turned away.

Galt strode over to the gatemen and barked orders. He fell back to the column as men behind him wrestled with mighty timbers, and turned the gate wheel. Winches and pulley systems slowly groaned and moved. The gates split in the middle and the gap widened.

The captain faced the four men. "There you are. Best of luck." He smiled, but the frost issuing from the man was chilling. "Kratoe," Galt said, as the Kratoe stepped forward and started walking. He-Dog looked at Galt in alarm.

"What are you waiting for, then? Escort!"

Without a word, He-Dog motioned for his companions to follow. They ran to the seemingly sleep-walking Kratoe, and encircled him.

"Galt!" someone yelled from above. "Galt!"

The last thing He-Dog saw was the figure of the captain turning to face Krajin, walking briskly toward him. The gates began to close.

*

Krajin faced his equal, who stood in front of a group of soldiers at his back. They weren't Krajin's boys. Krajin's station was the outer walls of Foust while Galt's was at the inner keep. Krajin's own soldiers eventually gathered round him, and if one were to gaze down upon the confrontation, one would see two distinct storm fronts colliding. All that was missing were the lightning and the thunder.

"Galt!" he said like an accusation. "Seddon above! You can't just open the gates when you feel like it! Why not just climb to the battlements and shout out a welcome to those damned dogs? I'll report this—"

"To whom?" Galt eyes smiled back. "The Kratoe? That was the Kratoe I just escorted out the front gate."

"What?" Krajin's face slacked in confusion, his meaty moustache slumped.

"Keep guarding your gate," Galt informed him. "You're doing splendidly."

Galt moved to leave, but Krajin reached out and grabbed the man's arm.

"Why would the Kratoe go out there?"

"Unhand me." Galt stared at the offending grip, but Krajin only squeezed harder.

"Answer me," Krajin insisted. "I haven't heard word from the inner keep in months except through you, and now the Kratoe decides to just leave? Under the escort of three men? What's going on?"

"I said," Galt repeated in a level tone, like a man knowing he had a weapon concealed on his person. "let go."

Krajin did so with some disdain.

"I don't know why the Kratoe did what he did," Galt said. "I only know my orders. And my orders were to obtain men to guard the Kratoe as he talked to the leader of that pack of dogs out there. No more. No less. Except I must now continue on with my instructions, which are to return to the inner keep."

Krajin did not take his eyes off the captain. "Something's wrong here."

"I don't care what you think." Galt flashed a sad smile. "You delay me here for no reason. I suggest you get back to your post and worry about your duty, and I'll worry about mine."

With that, the captain turned and marched away, back to the inner keep. Krajin watched him go. Galt's arrogance bothered him and this wasn't the first time Krajin had been left in the unknown regarding the Kratoe's thoughts and instructions. The Kratoe wanted to talk to the beastman leader? Krajin's head felt as if someone had struck him with a very heavy mace. That was unheard of. Why do such a thing?

He heard the screaming from beyond his walls, and decided that he was needed on the battlements.

*

He-Dog looked ahead and set his jaw hard enough to risk cracking it.

Ahead was a beach of white desert sand, dotted here and there with bones and debris from past assaults, and the ever shifting, teeming wall of beastmen staring at them as they approached. The Kratoe lifted one skinny arm ending in a streaming white cloth. A breeze found it and lifted it weakly, but it was enough to mark their intentions. Or so He-Dog thought. He quickly got in front of the Kratoe and hefted his round shield while the other stood at his sides. He-Dog didn't reach for his dog skull sword. Nor did Chop reach for his own weapons. Balless carried his monstrous mace in one spiked fist, near its head, and He-Dog felt the anxiety of being in the open facing down an army of savages. As far as his eyes could see stood a poised mass of bad intentions, all fixed on the four men crossing the scarred sands. Hoots and howls of warning went up, and He-Dog knew if he looked back now and saw the comforting heights of Foust's walls, saw the many shadows watching them in silence from above, that he would probably start running back.

"Seddon above," he muttered without thinking.

"Good day for it," Balless said merrily.

Both He-Dog and Chop regarded the man.

"Good day for what?" He-Dog grunted as he turned back to the horde's nearing front ranks. The fact that nothing was coming at them just yet heartened him.

"Whatever's to happen," Balless answered.

He-Dog chuckled in spite of himself. It helped control his nerves.

At the center, the Kratoe seemed oblivious to them all.

"Don't see the koch," Balless commented. Neither did the others. "What happened to it?" he wondered aloud.

He-Dog could see the tops of grey pavilions, ballistae, even catapults, all pointed toward Foust, and of course, what seemed like all the beastmen in the world gathered in before him. But he couldn't spot the wreck of the wagon that brought them to the city.

Halfway to the front ranks of the beastmen, the Kratoe stumbled against Balless. The big man helped him regain his balance. He-Dog turned and looked questioningly at the Kratoe and for the first time, looked into his eyes. They were large, dark and luminous and were not the eyes of one fit in the head.

Without a word, the black robed man steadied himself, and pushed on. Balless looked suspiciously at He-Dog, but neither spoke as they kept walking with the Kratoe at the center.

"Wonderful day, today," the Kratoe said, dreamily.

Wonderful for somebody, He-Dog thought. He also thought the Kratoe's voice sounded different.

"Simply wonderful," the man spoke again and waved the cloth.

He-Dog believed the battlement heights behind them all had become as still as that brief space of time just before something incredibly bad happens.

"Hot," Balless muttered.

"Yes, quite hot," the Kratoe agreed and then fell silent once more, the fluttering piece of white held high above his black robed head.

"Aeeeurrrrg," Chop said.

Not even the Kratoe paid him heed.

The party was three-quarters of the way across the sands when the beastmen began to howl, bark, and ring out curses that sparkled in the hot morning air. He-Dog clenched his jaw again and fought down every urge he had to draw his sword. Chop walked just behind him on the Kratoe's right, Balless on his left.

"Stay watchful now," the Kratoe slurred in his strange voice, and He-Dog again wondered if the man was drunk. The troubling thing was, He-Dog could usually smell the after-reek of wine or ale on a person who partook of it. There was no such odor from the Kratoe, so what affected him so?

The screams and curses became even louder, and the noise crashed over the tiny band like an avalanche.

Nothing will happen, He-Dog repeated to himself over and over as he came into full view of the twisted faces of the enemy, lining up on the edge of sand that marked the range of Foust's arrows and catapults.

"I seek your king!" the Kratoe bawled over again and

again, startling He-Dog for a moment.

He-Dog imagined that, underneath all of those black robes, there was a city ruler as red faced and sweaty as raw meat on an open flame.

The wall of moving flesh before them shimmered and shifted, not four strides away, and the chorus of beastmen became even louder. Fists waved axes and mauls above horrible heads. Spears and clubs jabbed in their direction.

He-Dog's mashed hand twitched, gripping the inner bar of his shield all the more. He stood directly before the wall of beastmen. He saw their snarling faces first. He saw their brutal weapons. If anyone was going to die, he would probably be the first. The thought was oddly comforting, but then he thought of what beastmen did to corpses and contempt rose in his gullet.

The mass parted into an uneven pathway, leading deeper into the army.

"I seek your king!" the Kratoe shouted in a drunken sounding voice. It was a wonder he could even stand in the middle of the three warriors, and He-Dog's head filled again with the thought of "why only three"?

The group of four moved forward. Beastmen on both sides pulsated with hate and bare weapons. They barked and screamed. Red, black, white, and green beastmen thrust their faces not a hand's width away from the Foust party and snarled. Jaws snapped. The Kratoe swung the white cloth above his head like a holy symbol warding off horrors from Saimon's abyss, screaming, *"I seek your king!"* again and again at the walls that sought to crush him and his three guards.

But none of them were touched. The beastmen came only so close as to voice their hatred and rage at the four men, shaking their fists and their weapons in their faces, but something kept them from bloody contact. He-Dog didn't think it was the white cloth of the Kratoe, and he snarled at the heat of so many bodies crammed about him.

They walked down the path as it parted before them,

moving past huge pavilions of war and crude siege machines. They saw one group of beastman off to the left, standing on something that lifted them above the throngs, studying the Kratoe and his escort darkly.

He-Dog looked back at his lads. As expected, Chop appeared ready to cut anything, and Balless smirked and nodded at the beastmen daring him. Over his shoulders, the path they followed had sealed up in a solid wall of beastmen teeth and steel. Above it all, appearing like high cliffs above a rough sea, were the battlements of Foust.

The Kratoe's body jerked and twitched at every sound. He-Dog could see the whites of the man's eyes for the first time, and he thought of a pig about to be slaughtered.

He-Dog looked at the open way ahead and smiled. It wasn't every day he got to see a ruler of a city about to let slip a cow kiss.

The beastmen herded them along until a great black tent of war rose up ahead, an island set apart from the other islands on a plain of madness. Two great, strangely silent reds pawed at the tent's folds and drew them back, and into its depths He-Dog and his companions escorted the Kratoe. Once the party was inside, the reds let the flaps fall back into place.

The smell of bad breath, unwashed hides, and smoke smacked their noses and even the Kratoe put a hand to his face. Two large reds armed with spiked mauls stood inside the entryway, their gazes hooded and lethal. A fire pit burned in the center of the room, and the skulls of dead beastmen decorated the walls, spitted on spears and grinning. Surrounding the fire pit was a multitude of barbarous-looking beastmen. Neither He-Dog nor Balless had ever witnessed the like before, and they had seen their share of the creatures. The beastmen seemed to be chieftains, and they sized up the four men in turn.

The escort walked to the center of the room, mindful of the roasted bones coating the sandy floor, and looked upon the beastman throne and the king who presided there. The huge red sat on a black stump raised on a mound of sand above the gathered beastmen. He was bare-chested, as was the beastman way, preferring to show off the might of his chest and arms. This particular creature had an overbearing lower jaw, and his fangs and tusks ringed his muzzle like a frightening fence. The beastman beckoned with a hand that only had three fingers.

A beastman as frightening as any He-Dog had ever laid eyes upon appeared at his side and pointed to the ground before the stump throne. The creature had a huge indentation in his skull, appearing like an apple missing a bite. They moved as directed by the beastman, eyeing the thing's battered red flesh. Even Balless' eyes widened at the sight.

Once in front of the throne, the beastmen sat on the ground, and the king studied them with interest. A stillness fell over the tent, broken by the sounds of hammers from outside.

With his fear apparently getting the better of him, the Kratoe thrust himself before He-Dog and bowed low before the beastman king.

"I am the Kratoe of Foust," the man announced to all within the tent. "And I have come upon your request."

The beastman king remained still, impassive. His jaws moved lopsidedly as he spoke. "I... Two-Bite. *Wuff.* King and War... Skull of beastmen."

"I have come as you asked, and I've done as you asked," the Kratoe said as he slowly straightened.

Two-Bite leaned forward. "These man-things?"

"They are," the Kratoe answered, setting off very bad feelings in He-Dog's guts and brain.

"Stand. There," the king commanded with a rough voice, and the Kratoe did so. He-Dog's guts churned at the way the man quickly obeyed.

The beastman king took in the black robed form of the Kratoe, and exhaled. "You," he said simply, slowly tilting his head to one side. "Kraw-toe."

Two-Bite snorted and stood up, towering over the smaller man.

"We… I've brought you the ones you wanted," the Kratoe blurted. "Here they are."

Hearing the words, He-Dog's face twisted at the apparent betrayal. "You ripe—"

Beastmen, thick and bearing weapons, gathered round the three men who rapidly placed their backs together in defence. The beastmen did not press them any further, and He-Dog did not lash out. Not yet.

"They're *here!*" the Kratoe stressed. "What are you waiting for!? Take them and let's discuss matters!"

In answer, Two-Bite grabbed the Kratoe by his throat. The man's eyes bulged and his hands gripped the beastman's wrists. A puff of breath left his lungs as he struggled to breathe.

"You. Stupid man-thing," Two-Bite rumbled. "Come here. Again."

The red king drew the Kratoe in close to him. "I show. You. Now."

"They're there!" the Kratoe struggled, sounding like a drunk man insisting upon something *right.* "Shh," Two-Bite said. "*Wuff.* Still."

The beastman let go of the Kratoe's neck and placed both hands on either side of his head.

"I know things!" The Kratoe shouted from a mouth mashed by the pressure of the two hands. "I know things!"

Two-Bite nodded, and pulled him closer. His mighty jaws hissed open.

"Wait! Wait! I'm not the Kratoe!"

"*Not the Kratoe,*" the words lanced into He-Dog's brain. The revelation stunned him. Who was he then?

"Not Kratoe?" Two-Bite questioned him.

"No! No!"

"Who you?"

"I'm a servant to the Kratoe!"

The beastman's brow furrowed in anger.

"Wait! I know where the Kratoe is! I know!"

"Where?"

"I brought the three men who kill—"

"*Where* Kratoe?" Two-Bite snarled.

The helpless man stared at the wet jaws flexing in his face. He breathed in the beastman king's foulness, and looked the creature in the eye. "Let me free and I'll tell you."

The beastman king hesitated for a moment, but then his features twisted into something feral. Without warning, Two-Bite bit deeply into the flesh that was the false Kratoe's face. He-Dog, Balless, and Chop tensed, but the beastmen surrounding them raised their weapons in warning. From where they stood, the three heard the man's agonized scream as the beastman king bit into his face once, twice, still holding him in place. A wet ripping noise tore through the chamber's gloom and the false Kratoe spasmed, shrieked, babbled that he would tell the king everything he wanted and shrieked again. Bone cracked. The man's legs kicked. Hands went from the beastman's wrists to his shoulders and fingers clawed into flesh, but he wasn't released. He dug his feet into the sand and tried to push away. The beastman held on. His jaws flexed and bit again and again, chewing inward, as if devouring a hard apple. The sound of more bones snapping. Blood pattered to the sand.

The man's movements slowed, slumped, and he finally hung still.

Two-Bite pulled the dead man closer, and before them all, devoured the remainder of his skull, cracking it open like a dog feasting on a bone. At some point, blood erupted from the Kratoe's neck, and He-Dog dropped his gaze. He probably should have stopped watching earlier, and he knew he would have nightmares—if he lived long enough to sleep. Balless watched, however, his usually beaming face now solemn.

Finishing the meal, the beastman king threw the remains of the false Kratoe into the dirt.

"I eat him again. To-night," the creature spoke, his jaws dripping red. He thumped his hand with its missing fingers into his chest and spoke in beastman. The tent roared in approval, then quieted. The beastmen standing between the remaining men and the king parted.

"You," Two-Bite addressed the three. "You kill... last beastman king."

Not He-Dog, Balless, or even Chop if he was able had anything to say to that.

"Now, I have. You."

"Kill us and—" He-Dog stopped. Foust wasn't about to do anything to help them, but he threw it out there anyway. "And... Foust will strike you all dead."

Two-Bite regarded the three men strangely. "Foust dead *now. Dead.* I have... have *plan.*"

"What plan?" He-Dog inquired, thinking it couldn't hurt to ask.

But the beastman king snapped his jaws and shook his head. "No... worry. You dead. Man-thing. Sooo dead."

He-Dog drew his sword and raised his shield. Balless brandished his mace. Chop's twin blades flicked out, ready to cut.

Two-Bite held up a hand. He barked a command and the beastmen around them withdrew a few steps. The king's eyes glittered in the light, and regarded the three standing before him.

"You fight, eh? *Wuff.* Good. Good. But... too bad."

The beastman barked out more of the guttural language.

He-Dog's eyes narrowed. Balless brushed against his shoulder.

"We fight here. We fight... under dead king's eyes." Two-Bite said and pointed to a skull. "But not yet. I show you... something."

He-Dog didn't like the sound of that. He looked about

the room and saw too many beastmen ready to close in on them from all sides. They would kill many of them, but in the end, the three would be swept away by the masses.

A beastman appeared at Two-Bite's side, and He-Dog's jaw clenched.

"This…" Two-Bite hit his fist on the helm that covered the beastman's head. The lower visor had been ripped away so that it would fit the head of the creature and allow his muzzle freedom. He-Dog studied the roughshod armor covering the beastman. Like the weapons they used, the armor looked heavy and crude, and didn't quite cover all of the warrior's body. The pauldrons protecting the shoulders appeared battered while the heavy plates covering the torso spotted dents and even holes in places. He-Dog realized that the armor was taken from a dead man and beaten out to fit a beastman's frame.

"This *Koja*," Two-Bite told the men. "This urrr… this *our* armor now. Make beastman strong!"

Koja. A beastman wearing heavy armor. The thought didn't please He-Dog in the least. Beastmen were bad enough to kill without armor. With it, they would last longer. He shook his head in loathing at the thought of hammering away at a *Koja*. A second, more disturbing thought entered his mind. Two-Bite spoke their language. How many others did that? Not many. He-Dog scoffed. Not many was generous thinking. *None* would probably be more accurate. This beastman was smart.

A smart king who led an army of armored beastman.

A smart king with a plan.

The thought made He-Dog even more uneasy.

Two-Bite raised his arm and the beastman with the dent in his head tossed him a huge battle axe. The king caught it and placed it head down in the sand. He leaned on the weapon and shook his own head.

"We fight… here…" Two-Bite said and bared his muzzle in a grimace. He shook his head again. Slower this time.

He-Dog's eyes narrowed. He sensed something wrong.

The beastman king straightened up and looked at the dark ceiling of the tent. Two-Bite shook his head a third time, and snarled. "We fight..." the king growled and spoke something in his own tongue. The beastmen in the tent turned their attention to their leader.

Who collapsed.

A roar of surprise and awe went up from the onlookers and several bolted to the fallen king's side.

Giving He-Dog the opportunity he needed.

CHAPTER 26

He-Dog lashed out with his dog-skull blade, killing one bare-chested beastman in a flash. The dark surge of bodies before him split, as some pressed forward to the fallen king, while those who guarded the three men were surprised, their attention divided. Balless brained one and killed another while Chop's blades opened up two of the creatures from chin to waist. With He-Dog in the lead, the three drove forward, pushing, cutting, and bashing any beastmen in their way. They bolted past the spears and the skulls atop them, and Balless snapped a pole in two with one swipe. The skull fell forward and landed in among the recovering beastmen. Guttural barks cut the air, raising an alarm, and several beastmen turned and roared upon seeing the three men at the wall of the tent.

He-Dog faced the dark, mottled wall of hides and made one downward cut. The tent wall burst open, and He-Dog smashed through with both shoulders. Sunlight blazed in his eyes while the fresh air energized him further. He entered a worn path between pavilions, and killed the first beastman standing before him, his sword slashing the brute across the chest and opening it to the innards. With a surprised cry of pain, the thing went down. Others appeared, and He-Dog pressed his attack, bashing one lout across the sensitive muzzle with the edge of his shield and sending curved teeth flying. He slashed another, drawing a bloody line from left hip to right shoulder. Chop appeared beside him, his blades swirling, slicing, and taking the lives of any beastmen still in their path.

A knot of the creatures halted at the path's junction, spotted the escaping men, and charged.

"Balless!" He-Dog shouted. "We are *leaving*!"

Behind him, Balless pushed through the tent slit with his savage grin still in place. A beastman followed him and the diamond head of Balless' mace took the creature square in the face. The creature dropped to the ground, widening the cut in the tent wall. The whole wall shuddered as a multitude of blades and spears pierced it and began savagely cutting their way through. Balless backed away from the cuts, and held his long-shafted mace at the ready. Clawed hands and bared teeth appeared in the tent wall. Balless looked over his shoulder, and caught the fleeing back of Chop. With a grunt, he turned to follow, aware of beastmen charging in from both sides.

Up ahead, He-Dog plunged his blade into the pavilion wall before him and slashed downward again, not knowing in the least what lay ahead, but knowing full well that taking the paths to his right or left would place him in a sea of beastmen. With a roar, he dove through his cut doorway. Chop followed. Balless hurried to keep up.

He-Dog entered a dark tent full of hanging skins and racks of spears. He pressed through it all, spotting a crack of light in the gloomy folds ahead. Chop stayed behind, his blades before him like sharp, silver torches. Balless entered and stood just inside the slit. When the beastmen pursuers came through, he swung with both arms and smashed his mace across the jaws of two of them, sweeping both creatures to one side. A third swung a war club at his head, which Balless stopped. His counterthrust drove his mace's spike through the face of his attacker.

He-Dog paused at the far opening and looked back at his companion. "Balless!"

The big man killed a fourth beastman, landing his mace against the bare chest of the brute and crushing in a ribcage. Another jabbed a spear at him, which he caught with one spiked glove. He yanked the weapon forward and brought the beastman through the opening, stumbling over the crumpled corpses. The creature fell flat on his chest and Balless drove his mace into its skull, cracking it open.

Outside, beastmen gathered and howled. Weapons punched through and ripped at the skins of the tent wall. His ruined smile in place, Balless waited for them to come.

"*Balless!*" He-Dog roared.

Hearing his name, the big warrior turned away from the collapsing wall. He started lumbering through the tent, swishing his mace to and fro and bringing down racks of spears as well as support poles. The damaged wall came down in a heavy huff on the pursing beastmen.

Chop's black mask regarded He-Dog, and he took the hint. Without looking, He-Dog pushed out the door. Chop followed.

Balless ran through the tent behind them, one end of the pavilion collapsing in his wake and howls of rage in his ears.

He-Dog emerged onto another street between the tents. He could hear the roars from behind, and to his left he spotted beastmen rushing toward the king's pavilion. He paid them little heed. The escaping warriors only had seconds. He took three steps and cut his way through a third tent. Without a thought, he charged into the darkness.

Beastmen rose, perhaps waking from sleep.

Chop appeared behind He-Dog and the two of them quickly, savagely killed the occupants of the tent, leaving dark bodies cut open and spurting blood.

Balless barrelled merrily into the tent. Beastmen pushed

through the slit opening in pursuit. Balless turned and swiftly killed them. Again, spears and axes cut through the wall, prompting him to chase after his companions.

He-Dog hacked his way through the far wall, grimacing as he did so. He glanced back. He wouldn't go anywhere without knowing for certain Balless was following. That weakness would be the death of him and he knew it. Then Balless burst through the cut in the folds, and he pressed ahead.

Grimacing, He-Dog saw there was yet another tent before him. Luckily, the opening faced him. He groaned nevertheless. Sooner or later, they were going to run out of beastman tents.

Behind him, Chop quickly attacked two beastmen rushing in from the right, his blades taking both creatures across their unprotected shins and sending them into the sand. Once there, he left them. There wasn't any time to kill.

Bringing up the rear, Balless bludgeoned both of the fallen beastmen as he passed over the writhing creatures. Screams followed him. It sounded as if the entire army had been alerted.

Gasping, He-Dog threw aside the folds of the tent and shield-bashed an emerging warrior, knocking the creature back. He-Dog swept inward, seeing the torches that lit the interior of the pavilion. Two braziers burned, the smoke rising up and away in a hole far above. Digging picks, shovels, and crude containers littered the floor. A crowd of beastmen roared at him.

Roar. He-Dog grimaced. He would give them something to roar about.

Plunging forward, He-Dog chopped the leg half off one warrior, and stabbed another through the mid-section. He cursed himself when he had to struggle to pull the blade free. *Slash or cut*, he reminded himself as he yanked out the steel. Beastman blood gouted, its distinct stink flowering the air. He stopped a shovel swinging at his head and hacked off an arm. A pick pierced the sand between his feet and he upper-cut with his shield's edge, whipping the head of his foe back. He ducked under another flailing pick and gutted the owner. Turning, he readied himself to face another attacker… and found Chop had already killed the remainder.

He-Dog grunted. To think, he'd ignored the swordsman.

Chop pointed a blade at the center of the tent. There, among four wooden pillars holding up the ceiling, lay a dark hole. Over it hung a crude winch and pulley system made of wood and rope.

Ignoring Chop, He-Dog pushed his way to the edge of the pit and gazed down. It was black down there. And deep. A single ledge lay several feet down with darkness to the right. How deep it went, He-Dog had no way of knowing, but since he had survived seconds longer than he had expected to among an entire army of his enemy, he was feeling lucky.

"Balless!" he shouted.

On cue, the brute burst through the folds. "Here!" he breathed.

"Tip that fire!"

Grinning like a wrecked skull under a cap of iron, Balless whirled and gripped the edge of the nearest brazier, made of heavy iron. Clapping his teeth together in terrible effort, the big warrior up-ended and set a small avalanche of hot coals rumbling across the tent's opening. Across the way, Chop grabbed a burning torch set into one of the many support poles and flung it at the wall. It caught quickly.

Beastmen came through the opening and howled in agony at stepping on the red coals. They danced on the spot, and Balless batted them away with his mace, each connection making a meaty sound that was music to his companions' ears. Gazing down into the pit, He-Dog took a breath and jumped. He landed on the first ledge, the impact making his teeth rattle, and peered into the darkness below. He could make out the next ledge from a light further down. Calling out to both Chop and Balless, He-Dog gritted his teeth and leapt into the dark. He crunched into a wall and felt rock shave his cheeks in an agonizing caress. He cringed and wiped his face on one shoulder. To his right, another drop, but torchlight from below brightly illuminated a ledge. There was a thud of boots above him, and he saw Chop crouched and ready. Without another thought, He-Dog leapt to the next rocky outcropping, wondering fleetingly just how deep the hole went. And where.

On the surface, Balless inhaled smoke and barked a cough. He knocked over the second brazier and smashed away one of the support poles. The thin wood buckled and splintered. He turned and broke another pole with one swing.

Beastmen entered the tent, snarling at him and using the fallen bodies as bridges over the scorching coals.

Balless whirled and cracked his mace off the head of the closest foe, breaking both skull and neck. He parried a spear and drove his shoulder into another brute. A backhanded swing removed the lower jaw of a beastman in a burst of blood, bone, and teeth. The creature dropped to his knees, holding his wound while Balless killed two more in similar fashion. Unlike He-Dog, Balless had no qualms about killing beastmen, smelly blood or not. He liked them simply because they did not stop until either they or their adversaries were dead. There was something to be respected in that kind of fearlessness.

Balless crushed the skull of the beastman whose jaw he'd removed, and brutally dispatched two more before he realized two walls of the tent were blazing. Smoke swirled and billowed, flowing out of the rips in the tent. Balless backed away from the dark shadows still charging inside. He almost tripped over two bodies before finding the open pit. Mashing his teeth together, he took one more look around the burning tent, and jumped.

Below, He-Dog pushed his way through a narrow cave where he had to partially crouch. Up ahead lay another brightly glowing torch. He spotted figures and groaned. Nothing was ever easy. Worse, he saw that the beastmen held iron picks. He came upon them in a huff, intent on killing each in turn. He stabbed the first one dead. He dispatched and almost tripped on the body of the second beastman, and the third one came close to plunging the iron tip of his weapon into He-Dog's guts. The pick gouged the rocky wall in a shower of fragments and dirt instead, and He-Dog jumped back before stabbing his attacker though the face. Then there was only one remaining.

Snarling, the beastman dropped the pick and charged.

He-Dog realized at once that the creature was smart; knowing that the cave was barely the width of its shoulders and seeing that He-Dog's blade was in the head of his companion, the beastman batted his dead comrade to one side and gripped the edge of He-Dog's shield. He-Dog couldn't free his shield or withdraw his sword in time, as the serrated edge of his weapon had stuck in the dead beast's skull. His fist came up as the beastman crashed into him, clamping the thing's jaws shut. Rough claws scrabbled at He-Dog's ribs, seeking to disembowel him, but the armor saved him. He-Dog brought his fist down across the muzzle of the beastman, smashing the sensitive nose. Instead of withdrawing in pain, the brute raged and swept him up under his arms, catching him by surprise and crashing his helmed head into the low hanging cavern. He-Dog saw stars and felt the ceiling rake against his helm as his foe pushed forward, snarling in pain and fury. He tried swinging his shield, but it caught in the low hanging rock. The beastman whipped him into the wall, and punched his midsection once with a blow that made He-Dog bark out in pain despite his armor. The creature pinned his sword arm and wet-looking jaws, poised at He-Dog's throat, opened with a hiss.

Chop stabbed the beastman with both swords, angling the steel upward to pierce both lung and heart. He-Dog's almost-killer stiffened, snorted, and slumped against him.

Squinting in pain, He-Dog regarded the black mask of Chop and nodded thanks. He considered himself a bastard, but he could be a thankful bastard at times. Retrieving his sword, he slapped the shoulder of the masked man. In the flickering light of the torch in the rocky corridor, he looked back the way he had come, searching for Balless. He motioned Chop for silence, and for a moment, all they could hear was the hiss of the torch and the deflating of the dead beastman's lungs.

"Where is he?" He-Dog wondered aloud.

Chop glanced back only for a moment. He pushed past his companion, and studied the end of the tunnel.

"Balless!" He-Dog called.

And heard a distant crashing.

Chop stood hunched over and studied the tunnel's end. He returned his swords to their scabbards and placed his hands against the rock.

"What is it?" He-Dog grunted, adjusting the helm on his head and feeling a trickle of blood from underneath. He sighed. More mending time.

The black masked man indicated he wanted a torch. He-Dog stepped back, mindful of the bodies at his feet, and took the torch from the wall. Chop took the light from him and held it to the end of the tunnel. There, in the upper section of rock and sand, was a black hole the size of a skull.

"Dying Seddon," He-Dog breathed. He heard someone approach from behind. Balless.

"Took you long enough,"

"*Urf!* Tunnel's small," Balless replied, bending over at the shoulders. "Topside's burning."

"Burning?"

"Aye. Gives us a few moments at least. Where are we?"

He-Dog pointed to the tunnel's end. "Figure we're going in the direction of Foust here. Looks like they've been busy."

Balless' brow crunched up in thought. "Tunnel's not wide enough."

"How wide do you want it?" He-Dog countered. "It's big enough for a single file of those dogs. And they might have dug into a cave or even sewers under the city. Lucky them."

"Lucky us," Balless grinned, exposing the few teeth he had.

Chop slapped his hands together and pointed to a pick at Balless' feet. The big man grunted and handed it over. Chop waved them back a bit and wound up. With a grunt, he pitched the pick into the rock before him, producing a puff of debris. He swung again and again, widening the hole as quickly as he could. When he tired, he handed off to He-Dog, who took his turn. No one spoke about what might lay ahead. They were well aware of what lay behind them.

False Kratoe. For all the gold we can carry. Lies. At least they'd been outfitted with armor and weapons. That took some of the sting out of the bargain.

Baring his teeth, He-Dog swung the iron pick with whatever strength he could muster.

CHAPTER 27

On the surface and still in his pavilion, Two-Bite took huge gulps of air. Around him, the earth spun and appeared in vibrant gashes of purple and gold. His beastmen gathered around like dark wraiths. Some reached out to him, but he commanded them back. He called for Turn-Bone and Axe-Jaw and two ghosts appeared by his side. Two-Bite grimaced and recognized his senses were skewed, but even as he thought it, he willed himself back to a distant point of awareness.

The beastmen around him asked him what was wrong. Two-Bite explained as best as he could, as the sand beneath him seemed to tilt and roll like the Big Water. He did not know what had done it, only that it felt like the juice the man-things called spirits. One of the wraiths spoke to Two-Bite, telling him there was no spirits of any kind in the entire war camp. The creature's voice sounded as if he stood days away, though the apparition floated right before him.

Two-Bite roared, fighting feelings of dullness and dreams that talked. He shouted that it was the flesh! The flesh of the man-thing whose face he'd chewed off. Even as he spoke, the truth of his words washed away the surreal tints of the world around him, and he felt his senses slowly returning. The wraiths took shape, the colors faded, and the world of ghosts drew back to reveal one full of growling beastmen.

Two-Bite stood and took huge breaths. He gazed upon the body of the dead man-thing and ordered that it be burned. Fighting dizziness, he looked around the pavilion and saw the dead warriors and chieftains. He spied the wrecked wall that allowed daylight to shine through. He demanded to know where the last three man-things were, to which a black replied that they had died in a fire.

Two-Bite demanded to see the bodies.

The black, a chieftain by his roughshod garb of bones and teeth, informed him that bodies could not be reached, as the fire still burned.

Smoke clouded the air and Two-Bite marched unsteadily from his damaged tent. The hot air filled his lungs and cleared his head further. He was grateful that the effects of the man-thing's flesh did not linger. Turn-Bone and an armored Axe-Jaw followed at their War-Skull's heels, as did the rest of the leaders. He followed the path of destruction. Chagrin swelled within Two-Bite's frame as he surveyed the dead and the damage caused by the three. Just ahead, over the half-deflated pavilions, a great fire raged, engulfing three tents. Warriors raced to and fro, attempting to contain the blaze by smothering it with sand.

Two-Bite's brain twisted in recognition. He asked the chieftains if they did not realize which tent was burning. He indicated the one he meant, and felt his blood boil when none answered. The War Skull turned on them all, his face growing darker by the second.

He looked at Axe-Jaw and commanded the Koja to be readied. Once the fires were beaten back, Axe-Jaw would take the armored beastmen into the tunnel. The same tunnel he planned to use to run under the walls of Foust. The same tunnel he knew had punched its way through to a deeper cavern, a cavern whose very breath had killed the crews digging in it, and had forced the digging to a halt. Only this morning, Two-Bite had ordered a new crew back into the shaft, to see if the cave's breath still killed. They had returned, but before he could command the digging to begin, the false Kratoe had appeared.

The false Kratoe. The more he thought about it, the blood of the man-thing had tasted off, as if poison of some kind flowed through his veins. But the three man-things—they were real. He could tell even as the cloud of dreams descended upon him and made the world strange.

Two-Bite suspected the man-things lived. He suspected that even now, they moved underneath his feet, toward the safety of Foust's walls. He did not know if they could make it to the surface, but he knew that these three man-things had twice escaped the wrath of the beastmen. They had killed Blood Skull. Perhaps they were charmed. Either way, Two-Bite could not risk having the existence of his tunnel revealed to the Foust defenders.

A sheet of flame rose before him and the smell of burning animal skins and beastman flesh filled his nostrils. Two-Bite knew in his gut the three man-things lived. They had the fortune of being ones not easily killed. He knew now what he had to do. With a gnashing of his jaws, Two-Bite barked the orders.

War had just begun anew.

*

From the walls of Foust, Krajin's eyes narrowed as he saw thick intestines of smoke rise from the center of the beastman army. Now and again, flashes of flame erupted from far off tent tops and cries of anger pierced the air. *Scream,* the captain thought to himself. *It's all they ever seem to do.*

"Koor," Krajin called out and his junior officer appeared at his side almost immediately.

"Captain."

"Get the word along the walls." Krajin glanced at him once before returning his attention to the land before Foust. "Prepare for an assault. Have archers at the ready. Make ready ballistae and catapults to let loose upon my command. Send a runner to the inner keep. Alert them that there may be action forthcoming. Go."

"Understood, Captain," and the young officer departed.

Krajin's eyes narrowed and his heavy moustache twitched. Ill feelings coursed through him and he'd learned long ago to trust them. First and foremost, he considered himself a protector of the people of Foust, slowly advancing himself over the years to his current position. He had taken an oath to defend the city with his life. Looking out over the burning fires, he grimly wondered if this would be the day when he would honor that vow.

*

When sand and beastman fury finally beat the flames engulfing three of their tents into submission, Two-Bite stood before the smoking ruins in full battle garb. A chain mail vest retrieved intact from a fallen man-thing covered his upper body, while pauldrons of thick metal protected his shoulders and gave him the appearance of greater width. A helm covered his head. In honor of the dead Blood Skull, Two-Bite wore some of the tooth necklaces and other war badges due a beastman king.

Two-Bite looked to his new Koja leader Axe-Jaw, and told him to use the tunnel below and make their way under the belly of Foust. Find and kill the three escaped man-things, but also find the way into the streets of Foust. Find their way to the high walls, and kill all they could. Two-Bite's jaws worked like a bloody trap after catching prey, and Axe-Jaw paid close attention to his War Skull's words.

"*Kill them all*," Two-Bite growled in the beastman tongue, "*and let us know when you are inside.*"

Axe-Jaw nodded his split muzzle, his eyes glowering out from the depths of his helm. He held a crude war club in both hands across his upper thighs. Gathered behind him stood the elite *Koja*, over a hundred and fifty strong from all of the gathered tribes, each covered in piecemeal armor taken from dead man-things. Some of the armor was in hard condition, making one wonder how long the armor had been in use or how badly it had been damaged before a beastman acquired it. There were other suits made from the forges within the camp, hammered together using man-thing armor as a guide. Frightening designs of heavy mail lashed together by metal pins, leather strips, and buckles covered the *Koja*, while helms of primitive makes protected their skulls.

Two-Bite told them to go as soon as the fire died down. He told them they would be waiting for their signs from above. He told them they were the spike that would kill Foust.

Then he left them for further preparations, shouting orders to the chieftains who followed.

Axe-Jaw turned back to the fires. Beastmen worked furiously to douse the flames. Soon, they would hunt.

CHAPTER 28

Balless made the hole big enough for Chop. The smaller man climbed in through the hole, and with a few more swipes, slabs of rock and dirt crumpled away to allow He-Dog passage. Extra hides and cloth material for torches lined the tunnel floor, and He-Dog put his blade away and gathered what he could. Stale air held a hint of sewage and it wrinkled He-Dog's nose. He waved the torch before him as Balless threw down the pick and handed Chop his mace.

"Hurry." He-Dog peered off into the darkness and wondered just where it was they stood. And what might lay ahead.

Balless pulled himself through the hole, grimacing as he came through. "I pity wenches," he grunted.

"I pity them too, to birth one like you," He-Dog said.

"Bit harsh." Balless frowned as he took an unlit torch from He-Dog. "How many of these do we have?"

"Six."

Chop carried two in one hand.

"Let's get on then," He-Dog said. "And watch your footing. The rock slopes down here."

"Think they'll be after us?"

"Aye. Think they won't?"

"Might not."

He-Dog shook his head. He had nothing to say to that.

They moved away from the hole with He-Dog at the front and holding the torch. The torchlight cast the underground world in orange, spiked with He-Dog's shadow. A deep earth smell laced with what He-Dog knew to be shite filled their senses.

"Smell that?"

"Aye."

"Shite?"

"Aye that."

"Sewers I wager."

"Far off, though."

"Aye," He-Dog said from where he hunched over at the front. Chop stood behind him like a dangerous silhouette, and Balless brought up the rear. Without another word, He-Dog led them forward.

Balless stubbed his boot against some rocks and sent them rolling downward. The noise crackled in the dark, and the echoes made He-Dog swing the torch back to the big man's face.

"I'm sorry," Balless muttered.

"You've woken any corpses down here."

"Sorry. You think there are corpses down here?"

"If there are, they're awake now."

"Sorry."

"Watch your footing."

Balless looked embarrassed.

"I mean it."

Balless nodded.

They kept on. It soon became obvious that the tunnel wasn't a tunnel at all, but merely the tip of the ear of a much larger cavern, and they were walking down its curve, mindful of where they stepped. He-Dog's foot slipped and he teetered for a moment, torch waving in the darkness. Loose rocks rolled away from him, their echoes crackling in the dark.

He gave a withering look to Chop and Balless. Chop's expression was hidden by his mask, but Balless shook his head.

"Not a word," He-Dog warned him.

The slope steepened, and soon the three had to lower themselves down from outcropping to outcropping until they came to a sheet of bedrock that stretched off into the darkness. He-Dog stopped and listened. The others followed his example, but could see nothing beyond their bubble of light.

He-Dog motioned to Chop for another torch. He took the fresh one and lit it from the old. He gazed up into the blackness, noting it was darker than night. He couldn't hear anything, and fear lit up his senses. Fear of unseen things in the dark. Fear of things with many legs, and a taste for warm flesh.

"Come on," He-Dog said to them, forcing the chill back from wherever it came.

"Where do you think we are?" Balless whispered. "Under the city?

Good question. "Maybe. I don't know."

"Can't hear anything."

"That's good," He-Dog grunted. "Means nothing is following us.

He looked behind and saw that beyond the rough bedrock only darkness prevailed. He looked upward, trying to see the slope they climbed, and couldn't see anything.

They kept walking until He-Dog stopped in his tracks. Chop almost bumped into him from behind. He-Dog looked back at the man and dropped into a squat. He kept the torch out ahead of him.

Chop straightened and searched the surrounding darkness. Balless bared his empty gums and the teeth that remained.

Bones. The bones of a man.

He-Dog's expression curdled.

Not a man.

"What is it?" Balless asked, moving to one side of He-Dog while Chop moved to the other. The three men stared down at the grim discovery. He-Dog got to his feet but held the torch high for the others to see, while he strained to see through the dark.

"Bones," Balless said and then saw that it was only the rib cage, skull, and right arm of a man, and that this particular man had possessed exceptionally long incisors. The fingers were cupped into a fist, but he could see the digits were unnaturally long, like thick needles. The skull was that of a man's but longer in the back, as if someone had grabbed a chunk of bone and stretched it.

The three stood and stared at the remains.

"What is it?" Balless whispered.

He-Dog shook his head. "And are there others?"

They shared a look. There probably *were* others. It was just their fortune.

"On guard now," He-Dog said, as he moved past them. "And no noise."

They kept on, pressing forward, and straining to hear anything lurking in the blackness.

"That thing reminds me of those other things we came across once, down in those jungles," Balless whispered.

Both Chop and He-Dog nodded.

They walked on, stepping as lightly as they did on a hunt. A sound perked their ears. In the distance, a *plink… plink… plink*. Soon, the bedrock beneath their feet became streaked with semi-dry sludge. The smell of excrement assaulted them, and He-Dog waved the torch to see what they had found.

"Sewers," He-Dog said. "Above us. There's a slope."

They could see the rise at the edge of the torchlight.

"What do we do?" Balless asked.

He-Dog thought about it for a moment. There might indeed be grates above, but the idea of coming up from the city's bowels was as appealing as being bathed in beastman blood. Something else hooked his attention and he focused on the blackness again. He hardly dared believe it, but he thought he felt a breeze from somewhere beyond. Another thing bothered him. He felt an urge to hurry build in his chest and his lower legs. A feeling brought on by the thought of pursuit. The Koja. Armored beastmen.

"Keep on." With that, he led them past the half-dried river of filth, and deeper into the unknown depths of the cavern.

*

Reducing the fires to sheets that flared only here and there, Axe-Jaw snarled and led his Koja through the hot spots to the hole. He roared commands, and Koja covered in leather and hammered iron bent to move away the debris. High above them, the sun beat down on their helmed heads, and Axe-Jaw himself felt how the new armor was not only heavy, but hot. He felt as if he were inside a pot, and it angered him even more. Around the camp, beastmen moved forward to Foust. They would be waiting for the Koja to penetrate the city from below, like a long spike thrust into soft guts.

With a guttural bark, the Koja removed the last few burning pieces blocking the hole. Axe-Jaw shoved them aside impatiently and peered deep into the smoking cavity. *They* were down there as well. The three man-things who had wrought so much devastation among the beastmen. They were down there and they were Axe-Jaw's to do with as he wanted.

Howling, Axe-Jaw raised his weapon into the air, a single bladed war axe with spikes on its head and opposing the broad slated edge. Many a time, he had plunged the same fearsome weapon into the unprotected stomachs of fallen foes, tearing out and twirling the grey and scarlet ribbons of their innards. He looked forward to meeting the people of Foust.

With the heat of the sun enraging him further, Axe-Jaw jumped into the welcoming blackness, and the mass of Koja followed.

*

They had gone beyond the sludge and were making steady progress into the cavern when Chop drew up and bade He-Dog and Balless to stop. He motioned for quiet. He-Dog had learned long ago to trust the smaller man's instincts and perked his ears to the dark.

There it was. A scrabbling somewhere to the right. No, He-Dog realized, all around them. A sound of movement and of many legs scurrying against the sheets of bedrock. He only hoped it was rats or some other such vermin. The bones of the thing behind him seeped into his mind.

He-Dog hefted his shield and torch and led the other two onward. The black mask hid Chop's expression, but Balless' was one of concern. He-Dog knew his companion did not like to be underground and fighting in the dark. Bad things came from fighting under those conditions.

The sound followed them, and He-Dog believed that whatever it was, it kept just beyond the protective circle of torchlight. With a grunt, he turned back and lit another torch and thrust it into Balless' hand.

"Both ends, 'eh?" Balless smirked.

"Don't want to be grabbed by anything, do you?"

"You think they'll try to grab us?"

He-Dog shrugged, but a worried looking Balless studied the burning torch and looked around.

"Smell something," he said.

He-Dog stopped again and took a breath, sniffing the air. He drew in a musky odor, pungent, like the sweat of flesh after years of exertion and never once washed. The smell made him scowl. Whatever they were, they made beastmen blood smell like flowers.

He waved the torch, thrusting it into the dark and

hoping it would uncover something to kill, but each time found nothing.

"Smells bad," Balless said from behind.

More skittering on rocks. "They're closer," He-Dog commented warily. He hated fighting in the dark.

"Aye."

Chop had his blades out. He-Dog lit another torch as his burned low. Over Chop's shoulder, he saw Balless trying to look everywhere at once with his torch, his heavy mace held at the ready in his other hand.

"Come on," He-Dog ordered and started walking.

"There's lots of them."

"I hear them."

"*Lots.*"

"I *know.*"

The sound came from ahead as well now, and the overpowering smell came close to making He-Dog gag.

"Wave that light around," Balless said. "It's keeping them back."

That was probably true. Any creature born into this subterranean night most likely saw quite well in it, and the torches were the equals of suns down here. Suns that burned out too quickly.

The smell grew, and He-Dog heard more claws on rock around them, as well as the low piping squeaks rats would make, except longer, as if drawing upon larger lungs.

They moved swiftly ahead, not knowing in the least where they were heading, and He-Dog wondered if they were going toward the nest of whatever was hounding them. The thought made him smirk. That would be a deadly jest indeed.

Chop turned this way and that, reacting to new sounds hidden by the inky blackness. In the rear, Balless waved the light to and fro while keeping up with the dark backs of the men ahead of him. In one swish of the light, he caught a glimpse of something, perhaps claws. But then it was gone, jerked back from the light as if it had never been. He did not leave the others to investigate. He-Dog would have his head if he did.

"Rock is rising," He-Dog said, feeling the incline under his boots.

"Where?" Balless asked, but got no answer.

The sound of pursuit increased ever so subtly around them, and He-Dog felt a growing sense of dread, which his hate fought to keep at bay. He pressed forward, swishing his torch left and right, feeling the presence of whatever it was crowding in from all sides, like a swarm of ants circling something sweet. He-Dog felt if he threw the torch into the darkness, if he really let it go into the cavern's night, he would see what surrounded them. Half of him, the spiteful half wanted to do just that, but the superstitious part of him pleaded not to, for fear of pulling more nightmares into his sleep. As he swept the light to the edges, he sensed something pull back, even though nothing was visible. His mind conjured up dark images of the bones left behind coming to ghastly life and clicking after them on limbs as long and as frightful as a spider's.

"Wave that light," Balless repeated from the rear. "It's keeping them back."

"What?"

"The light's keeping them back."

"Who?"

This time, Balless didn't answer. Glancing behind, He-Dog could plainly see the worry on his face as he jigged this way and that, swishing the fire and making it crackle.

"This way," He-Dog commanded, and did as Balless asked. It wasn't a bad idea.

The incline gradually became a steeper slope and they headed up. The smell became impossibly stronger, and they felt each breath laced their lungs with a foulness not even Sergius would be able to make well. Chop did not seem affected in the least and He-Dog thought perhaps he would buy himself a mask if he ever saw the light of day again.

"Watch your step," He-Dog said, louder now, for the sound of claws squealing on bedrock grew louder, closer. Waving his torch and extending his arm, He-Dog caught glimpses of talons, long, curved, and tough. He discerned movement in the inky dark, blackness moving against a wall of night. Indistinct shapes, but they were there. They were there in force.

He felt pebbles underfoot and envisioned himself falling, saw the torch dousing and the shapes pouncing. That would be that. Whatever was closing in was numerous enough that, once that first thing grabbed for him, they all would. Those curved claws, sharpened and worn by years of scratching rock, would hook into his armor, his flesh, and his organs, tearing him open like the peel on ripe fruit.

Out of the darkness appeared a portcullis. He-Dog's eyes nearly burst from their sockets. He put his shoulder to bars spaced close enough that he couldn't fit his arm through. The grate covered a small hole in the side, barring everything. He-Dog thought that it was the hole to another sewer, but the light revealed a passageway on the other side.

Behind him, Balless grunted as he swished the light back and forth. Chop stood by his side with his blades both out and ready.

He-Dog rammed an armored shoulder into the bars, but they did not move. He strained to see around the edges, and saw that pins secured the portcullis in place. Grunting his frustration, he shoved his shoulder against the bars once more. Then again, feeling them rattle but not yield.

"Let me." Balless switched places with He-Dog. The slope placed them all on treacherous footing, and as He-Dog got behind Balless, the torchlight revealed a rising embankment of eyes squinting against the light, glittering in the darkness. Hissing could be heard, which He-Dog believed meant an attack was not far off. Chop stood at his side, his swords angled downward like bare spear tips, but not even the swordsman's incredible speed would throw back the gathering tide.

"Balless."

"What?"

"Hurry."

"*Urf.*" Balless threw his torch back over their heads and slammed his shoulder into the portcullis with another grunt. He reared up his mace, aimed at one point on the door, and smashed. Sparks flickered.

Balless' torch turned over in the air and landed far beyond, illuminating the squirming spiny mass of metal grey backs of hunched-over things. There were squeals of pain and bodies near the light drew back from where it landed. Spidery arms lashed out, and the torchlight weakened. More squeals, more flailing arms, and the light fluttered and winked out.

All to the drum of Balless' diamond shaped mace.

The big man drove its spike into a groove and heaved. Metal groaned. He took a breath and stabbed again into a joint. With whatever power he possessed, Balless pulled and pushed, working the spike of his mace further into the metal and feeling the slow movement of metal bending to his will.

Behind him, a claw reached out of the darkness on Chop's left and reached for his boot. The swordsman slashed it away, making the limb shiver as it disappeared.

More limbs reached for them, testing, prodding, as an old grandmother might pinch a child's cheeks.

He-Dog and Chop got busy.

Balless heaved his weight against the door again, feeling a corner give. He kicked at the metal in the lower right section. He pushed. He dropped low and placed his shoulder to the bars while finding solid ground with his boots.

A claw swiped at He-Dog's face. He thrust his torch at

the limb and burned it. A pain-filled shriek stabbed the gloom.

A hand slinked out of the inky air and Chop lopped it off at the wrist. Black blood spurted and the fingers danced for a second before tumbling out of sight.

Balless bared his ruined teeth and *heaved*. The section of bars buckled inward with an iron groan. He pushed until he thought it wide enough for him, and then forced his shoulders into the gap. It caught him and held firm, but he wormed his way through, his grin returning.

"He-Dog!"

Limbs ending with claws pawed at him now, batting at the light. He-Dog looked over his shoulder and saw Balless beyond the bars. He whipped the torch across the slope one last time and handed it over to Chop, who took it in the same hand as his right sword.

They would have to be fast, He-Dog knew, and he dove into the hole. His armor caught in places, but Balless pulled him through, kicking and grimacing and hating every moment.

"Chop!"

The swordsman backed up. The stench from the creatures was breath-stealing, and the torch kept the tide from rising any further, but He-Dog could see the masked man had no chance of getting though that narrow hole before the things in the dark grabbed his ankles and pulled him back. He-Dog bared his teeth.

He was as good as gone.

Chop screamed, a blood curdling sound that made the hair on both men's necks stand up, and the black mask dropped the torch while spinning and diving through the gap in the portcullis. His armor hooked in the metal and rock but He-Dog grabbed for him and pulled, pulled even as Chop's legs kicked and scrabbled and pushed against the multitude of clutching claws as if it were a living wall.

Chop's eyes locked with He-Dog's, and he saw the swordman's fear in them as the things beyond the gate swooped in. It would be now, now even as he was close to safety that he would be pulled back into the dark. Claws scratched Chop's bronze greaves and tried to grab his ankles, but He-Dog would not let his companion go so easily. He yanked Chop through as the torch light fell away. Balless was there, swinging his mace and crushing the things struggling to get through the opening in the grate. Shrieks and squeals of a nature none of them had ever heard cut the blackness. Balless swung his mace, pulverizing any flesh that sought to come through. The bars were narrow enough to stop whole hands, and there was one last glimpse of torchlight to see rows upon rows of claws spring through the gaps in the metal like a mesh of wriggling, hooked daggers.

Balless continued to smash, pulping limbs trapped in the pried back hole of the portcullis and breaking fresh ones. He-Dog pulled Chop away from the opening and fumbled for a torch. He realized he had nothing with which to light it.

"Close it, Balless," he barked.

Balless grunted in reply, bringing the diamond-headed mace down and down again. Screams went up from beyond the grate, and a whispering noise He-Dog suspected to be the lapping of tongues against the iron of the door. Like men dying of thirst, so ravenous were the things for blood.

After a while, Balless put his boot to the iron, smashing more claws.

"Leave it," He-Dog roared. "And follow the wall."

"Where?"

He-Dog didn't bother replying because he didn't know. All he knew was that air flowed through this tunnel, and it was built and fitted with stone in places.

"This way," he called, and thought he heard Chop shout behind him, letting him know he was there.

Behind them, Balless held the line at the door, allowing none to pass, and smashed on in utter darkness.

CHAPTER 29

Under torchlight, the gleaming column of Koja slowed when they came to the steep slope dropping into blackness. Axe-Jaw cautioned his followers to move slowly, and not be overeager. It was warm beneath the earth and the air smelled bad, but they no longer cooked in the sun, and that was good. They descended farther into the cave, and Axe-Jaw realized he didn't know how far down they were. Not that it mattered much. They would find their way back up.

They came to a plain of rutted bedrock and forged ahead, searching for signs of the three men, or of a way to the surface behind Foust's walls. There was some shock when they found the bones in their path. Axe-Jaw, for one, thought they were a beastman's bones, an ancient cousin to the surface tribes. Axe-Jaw had heard stories of such creatures and their thirst for warm blood. He recalled being told of a time when enslaved beastmen worked the mines of Foust. Slaves to the man-things who were sealed in the catacombs for forgotten reasons. Whatever the case, the things did not die as the man-things had hoped. Instead, they thrived, living off each other when necessary, and other things in the deep dark of the mines. Axe-Jaw had even heard of stories of them reaching the surface, but finding the sun too bright to bear, and retreating to the blackest pits, which were now called home. They would not go back until they took meat with them. However, they were not particular in the least about what kind of meat. They feasted on whatever was unfortunate enough to be caught.

The elders of his tribe had a name for such beastmen. They called them the Mar Fahten— Children of the Deep Earth.

Axe-Jaw gave the command to move on. The air smelled like shite, and he was aware that the man-things liked to squat over holes in the earth. Before long, he found a riverbed of dried sludge, his sensitive nose quivering at the aroma of the city's waste. He saw the sign he was looking for: tracks. Boots of man-things, leading into the gloom of the cave.

Axe-Jaw's nose smelled something else to his left. Waving his axe, he proceeded in that direction, deviating from the tracks and feeling the rock rise beneath his feet. The incline wasn't as steep as the previous one. He heard the mewling of the Mar Fahten, but he paid them little heed. The Koja were more than ready to deal out death if their distant cousins felt up to it. As they didn't care who they feasted upon, the Koja cared little about killing something that lived beneath them.

Climbing upward, Axe-Jaw suspected that they were inside the walls of Foust. He turned and motioned to those behind to stay quiet, and made it clear he would brain any who disobeyed. With that, he edged further, cautiously, mindful and sensing closeness to the enemy. He came to a wall with a trickle of scum water dripping over the edge of a wide hole. Axe-Jaw thrust his torch into the dark. There was stonework beyond, and filthy smelling water. He recognized it as one of the veins of Foust that collected all of the man-things' shite. He had never actually seen one before, but he'd heard of them.

With a low growl, Axe-Jaw hauled himself into the sewers of Foust, and the Koja followed.

The brick tunnel ahead forced the beastmen to walk hunched over at the waist, wading through filthy water. Axe-Jaw wondered if the Children had made the hole to access the streets of Foust for late night hunting. Whatever the reason, the Koja used the sewage system, sloshing and slinking beneath the streets of the city.

Here and there light spilled down from open grates, and Axe-Jaw saw either passing man-things, or structures of their design. These grates were too small and surrounded by brick and stone.

Then he arrived at the opening he sought—a huge aperture in the stonework, divided by thick wooden beams into sections. Several holes allowed light. It would be an easy thing to punch through wood.

Axe-Jaw beckoned the Koja behind him. Blood-Grin wielded a heavy maul. Axe-Jaw told him what he wanted done and got out of the way.

*

The public latrines were empty this afternoon, a rarity unto itself, but it gave Balven a break with the scrub brushes. Ordinarily, he would take the chance to clean around the open seats in the alcoves, but there was a decree to conserve water, so he did nothing except endure the stench that came with the job. He wanted to place wooden covers on each of the holes, and thought it would reduce the reek of excrement, but that would only happen after the siege reached its conclusion, as all able-bodied carpenters were at the walls. Balven couldn't handle a hammer, nor did he have any interest in learning how. It wasn't his job. Public voiding was his lot in life, and the eight latrines that he was employed to preside over were his domain. It wasn't a bad job. Keep the premises clean, hand the scrub brushes to the patrons when they needed them. It kept him off the walls, and out of harm's way. He was as much a warrior as a carpenter, and in a way grateful that his small frame kept him out of a suit of mail. Wearing armor and potentially getting killed was not Balven's idea of fun.

He heard scraping coming from one of the latrine's alcoves, and paused in thought. Sewer rats, no doubt, trying to get up and into the street by way of the latrine. He got up from his seat at the edge and picked up his rat stick, a heavy piece of wood the length of his arm with a nail driven into one end. It was enough to deal with a sewer rat. Balven quietly approached the latrine. He leaned over the open hole and saw something move in the dark. Something big. Balven brought his rat stick to bear, his long face pensive. It was fortunate that he would kill the creature when there was no one around. Rats in the latrines did nothing for some folks' voiding.

He heard a crash and leaned back, looking at the other alcoves. Another crash and something long and weapon-like jutted into the air. Balven backed away from the latrine and walked cautiously toward the noise. He heard growling and grunting, sounding something like a cross between a dog and a pig.

Balven turned the corner and froze in place.

The beastman emerging from the ruined latrine stared at him. Their eyes met. Then the creature's maul came down upon Balven's unprotected skull. The swing was a clumsy one as the beastman was somewhat restricted in the narrow confines of the alcove. It was still enough to drive Balven to the ground. Stunned, but far from dead, Balven rolled over in a soup of pain and watched, bleary-eyed, as the beastman extracted himself from the bowels of Foust. Even worse, others emerged.

The attendant tried to rise to his knees, but his limbs did not respond to his summons. Nor did they respond when the beastman with the maul stood, gleaming in the light. The thing shook out his maul, the movement registering in Balven's senses, but nothing more.

The beastman lumbered over to where Balven lay, breathing shallowly on the warm bricks. The head of the maul came over his skull, and lifted. Balven tracked it as best as he could with glazed eyes.

It came down with explosive force.

*

Axe-Jaw wormed his way up through the hole and extracted himself. He brought up his axe and moved to a corner while other Koja crawled free of the alcoves and assembled in the small area. The Koja leader peered around one corner and saw that good fortune was with him. There, straight down a narrow street occupied by a scattering of man-things, loomed the walls of Foust. Barking commands, Axe-Jaw waited until the bulk of his force crowded behind him. He led them out into the street.

A door opened and a man-thing appeared on Axe-Jaw's right. With a snarl, the Koja leader threw his enemy into the street and brained him with one cut. Other people stepped out of their homes and into the path of the advancing beastmen. The Koja dispatched each of them in bloody fashion, keeping the distant walls in sight. They did not deviate from their path, as Axe-Jaw had warned them to stay close and quiet until the last possible moment. Surprise would be everything.

*

Walking up an alley, Jun-Jun and Jawbone looked for the one-eyed bastard who killed had Sabo. In a rage, Karast had sent them out to search the city for the man and the bitch with him, but they hadn't found their quarry. They were in the city, that was for certain, but as Jun-Jun pointed out, it was a big city.

Karast stayed in the Hole in case of customers or, even better, in case the need for Tar brought Sabo's killers back. Both Jun-Jun and Jawbone thought that Karast would have the greater luck in catching them. Still, they owed Sabo for the years of favored employment, so the two brutes searched.

Up ahead, screams rang out, causing Jun-Jun's silver boy-mask to look up. Both men hefted their weapons. They moved to the mouth of the alley, which opened to a wider street, and stepped out with steel bristling. There were very few soldiers in the city itself besides a patrol or two, and the men had thus far managed to avoid them.

Behind their masks, the faces dropped in horror at coming face to face with a rush of armored beastmen.

Though involved with a shady trade, Jun-Jun and Jawbone were both warriors. The abrupt appearance of the beastmen left little room to run, unless they wanted to be killed from behind. There wasn't even any time to properly react.

The beastmen overran the two burly men. A maul smashed into the silver face of the boy, driving Jun-Jun to his knees while an axe took his weapon arm off at the shoulder. Jawbone had his thigh crushed by a mace a second before an axe swiped his grinning grill from his face. The beastmen smashed them into the dirt and sand and trampled over them.

Leaving behind two wrecked forms.

*

The beastmen continued down side streets. Some women screamed upon sighting the brutes while other shouted warnings. The men folk ran and slammed doors. Axe-Jaw did not know what they said, but he liked the screams. What he really wanted, however, was more warriors to kill.

Fortune remained with him.

A patrol of Foust soldiers crossed their path. One man in the rear turned and bolted for the wall. That was fine with Axe-Jaw. He was tired of being quiet.

Raising his weapon, the Koja leader roared and those congesting the street behind him took up the bestial cry.

*

Outside the wall, the massed beastman army waited impatiently for the fight to begin. An impassive Two-Bite watched the walls, waiting for the signal to commence the attack. Behind him loomed the unarmored form of Turn-Bone. Not all of the beastmen wished to wear metal and Two-Bite had given up trying to convince him otherwise. Around them stood the terrible strength of twenty-nine tribes, poised and eager to take the fight to the walls of Foust. The War Skull looked beyond his private guard, taking in the *whuffing* forms of other savage reds, dangerous blacks, cruel whites, and cunning greens. Axes, swords, war clubs, mauls, and maces were held closely, tightly, and eager to take the lives of the man-things. Ballistae and catapults, crude but effective machines of war, were pushed to the front of the army, their crews ready to push them into striking range at Two-Bite's order.

And there was the koch.

The koch that had taken the life of Blood Skull had impressed Two-Bite. He appreciated the sheer power of the machine and its tough hide. The man-things could not reach the wagon and so it lay there on its side for weeks, allowing Two-Bite and his cohort time to inspect the monster. Though red beastmen had the reputation of being the most savage, Two-Bite knew his tribes had thinkers as well. He knew careful thought was just as powerful a weapon as lunging headlong into an enemy, and he recognized the potential of restoring the koch to its former glory... with a few adjustments.

The koch stood among the beastmen, its wheels and

armor plating repaired where necessary. The spiked roller had been removed. Slabs of wood roofed the poles in front of the koch, where horses once pulled the vehicle. Now the wood would protect the sixteen beastmen who would pull its bulk to the gates of Foust. Beastmen would push from behind as well to get the monster moving. Once it was underway, they would fall back.

The sound of horns perked Two-Bite's ears. He gripped the double-bladed axe, flexing his remaining fingers.

It was time.

Two-Bite bellowed a command and the crew assigned to the koch began to pull. Their labored grunts reached the War Skull's ears and he was pleased. The army parted and the koch rolled onto the white sand, making a straight line for the gates and trailing a chain leading back to the beastman lines. More horns rang out and Two-Bite roared. The beastmen around the king shouted and the whole of the army took up the cry, blasting the city with a wall of blood-curdling intensity. War drums from behind the lines struck up a fearsome beat. Foustian arrows *pinged, panged,* and *whuked* off the thick hide of the koch. Spears struck and stuck out of the wood as it closed with the wall. Two-Bite watched men high above take aim at the approaching beast; some even lit arrows of flame and loosed them.

This was even better than Two-Bite's original plan.

The arrows struck the shell and began to burn. Smoke rose from the roof. Thin wisps of grey snaked upward. The beastmen continued to scream and the koch smashed into the bronze and wooden gates of Foust. The crew pulling the monster stooped out from under the slabs of wood and ran back. All except three. Those three went inside the beast, and lit the oil, kindling, and animal skins packed within. Flames erupted from the belly of the Koch, and the three beastman ran back to their lines. Arrows studded the sand on either side of them, but did not strike.

Smoke rose. In seconds, it thickened, blinding the

archers on the right. Two-Bite did not know which way the wind would blow, but paid it little heed. His catapults and ballistae were rebuilt, repaired, and numbered in the dozens.

At his command, his beastmen pushed and pulled them into range of the walls.

As well as a battering ram.

Missiles from Foust's defenders rained down on the siege weapons, but the beastmen had shields—another of Two-Bite's ideas—which they raised over the heads of those laboring with the machines. Arrows found and killed beastmen all the same, but as one dropped, another filled the place and bent his back. In what seemed like no time, the machines closed with the walls, and Two-Bite noted a lack of catapult shot from Foust. Axe-Jaw had done his task. He hoped to see his friend soon.

Fire danced and raged over the husk of the koch, its flames licking at the gates while dark smoke piled into the sky, ruining the archers' sight. Below, the beastman catapults were readied, stone shot and wood set afire, and let loose. Balls of flame trailed fluttering smoke across the sky and flew over the battlement heights. Some pounded the battlements of Foust, smashing free stone merlons and knocking them back inside the walls. A sleet storm of arrows fell to earth, killing beastmen without shields and nailing their corpses to the earth. Another command from the War Skull and a thick tide of beastmen charged the walls. Several bore ladders high enough to scale the heights.

*

Within a courtyard of Foust, Axe-Jaw cut down a soldier and opened the throat of another with a back-handed cut. Blood-Grin smashed a soldier off his feet and crushed his helmed skull with one savage blow. The Koja tore into any soldiers facing them, made quick work of the man-things in brutal fashion, and pressed on toward the gates and the wheel which would open it. Some of the Koja sprang on the catapult crews and killed them quickly, but the main force charged ahead.

Commands rang out and a thick group of soldiers formed up before the gates, setting spears into the sand and waiting for the beastman onslaught. They did not wait long. The Koja smashed into the line, breaking it and lashing out at any man within weapon range. Some spearmen ran a few beastmen through, but the creatures were soon overwhelmed. Soldiers ran to reinforce the gates as a feeling of desperation mounted in the air. Catapult shot and ballista spears crashed down on the defenders. Some of the burning shot crashed down on rooftops, while others crushed soldiers to the sand. Ballista spears skewered some men at an angle, killing them instantly.

Being as close to the wall as they were, the Koja escaped most of the carnage. A merlon fell close to a knot of the armored beastmen and shook the ground. Axe-Jaw killed a last soldier and reached the gate wheel. He pointed to the timbers bracing the gates and Koja sprang to wrestle them away. Gesturing with his free hand, he motioned for another knot of Koja to hurry. They rushed the great wheel and turned it. Axe-Jaw took in the courtyard and noted sword-and-shield-bearing soldiers rallying to the gate. Horns sounded thoughout the city.

Leaving a score of his Koja to open the gates, Axe-Jaw charged forward, leading the remainder of his force to close with the approaching defenders. They met only strides away from the gate in a frightening clap of metal on metal.

And then the blood truly began to fly.

*

Outside of the walls, beastmen hoisted ladders through the smoke and slapped them against the battlement heights. Screams cut the air as well as spears and arrows, and beastmen scurried up ladders that strained under their combined weight. Another flurry of burning catapult shot hissed though the air, with two slamming into the walls in a burst of sound, brick, and dust. Foust archers and spearmen let loose shaft after killing shaft and beastmen fell from the ladders in droves. Two ladders eventually breached the heights, and a thin stream of screaming beastmen reaped the closest defenders.

Two-Bite saw the ladders deliver their attackers. He shook loose his battle-axe and slapped his helm. Behind him came the dark shape of Turn-Bone lifting a spiked war club of monstrous size. The rest of Two-Bite's guards followed their War Skull.

Over the din of battle, the crashing of the war drums, and the crackling of the burning koch, Two-Bite heard a roar from his army as the gate cracked open. Without needing any command, beastmen pulled the chain hitched to the chassis and hauled the flaming wreck back to allow their brethren space to charge ahead. They swarmed through the gate, and Two-Bite waved his remaining forces forward.

A black wave of beastmen rushed the gates, their battle-cries blasting the air, and the mighty walls of Foust seemed to slouch and shudder. Warriors crowded into the widening crack of the gates.

Horns called across the walls and from the interior of the city, blaring out the notes the people of Foust dreaded to hear.

The walls had fallen.

CHAPTER 30

Even in pitch black, the passage wasn't difficult to follow. Whoever dug it out had built it narrow. For that, He-Dog was thankful. There was less of a chance of going astray in the dark.

Behind him, Chop groaned something.

"Head this way until we can't go any further," He-Dog responded, not knowing in the least what the swordsman meant.

Chop moaned again. He-Dog frowned. He couldn't be bothered to reply.

They moved on, feeling the passage arc upward, when He-Dog caught a whiff of something that made him almost smile. Air. *Scented* air.

"Slow down," he told Chop, and reached out with his hand. He felt the two walls, a low ceiling—all cool brick— then the end of the tunnel, flat and made of brick. He placed an ear to the surface. He dropped his shield and placed both hands against the stone. With a breath, he heaved against it. Something shifted, ever so slightly, and a crack of light formed a line at one edge of the tunnel. He shoved again, but there was something keeping the door in place. He jammed his fingers against the crack, wishing he had something thin enough to use as a pick. He wedged his sword into it, but it wasn't enough.

"We're here," He-Dog muttered. "But no further."

Quickly He-Dog ran a hand over the four sides of the passageway's ending. There had to be a way in for people from this side. Who built secret passages with only one entrance? The thought befuddled him and he ran his hands back from the surface, feeling his way as best as he could in the dark.

After a few moments, he found what he was looking for. Perhaps a forearm's length from the door, on the right side, was a hole and inside was a lever. He-Dog tried pushing it up then down. Nothing. He pushed it one way, then the other, and there was an audible click deep inside the wall. Half-expecting something bad to happen and not knowing why, He-Dog released the lever and lowered his hand. He placed a hand on the surface of wall ahead of him, tensing to leap back if necessary.

He pushed and the door swung open. Light flooded the brick tunnel.

"Aye," He-Dog breathed, squinting against the light. "Come on, then."

Chop followed him into the room.

They both stood and stared.

The chamber was large and made of dark wood and shining bronze. The thick timbers appeared especially expensive given the nature of the land and the lack of growing wood nearby. Like fingers, the wooden beams reached up, forming a domed ceiling that met in a thick circle high overhead. Both the wood and bronze gleamed in the room's light, and He-Dog saw that the sun blazed in through slits in the walls, except for the one where they emerged from the tunnel. A huge bed dominated the center of the room, lavished in pillows of exquisite material A fine mesh of sheer, silken cloth draped the bed in a shimmering gauze, no doubt keeping any and all insects at bay. The two men stepped into the room, marveling at the display of wealth. A mural cut from stone decorated the wall opposite the bed, depicting a scene of beach, sun, and trees.

Chop wandered to a desk and chair, and began opening and closing drawers. All were empty. He-Dog discovered an alcove to the right of the secret passage, and found elaborate trunks and chests as well as mirrors. Fancy pegs studded one wall, yet everything was bare of any clothes, as if the place had been picked clean.

Chop grunted loudly, catching He-Dog's attention. The swordsman pointed. To the left and right of the mural were archways draped with thick curtains. He-Dog walked to one while Chop faced the other. They went through the arches at the same time and saw the throne and audience chamber, with the same spouting fish taking up the middle of the room.

"We're back in the keep," He-Dog muttered, getting a dark look from the black mask. "But no Kratoe."

"He-Dog!" Balless bellowed from inside. "You there?"

He- Dog stuck his head back into the Kratoe's bedroom. Balless stood before the secret passage and beamed.

"Finish them did you?"

"A little." Balless nodded. "But when I pulled away they followed. They followed me right up to the door here, but then they fell back. Didn't like the light."

"Guess where we are."

"I can't guess. Where?"

"In the Kratoe's bed chamber."

Balless looked around. "Bit bare isn't it?"

"It is, it is a bit bare," He-Dog said. "Why do you think that is?"

A great frown crossed Balless' features, like a dark cloud stepping in front of the sun.

"He's gone?"

"He is."

"You killed him?" Balless brightened.

He-Dog shook his head. "I did not. But I certainly want to talk with him."

"Aye that," Balless agreed, but he wasn't sure what they'd talk about.

He-Dog motioned Balless and Chop to follow. He led them into the audience chamber and around the fish fountain. They opened the doors to the chamber and were surprised yet again to find the corridor leading to the place deserted.

"Something's wrong," He-Dog said simply, feeling his guts churn. The staff and guards of the palatial keep were gone. The hallways branching off from the main corridor were deserted. Open doors revealed peopleless rooms scoured clean of valuables.

"Place's been looted," Balless commented.

He-Dog nodded and felt a mite unhappy about that. He would've enjoyed being in on the looting.

They kept on, their puzzlement growing. As they approached the barricaded high double doors that led outside, He-Dog heard it. The noise grew louder as they got closer, and it made the three of them tense up.

Fighting.

Heavy fighting.

"Help me here," He-Dog said to Balless, and they removed the three timbers barring the doors from the inside. He-Dog pulled one door open, hearing the groan of the hinges and seeing the sun shine in. They peered into the courtyard of the inner keep. As He-Dog expected, it was empty. Stables stood to the right of the bronze and wooden gates, also barred by thick timbers, and he could hear the restless horses within. He ignored them, and ran to the nearest flight of steps leading up to the battlements. Balless and Chop followed.

Reaching the top, the three peered out over the city. In the distance, black smoke rose into the air to the grim pounding of beastman drums. He-Dog could smell burning wood. He thought he could even see the outer walls and the fighting there. Beastmen, he sighed. No more stubborn race ever existed.

"What do we do?"

He-Dog looked on grimly. Good question.

"You there!" a voice shouted out from the streets below.

He-Dog looked down to see a gathering of citizens approaching the closed gates. One of the men in the front, dusty and carrying a sack over his shoulder waved and shouted again. "Open the gates, you bastard! Open them before they kill us all!"

That brought He-Dog back to reality. He turned away from the battlements and quickly descended the stairs with Balless and Chop at his back. Grunting, they removed the timbers locking the gates, and pulled them open. They had only just made a crack when the people gushed in and milled about the courtyard.

"Where's the Kratoe?"

"Where're the guards?"

"What's going on?"

He-Dog stood back and studied their frightened faces. There were whole families here, and he spotted Sergius with his two daughters among the crowd looking back at him. More people rushed through the open gates and some of the men ran up the steps behind He-Dog, to peer back out over the battlements.

"Who are you?" One short man pushed himself to the head of the mob and pointed a finger. Another man stood behind him, a brute who actually wore a black mask. He-Dog looked to Chop for an explanation.

This time, Chop ignored him, staring at the man in the black mask, who stared right back.

"Who are you, I said," demanded the short man again.

He-Dog said nothing. He looked back to the gates and watched more people rush in. Balless stood by his side, holding his mace with his mouth slightly open. More and more citizens of Foust entered, backing the three of them up until they stood before the open gates of the keep.

"What of it?" the short man demanded again.

"Where's the Kratoe?"

"The beastmen will be here before long!"

"Shut the gates!"

"There are soldiers coming!"

The mass of people looked in the direction of the gates. Running up the streets in full retreat were a group of Foust soldiers. Perhaps two dozen of them. Within moments, they pressed into the rear of the gathered crowd and forced their way to the forefront of the gathering.

He-Dog tilted his head in greeting. He knew the lead man. Knew him well, in fact.

Bowlak.

*

The people stepping over him caused him to open his eyes. Thankfully, his senses were returning and Borus saw the outer gates of the keep open. The citizens of the city pushed and shoved their way inside. He sat there slowly blinking, with his back against the wall, and flinched when he heard a great cracking coming from far behind. He attempted to rise. Couldn't.

Mage.

He looked at her dust covered face and, for a moment, felt a stab of fear the likes of which he'd never experienced. He wiped the grime from her face and patted a cheek. Nothing. Getting his legs out from under her head, he set her down, patted her cheek again, and placed an ear to her chest. Lords above, he couldn't hear a heartbeat. He rose above her, wondering what to do, and felt his throat constrict in mortal grief.

She coughed.

It was weak, but she coughed and cracked open her blue eyes, even more striking in the light.

"What?" she croaked.

"Nothing." Borus smiled weakly. "Can you get up?"

The space between her eyes furrowed. "If you help me."

"There's something happening."

"What?"

"I don't know. Can you hear?"

Her eyes looked in the direction of the inner keep. "Can't see. But… yes. I hear people… shouting."

"I do too."

He heard something that made him pause in surprise.

"Close the gates!"

*

"The beastmen will be here in no time." Bowlak said though his mouth of bad and missing teeth. "Who here is a soldier?"

Of the mass of people gathered, none came forward.

"Right then," Bowlak said, lifting his chin. "I'm a Koor with the Foust guard. Close the gates!"

Half of his force rushed to do just that.

"The beastmen are behind you?" someone asked.

Bowlak nodded. "They were and they'll be here eventually, after they've sacked the outer city and killed whoever is left. We'll hole up here."

"Is that your plan?" Sergius appeared with his daughters in tow.

"Aye, is it?" asked another.

"It is."

"We'll never last in here," Sergius said. Several of the people around him looked ready to wail.

"No choice," Bowlak said, his straw like hair hanging out underneath a helm that He-Dog thought didn't fit him. "There's nowhere else to go, but we'll arm those of you who can fight and make every foot count."

Serguis appeared shocked. "Arm who? Look about you! Most of us are women and children! And I'm fifty-seven, by Seddon's grace!"

At the exchange, Balless squinted and spotted a face in the crowd that he recognized. The little girl of five. He gave a tiny smile and nodded at her. The girl clung to her mother's arm, but she saw the gesture and timidly waved back.

That made Balless feel good.

"You can fight." Bowlak jutted his chin toward the healer and his daughters. "Certainly this one can." He indicated the big man wearing a black mask like Chop's.

"Me?" Sergius' eyes bulged. "I can't fight!"

"You will if I say so," Bowlak warned him. "And anyone else I see fit. And you three…" Bowlak trailed off. Behind him, the gates closed with a loud clap.

He-Dog had wondered when it would get around to him.

"You," Bowlak repeated, his eyes narrowing and his mouth becoming an ugly gash of hate. "I'll kill you."

"You will not," Sergius declared, looking at the Koor in surprise. "You just said you'll arm those who can fight. Look at them. I think it's obvious what they can do."

"These men killed—" Bowlak began.

But Sergius would have none of it. "Are you still on that? He didn't kill your soldiers! If you want to be angry with anyone, it should be—who's your captain again?"

"Krajin."

"Where is the good captain?"

Bowlak cast a poisoned look in He-Dog's direction. "Dead."

"What?"

The Koor reached up with one hand and scratched at his chin. "Got himself caught by the beastmen. He's dead. If he's lucky, it'll be quick. If he's unlucky, he'll be in pieces."

The news visibly dampened the expressions of the surrounding people.

"We're stuck here," Bowlak said to them all. "So we

may as well fight while we can. If you die in battle, I can guarantee you it'll be far better than if you're taken alive."

"Trapped," Serguis breathed, placing both hands on his near bald head. His daughters crowded him from behind. The people appeared stunned by the news and the realization that the inner keep wasn't a safe haven after all. It was merely a delay of the inevitable.

"Where's the Kratoe?" Sergius finally asked, looking around.

"Gone," He-Dog informed him.

All attention focused on He-Dog in that moment, and he had to admit he liked it. Balless and Chop stood just behind him, waiting and ready.

"Gone?" the short man asked.

"Look around." He-Dog gestured. "You think you could get in here otherwise? If he was here? Hm?"

Stunned silence.

"And if there were any officers about, you think they would've allowed this dog here to take charge?"

Bowlak visibly bristled at the insult.

"All gone," He-Dog informed them. "And you're all dead."

The faces before him paled and slackened. Old men and women appeared on the edge of open panic. Sergius looked somber, his eyes drifting to the ground as Hesel and Samil clutched at his sides. Bowlak simply stood, glowering at the three warriors.

The time was ripe. "But you don't have to die…" He-Dog said.

"What do you mean?" one man blurted. "What do you know?"

"My lads and I know how to get out of here."

"Where?" they demanded in near unison. "*Where?*"

"For a price, we'll take you away from this place."

Stunned silence again.

"You're joking!" Sergius exclaimed, his eyes wide.

"Vulture!" the short man shouted.

"Mercenary!" someone else cried. "Sinder!"

"Heartless topper!"

"Kill him!"

Balless stepped forward, his mace coming into view. Chop appeared on the other side of He-Dog, who simply stood and hooked his fingers into his belt.

"Don't think that's wise," He-Dog declared in a quiet voice. "Do you?"

Bowlak drew his sword. "You'll lead us out of here," he warned.

"Wait." Sergius waved him down. "Wait," he sighed. "How much?"

Bowlak could have killed the healer with a look. "You're not buying—"

"I have daughters to think of!" he barked, startling the Koor into silence. "We all have families. If this man can get us out of here, I'm willing to pay."

"My lads and I will get it out of him," Bowlak said.

"Then we'll fight." He-Dog nodded and marked him with a defiant glare. "And after you're dead, we'll take whoever wants to go."

Outside the keep, someone pounded on the gates.

"Who is it?" Bowlak bawled to some of his soldiers who had climbed the steps to the ramparts.

"More people," they called back.

"Don't open the gates," Bowlak ordered.

He-Dog smiled coldly. "Now who's heartless?" He winked at the Koor.

"I have twenty men with me," Bowlak spat out. "And we'll take you down, my lad. Right and proper."

"You don't have the time. The more we stand here talking, the closer they get."

"Pay him!" someone shouted.

"Yes, Seddon above, do it!"

"Pay the heartless bastard!"

"What do you offer?" Sergius said, ignoring looks from Bowlak and the short man.

He-Dog shrugged. "Pay your way in gold, and we'll get you to safety."

"Some of us don't have any coin!" someone shouted.

He-Dog hadn't thought of that. There was no need to be a bastard about it. Some gold was better than none. "Alright. I have a number in my head. Collect that number and we'll take the lot of you."

"And you'll take us out of here?"

This was getting on He-Dog's nerves. "Aye, we will. But you better hurry else we change our minds."

"What if we don't pay and just follow you wherever you go?" a voice called.

He-Dog kicked at the sand under his boots. "You're not thinking. Who do you think you are, eh? And who do you think the beastmen are? You think they'll stop coming after you? After this? They won't. As soon as they find your scent, they'll be after you. You want to follow us? You're right, I can't stop you, but I sure as Saimon's hell won't help you if you fall behind. These guards might, and they might not. But these soldiers, they know who we are. They know we came through that bloody mess to get here. We got in. We'll get out."

He-Dog paused then to let his words sink in.

"You want to survive this? You speak to me."

"How do you want the coin?" Sergius asked, and this time, no one challenged him.

"I said already. Once more, and listen this time. I have a number in my head. Collect it yourselves. If you can fight, that'll be your passage paid, so the soldiers are fine in my eye. But the rest of you, it's your burden to pay for the ones who can't. Decide among yourselves, and get the coin to me when you have it. The faster we have it… "

He didn't finish. He knew his point punched home.

"And let those outside in as well," He-Dog said to the soldiers near it. "That could be extra coin for us."

Looking uncertain and mad because of it, Bowlak nodded to his men to do just that.

The gates opened and a second surge of citizens came through.

*

The people shoved and pushed Borus as he staggered through the gate, holding Mage in his drooping arms. He'd thought he had more strength, but reality claimed otherwise. His energy faded with each step, and he when he got through the opening, he stumbled to his knees. Soldiers tried to take Mage away from him, but he refused. He did allow them to help him get out of the way while they closed the gates.

Borus saw Balless, and then the others. His core froze despite the heat.

*

Sergius came forth with a small sack and offered it to He-Dog.

"How much is in there?" He-Dog asked him.

"I don't know. I didn't count, but it's what people could give, in any case." The older man's silver tuft of hair was in need of a wash.

He-Dog opened the sack and peered inside. There was a modest collection of gold and silver in there, lighting up the cloth and twinkling at him. He closed the drawstring with a yank.

"You got the newcomers?"

"Yes."

"Then it'll do," he declared and looked at the gathering. "We'll take you. Line up as best as you can. You there, soldier!"

"Bowlak." Sergius supplied, but He-Dog didn't use the name.

"Gather your men around the people. Keep them in line."

Bowlak did not appear happy with the situation, but he turned and did as told.

"Alright." He-Dog turned his menacing countenance toward the bulk of the crowd. "Line up! Hurry now! We'll be going inside the keep. You men in the rear bar the doors when we're all in. The rest of you, if you have water skins or the like, get them ready. We'll get water inside. You'll need it."

"What about the horses?" someone shouted.

"We can't take them where we're going," He-Dog answered. "So free them from the stables if you care."

Bowlak's face hitched in confusion. "Where *are* we going?"

"To safety," He-Dog answered. With that, he turned and marched into open doors of the palatial keep. Balless, Chop, and Chop's larger twin followed at his heels.

The refugees of Foust, all hundred and eighty-three of them, walked after the warriors.

"To safety?" Bowlak grumped, watching the people file by. "Where?"

CHAPTER 31

He-Dog led the column of people back the way they had come, toward the audience chamber of the missing Kratoe where the open doors gave a sense of desertion. He-Dog heard the people gasp behind him. Perhaps none of them had ever set foot within the inner keep, let alone the audience chamber. *"Gone,"* he heard some of them say. *"They're all gone. But where?"*

He-Dog didn't know the truth, but he had suspicions.

"What do you think?" Balless asked at his side.

"I think the Kratoe ran," He-Dog answered. "Down that passageway we came upon. I think he had that tunnel made a long time ago just in case of something like this. And I think he's heading for the coast."

Balless appeared to think about it, his face becoming pensive. "So, when we went out to the beastmen?"

"Time to escape."

"Ohhh," Balless snarled softly. "The *bastard.*"

"The bastard," He-Dog agreed.

"We going after him?"

"We took coin from these people. Said we'd get them to safety. Right now, that might be following the Kratoe's tracks to see if we can catch him."

They came to the fish spitting water into the air.

"Alright, "He-Dog bellowed. "If you have water skins, fill them here and be quick. If you don't, find something that will carry water. Food too, if you can find it. Beyond that wall is a bed chamber full of skins and such. Take anything that can be used as torches and anything else that will burn. We're going underground. Now hurry."

Bowlak walked up to the three mercenaries. "Going underground? Where?"

He-Dog didn't care anymore. "There's a passage just beyond that wall that took the Kratoe away from here. He's left Foust. He's left it to fall and these people and you to the beastmen."

Bowlak's mouth hung open. He seemed to have just as many missing teeth as Balless.

"Hm." He-Dog nodded, but he was glad to see Bowlak was not challenging him. He might have need of the soldiers later. "I don't know where this goes, but I think anywhere is better than here. Agreed?"

Glowering, Bowlak kept silent.

"How many men did the Kratoe leave here to die?" He-Dog asked him. That made the Koor officer snort and turn away.

"He's angry," Balless said.

He-Dog shrugged. "How would you feel if I left you to savages?"

Balless smirked. "You wouldn't do that," but his expression softened into uncertainty.

"Oh yes, I would," He-Dog informed him with a dare in his voice, and left Balless to stew in uncertainty.

"Drink what you can now!" He bellowed at the people around the fountain. "I don't know when you'll be able to drink again."

He-Dog watched them pushing, shoving, and filling anything that would hold water. He had a suspicion that they would need every drop, and whether or not they would survive would depend on each other. If he was right, and he suspected he was, the cave below went under the hills and mountains behind Foust, probably coming up on the other side. The Kratoe was most likely heading for the coast three days away and the village there. More precisely, the docks. The thought made He-Dog boil. When could he have left Foust? At what time? He-Dog shook his head in dark appreciation of the Kratoe. The man was smart. Draping his double from head to toe to take away any suspicion and sacrificing a few guards to make the ruse stick.

"Hurry, you shaggers," he roared again. "Else I leave here without you and leave you to the beastmen!"

That hurried the people and a flurry of activity broke out. He-Dog was pleased. He'd have to remember to make more threats to light a fire under their arses. Might even work on Balless, for that matter.

He saw the big man at his side with a lopsided grin in place.

And maybe not, He-Dog thought.

*

As He-Dog stood thinking, Chop confronted the man with the black mask. He reached out a single hand.

The man called Karast said not a word. Instead, he reached out and clasped Chop's offered arm tightly, and in the manner known to only the warriors of his particular order. Chop nodded once, and stepped back. A moment later, he wandered off to another part of the chamber, and Karast followed.

*

In another part of Foust, beastmen roared, bit, clawed, and feasted on raw human flesh. The sand soaked up enough blood to turn it all into a runny mess that sucked at bare toes. Beastmen ran amok, killing citizens where they found them, punishing and killing soldiers if they came upon a cornered knot. The smell of blood, excrement, and steaming viscera filled the air and choked human prisoners until their captors killed them without any reason, other than to simply wipe them from the land.

Two-Bite stood in the courtyard of Foust's outer wall, basking in the smoke and cries of terror. He let his minions have their amusement, for it was the duty of a king to allow his followers some entertainment after a hard-fought victory. He looked around, saw beastmen raping the man-things' females, and saw the sport in it. He saw their children bashed against walls and eaten like delicacies. He saw man-things slaughtered for the shocked expression that crossed their faces just as their throats were bitten out. And he heard the guttural howls of pleasure from his followers, basking in blood up to their elbows. He personally intended to eat his fill of them later in the evening in a great victory feast.

After so long, the man-things had finally fallen.

He roared for prisoners to be brought to him. Soldiers, if there were any nearby. Over his shoulder, the imposing figure of Turn-Bone stood silent, his spike club coated and dripping with the blood and fleshy matter of the fallen.

Reds dragged three soldiers to the War Skull and forced them to their knees. All three had been in a fight. Their armor was torn and their bodies bleeding. Blood caked the faces of all three and their eyes were glazed and fearful. Beastmen crowded around and the figure of Axe-Jaw appeared.

"You." Two-Bite pointed a talon at the nearest prisoner. He approached the prisoner, flexing thick fingers ending in claws. He took a hold of the man-thing. The prisoner's eyes bulged as the hand fixed on his throat.

"You. Tell I. Where Kratoe?"

"In the inner keep," the man croaked. *Too easy*, Two-Bite thought, and ripped the man's throat out anyway.

"You," Two-Bite fastened his bloody hand on the

throat of the next. "Where Kratoe?"

The man started to hitch and lost control, tears and snot bursting from his face. Not even Two-Bite liked to see a man-thing in such a state, so he killed him with one crushing fist.

Blood pooled around their feet, and Two-Bite noted how rich the color looked in the sand. Like something extremely valuable. With that thought, he clasped the throat of the last soldier, a fat man in shreds of armor. A large bush of hair covered his mouth, and he regarded the king with an exhausted but defiant air.

"You look tough," Two-Bite grunted.

The prisoner said nothing, but grimaced in the king's bloody grasp.

"Where Kratoe?"

Krajin sighed. He had mustered his troops and fought to protect the people as best he could. He fought even as the armored beastmen came upon them from behind, slaying several of his troops. It was his bad fortune to be knocked senseless and wake up to this. To wake up and see this once beautiful place smoking and falling to rubble, to hear the sound of dying citizens. Before him, the beastman king, for this could be no other, tightened his grip around Krajin's throat. He could feel the creature's powerful fingers and nails dig in. The captain of the outer walls took a deep breath of air heavy with smoke and blood, and closed his eyes.

The beastman king scowled questioningly for a moment before finally understanding.

Then ripped.

Standing over the three corpses at his feet, Two-Bite looked toward the city. Deeper. He must go deeper. He must rip the heart from the city and feast upon it. He knew he had to do this, else the man-things would only return to fight. Not that it bothered Two-Bite. It only meant more fighting, and more food. But something bothered him.

He gestured for Axe-Jaw to come closer. The leader of

the new Koja had done well, and Two-Bite told him so.

Axe-Jaw accepted the high praise, and took the opportunity to inform his king that the other man-things were below the city, trying to escape.

Two-Bite wanted to know if this was true, and snarled out the question.

Axe-Jaw reported that it was, indeed, and that he had seen the tracks below.

This greatly interested Two-Bite and he gave new orders to his Koja leader. "Go below the city and find them. Take the Koja with you. And Turn-Bone. Find the three and bring them back, dead, alive, or with bites taken out of them."

"But bring them back."

"To me."

With a snarl and a particularly vile oath, Axe-Jaw swore he would do just that. The Koja leader roared, and the remaining hundred answered him.

*

On the other side of the mountain, Galt emerged with a handful of warriors. He dropped his torch to the sand, not needing it any more. The sun blazed down and damned near cooked his eyes in his head after hours of darkness. The grunts from the lads following him voiced similar sentiments. Galt stepped away from the exit and inhaled desert air. Before him, Brakuss and a few others waited with the horses that would carry them to the coast, and the waiting ship which would take them away from this extension of Saimon's hell. Empty wooden stages filled a deep, sand-golden grotto. The raised platforms had once held crates of supplies up off the desert sand. Supplies destined for a lusher climate. The Kratoe had already gone a day earlier, but no matter. Galt eyed the two roads leading from this place. He'd be joining the old bastard soon enough.

Then they would go about carving out their own empire, one to rival the likes of Zuthenia and eventually consume it.

But that was for another day.

"Brakuss!" Galt bawled. At once, the armored man led the captain's horse to him. Galt took the reigns and mounted, glad to have the animal under him.He watched the last few men reach their own horses. Twenty of them, the last of the cadre the Kratoe left behind to populate the inner keep.

Brakuss handed his commander a water skin and Galt drank without thanks. He lowered the skin, lips wet and red, and regarded the mountain in whose shadow they stood.

Seddon above, he was glad to leave this place. Let the beastmen have their rock. He was destined for better places than this, with whatever wealth the Kratoe had managed to steal from the Zuthenian mines below.

Galt sighed. Time was wasting, and there were new worlds waiting to be conquered.

"Behind me," he ordered as he steered his horse into the lead. "And by Seddon's rosy ass, don't lag or I'll stab any punce that does through their eyes and leave them with their guts curing in the sun."

With that, Galt and his warriors rode for the coast.

Forever leaving Foust... to the dogs.

CHAPTER 32

He-Dog waited until his patience left him and then he took matters into his own hands. He informed the people that they were leaving, and led them into the Kratoe's empty bedchambers. The people stripped the place of its priceless cloth, blankets, skins, and mesh nets. All would be used as fuel for the fires to light the way through the tunnel. He-Dog ordered them to not make a sound, lest he beat the offenders senseless and leave them behind. He told them to follow him into the dark, and to not stray from the path or the light. The warriors, he commanded to space themselves among the people. He warned them all of the portcullis, and to be careful of it, but gave no reason why.

To all of this, they gratefully agreed.

He-Dog, with Balless behind him, lit a torch and went through the secret door. The long line of people followed him.

Time stretched on, and when they had all passed into the passageway, a silent Chop and his new companion stood and regarded the empty bedchambers. Chop finally turned to Karast and gave him a nod, and Karast retreated into the tunnel, his huge double bladed axe held in his fist. The swordsman followed him.

A moment later, the secret door to the Kratoe's bedchamber closed without a sound.

*

With a sense of urgency only felt when something hunted him, He-Dog dove into the depths of the tunnel with his torch held high. He carried his shield and had put away his sword for the moment. He didn't like going back into the tunnel, but their time in Foust had come to an end. It was the tunnel now, or death.

At that particular moment in time, He-Dog hated the thought of death.

He pushed on, grateful for the light illuminating the way and the tunnel's brickwork. They eventually came to the portcullis and the mess of mashed limbs and skulls upon the floor.

He-Dog slowed down and drew breath. The creatures' gray flesh shone in the torchlight. Claws and fangs littered the floor, and He-Dog saw perhaps five bodies blocking the way, trying to squirm inside the small opening when they were smashed by Balless' mace.

"Ugly," Balless muttered. The things *were* incredibly ugly in death. Something tugged at He-Dog's mind as he studied the creatures' faces, something familiar about the beasts that he couldn't quite place. It bothered him. In the end, he gave up trying to figure it out.

"Stay clear of the gate there," He-Dog said to the nearest people. "Pass it on down the line."

"Else something might grab you." Balless grinned.

"And eat you," He-Dog added, rare amusement lighting up his face. Then it was gone in an embarrassed scowl. He motioned to Balless to get moving again, and the line of refugees lurched ahead.

"You did some work on them," He-Dog said to Balless.

"They wouldn't stop coming."

"But they did."

"The light drove them back." Balless grunted. "They followed me right up to that door in the bedchamber."

"Determined toppers."

"Or just hungry."

He-Dog grunted at that. He wondered if the ones that had slipped through were nearby. He supposed they would find out soon enough.

They continued until the brick faded to natural stone running at a downward slope. He-Dog's torch began to wane, and he stopped to wrap animal skins around it. He had no idea where they were going, but he hoped that they reached the end soon. He had no desire to be left stumbling about in the dark earth when the last few torches burned out.

The passageway flowed deeper into the earth, and stone teeth hung from the ceiling and rose up from the ground.

"Where are we?" Balless grunted. His face looked hellish in the torchlight.

"In a cave," He-Dog answered.

"Another cave?"

"This one's bigger."

"I don't see any walls."

"Nor I. I don't like that."

"Why?"

"Those things could be here. Just waiting for us at the edge of the light."

"They made noise last time."

"Keep that in mind. And pass it on down the line. I'll try to find a trail if I can," He-Dog finished and resumed looking ahead, his eyes fixed on the rock and sand before him. He listened, and heard only the rumble of Balless as he delivered the message.

"Are we lost?" he heard someone ask Balless, but he didn't hear the reply. He didn't have to. Being lost would be far better than the other horrors that might pursue them. Because he knew *they* were coming. He didn't know how *they* knew about them, but his gut told him: they *were* coming.

And if they catch us, He-Dog shook his head. He doubted if he would be able to save a mere handful of the people behind him. Not in this place.

That thought made him walk faster.

*

Back in Foust, Axe-Jaw found the latrines he and his Koja had come up through. Standing next to him, tall, powerful, and as bare of armor as a cub's arse, was Turn-Bone. Axe-Jaw didn't want Turn-Bone to come with the Koja as he already felt the command was his and his alone. He didn't need or want Turn-Bone thwarting or undermining his orders. But, Axe-Jaw thought as he lowered himself into the fragrant gloom of the sewers and called out for torches, so far Turn-Bone showed little inclination of doing anything. That made the leader of the armored beastmen feel less threatened. All knew aboutTurn-Bone, and Axe-Jaw knew that Two-Bite wasn't the least bit threatened by the silent beastman; thus, there was no reason for Axe-Jaw to feel that way. Thinking further on it as he led the way deeper into the sewers, back toward the hole that led into the caves under Foust, Axe-Jaw realized what a complement Turn-Bone would be to the newly formed Koja, especially if he could convince that dented skull of his to join them.

The column of armored beastmen, with the grim exception of Turn-Bone, sloshed in sewage water, waving their torches while moving forward. Weapons, still bloody from the battle above, swung at their sides. Axe-Jaw arrived at the hole, and thrust his torch within. With a snarl, he tossed the torch into the cavern, watching the light fall to the not so far away floor.

He told the ones who followed him to keep close. He

reminded those who carried torches to hold them high so that the others could see. He ordered them to be mindful of the Mar Fahten. He knew they were below, waiting in the dark. If they wished to fight with their distant surface cousins, that was their choice. The Koja would kill anything.

With that, Axe-Jaw climbed through the hole and descended toward the torch. He reached it without incident, and picked it up with a growl. The others caught up, and he shushed them with a curt wave of his spiked axe. He turned his helmed head and strained to hear. Nothing.

Growling, Axe-Jaw struggled to get his bearings. He searched until he found the riverbed of sludge, and moments later, he found the footsteps leading off into the dark, deeper into the cave. He gestured for the rest to follow, a long glowing worm of a procession bearing savage weapons, slipping its way through the sepulchral blackness.

They heard the chattering and the scrabbling of claws on bedrock. Even the stoic Turn-Bone stopped in his tracks to listen to the noise surrounding the advancing Koja. Axe-Jaw heard the sounds and bared his fangs.

The Mar Fahten had found them.

Axe-Jaw told his Koja to stand ready and not to go outside of the light. He ordered them to form circles around the torchbearers. He warned the torchbearers to stand within the ranks and hold the light up high. Axe-Jaw grinned and bared his fangs. He faced the gloom and hefted his spiked axe. The noise surrounded them, and the leader of the Koja knew he'd never heard the like before. The Mar Fahten stayed to the dark, but their presence drew closer as the sound of their approach grew louder. The mewling intensified, and Axe-Jaw swished his axe before him, loosening up his arm.

The sound got even closer, an ugly rush of hate and hunger, swelling in the dark like something lost and infected.

The Koja snarled and tightened their grips on their weapons: axes and mauls, great swords and war clubs. They faced the dark and welcomed their long lost cousins.

Shapes teemed just within the veil of black, thick and swearing at the beastmen standing within the torches' glare.

Axe-Jaw could see them—like shiny figures struggling in oil—holding just beyond the torchlight. They shied away from the postures of the Koja. The Mar Fahten seemed to dare them to drop their light. "You may keep the weapons," the Mar Fahten seemed to challenge, "for what little good it will do. Just douse the light."

Their deep earth cousins cared little whose flesh they feasted upon as long as they feasted. Knowing this, Axe-Jaw scowled and drew back his axe. He looked at the dour Turn-Bone, who stood ready with his massive, spiked war-club. He also appeared to have had enough.

Very well, Axe-Jaw thought and roared a command.

A hundred beastmen shouted back, momentarily drowning out the Mar Fahten.

And the Koja surged forward at the dark.

*

"We have to stop," someone blurted out in the dark.

He-Dog scowled at the voice.

"Please, we can't keep up this pace."

"We're exhausted."

"We've been walking for *days*!"

That made He-Dog scoff. *Days*, his arse. They had barely begun! Still, he stopped and surveyed the dark. All he could hear was the sound of the people rustling behind him. He supposed that was a good thing. He nodded at Balless.

"Alright," Balless announced. "Take a rest. But stay in the light."

The sounds of relief rippled through the line all the way to the back.

Balless left He-Dog's side and walked among them, his mace ready as he looked between the people on his right and the black oblivion on his left.

"That's him, momma," he heard a little voice say. He saw the little girl to whom he had given food standing with her mother. Balless's face lit up in appreciation. The little one's mother wasn't bad looking.

"Are you the one…" the woman trailed off, clutching and nodding at her daughter. The resemblance wasn't all there, but the mother possessed the same straight hair parted in the middle. The same dark eyes.

"Aye," Balless said. "I'm he."

"Thank you," the mother said. The little girl smiled at him.

Balless shook his head. "Not at all. I know," he thought for a moment, "what it's like."

"You saved us then," the mother went on, her dark eyes bravely staring down the fear Balless detected in them. "And I'm certain you'll save us now."

"We will." He smiled. "We have a bargain, after all."

"To get us to safety?"

"Aye that," Balless rumbled.

"You promise?" the little one asked him. Balless liked the pipe sound of her voice.

"We promise."

"Promises are important."

Balless nodded. "They are. Remember that."

"Where are we going?" the little girl asked.

He thought about her question for a moment then nodded. "Out."

That brought on a few blinks and looks from the people standing nearby.

"Out?" said one man loudly. "Where's out? By Seddon's rosy ass, we could be here in the dark for days… oh…"

He trailed off as Balless fixed him with a gaze that suggested he didn't care for the man's tone or opinion. Especially not in front of the little girl and her mother, both of whom were displaying more courage than a grown man. Balless scowled ever so slightly, and got his message across. The man shut up and looked away.

"Out," Balless repeated to the little girl and her mother. "We've struck a bargain… and we do what we can to hold up to it."

"What if you can't?" the little one asked in a tone that made Balless think of broken promises. Her mother shushed her, for some reason Balless could not understand. It was an honest question.

He looked down at her tiny frame. "Then we…" He saw the look in the mother's eyes. A pleading, behind her brave front. "We will…"

Balless paused. What would they do? Then it came to him.

"We'll give you your gold back."

"We gave the gold coin you gave Yuti," the mother said.

"Did you, now?"

The little one, Yuti, nodded. Balless liked this child. "Then it was gold well spent."

With that, he nodded to the mother, hoping he'd made her feel somewhat better. He smiled at the little girl as well, who smiled back. Balless got a glimpse of well-formed and all-present teeth. That was good.

Balless scowled again at the man watching him, the same one who had piped up and come close to scaring people. The mouthy one dropped his gaze immediately. Rightly so. Balless fumed. He'd hate to have to slap a customer around. That would be just all'round bad for business.

Balless moved further down the line, nodding at people who met his fearsome features. He nodded to Bowlak, who only glared back. He walked on, passing Foust soldiers at various points until he met Sergius and his daughters. Both women appeared glad to see him, and even the healer gave him a pleasant look. Balless' eyes lingered on the ladies for a moment, before Sergius cleared his throat and spoke.

"I see you're well?"

Balless regarded him and shrugged. "Right now. Daresay we could be dead in the morning."

Sergius shrugged back. "Daresay you could," he agreed sardonically. "Tell your friend that this rest was needed. There are some older people here as well, as you can see. We can't move like we used to."

Balless listened, but he knew what He-Dog's thought would be on that. "Where's Broken Legs?"

"Ah," Sergius shook his head. "When the beastmen were coming over the walls and surging up the streets, I hurried my patients out of there. There weren't many, but those who could walk or run did so. Anak—Broken Legs––couldn't move anywhere. He asked for…" Sergius' face tensed. "He asked for the axe you took from my table when you were on guard those nights, and a few other bladed tools. I couldn't carry a man of that size, and he decided to stay… so…"

"You left him," Balless said simply.

"I did," Sergius said, appearing deeply troubled by his choice.

Balless did see what the trouble was. "Fighters—soldiers get left behind all the time. Broken Legs knew that. Sounds to me he died as he wanted."

Sergius regarded the big man with hope in his eyes. "Do you think?"

"Aye. I could be wrong." Balless cocked his head. "But I don't think so. I'm sorry I hit him when I did."

"Well," Sergius said. "You tell He-Dog what I told you."

Balless nodded and moved away, feeling uncomfortable. He wasn't sure what the healer was talking about. Did he mean Broken Legs? Or that thing about old people? His brow crunched up in thought, trying to remember just what it was about old people. Then he arrived at the back of the line and the two soldiers bearing torches.

"Who're you looking for?" Balless asked.

"The two men—one of them with you."

"Black mask?"

"Aye."

Balless nodded and peered into the dark. Chop was in there somewhere, and he had with him the one who wore an identical black mask, before Chop had his all ripped to Saimon's hell. A right big bastard as well, if Balless remembered correctly. He didn't envy either of them being behind them, or wherever they were in the surrounding blackness, but he hoped that the little swordsman got back in one piece.

"Keep a watch out then," Balless said, more to himself than the two soldiers.

With that, he returned to He-Dog.

CHAPTER 33

The Mar Fahten withered against the sudden attack of the armored Koja, fleeing back into the greater depths of the dark. Around the line of beastmen lay the crushed and bleeding bodies of several Children of the Deep Earth. Axe-Jaw killed three of them personally before the creatures retreated. Retreated, but did not break.

With blood staining his chest plates and pauldron-covered shoulders, Axe-Jaw peered into the blackness before him and heard the outraged chirps and squeals from their distant cousins. Axe-Jaw looked at Turn-Bone. The big beastman had left a trail of three dead behind him as he rushed forward, swinging his spiked club at what the torchlight revealed. They all stood in the blood and guts of the fallen, and Axe-Jaw heard that none of the Koja had been taken by the Mar Fahten.

Shouting and waving his axe in the air, Axe-Jaw made it clear that they did not fear the Mar Fahten. He ordered his Koja to form up and move ahead.

The darkness beyond the riverbed of sludge exploded.

Creatures, their flesh made gray by the years spent under the earth, lunged at the front of the line, and Axe-Jaw lashed out in pure reflex to cave in the head of one.

Others came at him, hissing, screaming, and clawing, and Axe-Jaw swung his spiked axe into the lunging mass. Other Koja stepped up and joined the fight, killing the Mar Fahten in droves and leaving a low pile of dead and dying. Axe-Jaw bared fangs as he took the head half off an attacker, then slashed open another, and bashed yet another with a free fist. He spiked one creature through the middle and had to kick it off or else lose his weapon. Others sought to attack but his Koja formed a wedge that flung the remaining frights back. And then, as soon as the attack began, they vanished yet again, into the ink.

Once more, Axe-Jaw bellowed a challenge and stood ready with his axe. A chorus of roars came back as the screeching Mar Fahten ripped into the Koja line. A savage fight ensued, was won, and in the end, the dark creatures retreated once more, leaving hundreds of dead.

But they took the lives of eight of the Koja, overwhelming the beastmen and driving them to their knees where the Mar Fahten used sheer numbers and claws and fangs to kill the intruders quickly. The Koja left the fallen eight, as commanded by Axe-Jaw. The beastmen who were the last to see the dark swallow up the unmoving carcasses of their brethren heard the hideous mewling from beyond.

And the sinewy rip of flesh and muscle.

Axe-Jaw gave the command to press forward. He ordered his warriors to stay within the light, insisting that the attacks were merely the hellions flinging themselves into the light blindly, trying to knock the Koja into the dark where the advantage would be the Mar Fahten's.

No sooner had he shouted the command than more forms flew out of the blackness, jaws splayed wide and screaming. Some of the Koja bashed the monsters out of the air with their axes and mauls. One even flew at Turn-Bone, and the big beastman swatted his attacker away in a bloody spray. Again the Koja beat back the Mar Fahten, but in the subterranean creatures' retreat, four dead beastmen were dragged with them.

Livid at losing any of his fighting force to such animals, Axe-Jaw roared and cursed at the ebony veil engulfing them. He vowed to come back to these caves and scorch it all with fire. He promised he would eat the very meat from their bones. He shook his spiked axe in fury at the gloom and the mewling and the scrape of claws on rock just beyond.

He turned about and met the dour face of Turn-Bone. The beastman nodded forward, indicating it would be a far better idea to simply get *away* from here. Fuming, Axe-Jaw gave the order, and his Koja pressed on. They formed up into tighter knots, ready for attack from all sides and more than a little anxious at the pure abandon with which the Mar Fahten threw themselves at the beastmen line.

The Koja did not hurry. Axe-Jaw would not run in the face of creatures who existed underneath them. He marched forward with his axe at the ready. If the Mar Fahten wanted to attack, he welcomed it. It would be simply one more chance for him to kill.

Onward they pushed, on bedrock now, and twice more the Children tried to sweep them away. The Koja smashed, hacked, and flung the creatures back into the dark, wreaking horrible devastation among the underground denizens. Turn-Bone killed too many to count, and even Axe-Jaw's arms began to weary from the sudden battles. The Mar Fahten claimed seven more beastmen, and the sounds of them ravishing the dead filled the living's ears.

They reached an upward slope, and Axe-Jaw pushed his warriors forward. He knew the value of high ground. His spirit sank when, after clawing his way up the incline, he found a portcullis barring the way. Axe-Jaw reared up and gripped the bars, shaking them furiously. Snarling, he whirled around and looked below, the torches from the remaining Koja lighting the slope quite well. His forces were strung out behind him, holding formation as he ordered, but he could hear the sound of their pursuers' claws and the snap of their jaws. Even as he watched, he saw long limbs flash out from the dark at the base, taking swipes at the knot of Koja at the bottom. The beastmen struck back with their great swords and long mauls, and howls and screams pierced the dark as the weapons struck and took a heavy toll.

Axe-Jaw faced the portcullis. He lowered his armored shoulder and rammed it into the door, making it shiver. He noted the length of pulped arms in a slot near the bottom's edge, but he knew none of his Koja could slip through such a narrow opening. He slammed his shoulder into the door again and felt it ring. He looked below and saw a single beastman being peeled away from the mass below, howling as he went. The others tried to save him, but a surge of arms emerged from the blackness, clutching and grabbing for more. He returned to the iron and felt a hand on his shoulder.

Turn-Bone.

Holding a greatsword in his hands, the massive beastman plunged the weapon's point into the crack of the portcullis and bent his back into it. Iron groaned. Rock fragments and dirt fell from the portcullis, and still Turn-Bone stood and strained, his eyes slits, his fangs bared.

Below, two more beastmen died in savage fashion.

With a shuddering groan and a crash, the portcullis fell away from the doorway. Axe-Jaw roared and pushed Turn-Bone through. He ordered them all up the slope and through the door, losing five more beastmen to the appetites of the Mar Fahten.

The tunnel beyond was narrow and split into two and on instinct, following his nose, Axe-Jaw pointed the way he wanted his Koja to go. He stood at the portcullis opening, slapping his warriors as they came screaming through. When the last one passed, Axe-Jaw took up rear guard, and smashed any and all of the foe who tried to come through the hole. The grim leader slaughtered until the rocks were slippery with blood and bodies, and he paused only for one of beastman to thrown down a torch, catching one of the Mar Fahten ablaze. The stench and fire from the burning dead held the horde back, their arms and claws swiping at the corpses.

While Axe-Jaw and his surviving warriors made their escape.

CHAPTER 34

"Balless," a weak voice called out to him on his way back to the front of the line. Balless turned to see Borus sitting on the ground with what appeared to be a dead woman in his lap.

"Borus?" Balless went closer. "You've gotten hairy," he said, pointing to the other's beard.

"Has He-Dog seen me?"

Balless thought about it. "No," he studied the man's thin face. "You've lost weight."

"I'm sick."

"Hm, she dead?"

The question appeared to startle Borus, and he quickly inspected his friend. He patted her face with growing urgency, whispering to the woman. She did not respond. Then, a slow hand reached up as if in surrender and her face scrunched up in annoyance.

"Oh thank Seddon," Borus breathed, and hugged her close.

Balless didn't say anything. He wasn't a smart man, but it was plain to see that the one-eyed champion had seen better days.

"Thank Seddon," Borus repeated and lowered the

woman.

"Anyone have any water?" Balless asked the surrounding people. Moments later, a man offered a water skin and Borus took it. Balless also summoned Sergius and his two daughters, and the healer eased the woman away from Borus.

"She's not very good," Sergius commented with a dour expression on his face. "But I'll see what I can do."

Borus nodded his thanks.

"Where have you been?" Balless asked the former archer.

"In Foust." The other smiled unpleasantly. "Good to see you."

Balless said nothing.

"Is He-Dog angry?"

"*Urf*. He's always angry."

"No, I mean about me leaving you in the infirmary."

Balless thought about it. "Don't know. Why don't you ask him?"

"No," Borus shook his head. "Not in this condition."

"Hm."

"Don't tell him I'm back here," Borus said.

Balless couldn't promise that. Things had a way of popping out of him without his knowing.

"Thank you for getting us out of the city."

Balless nodded and, thinking the conversation done, moved to the front of the line. He found He-Dog bent over with his torch in hand, studying the ground before him.

"Signs everywhere," He-Dog informed him.

"Borus is back there."

"What?"

"Asked me if you were angry with him."

He-Dog stood up. "He's back there?"

Balless nodded. "Looks sick. Got a woman with him, too. She looks in even worse shape than Borus."

"A woman?"

"He looks fond of her." Balless said.

Borus? Fond of a *woman?* At one time, the notion might have made He-Dog laugh. Not now, however. He looked back over the people and shook his head.

"Are you sure about that?"

"Aye that."

Borus fond of a woman. A true wonder. And trying to escape with her to the coast.

"Not angry with him," He-Dog stated quietly. The old Borus would not have cared one shite about what He-Dog thought. That, in itself, was something of note. If someone as full of hate as Borus could find a woman to change him, he supposed that was a good thing. And He-Dog knew there were too few good things in the world. He wasn't going to ruin it for the one-eyed man.

"Rest time is over," He-Dog said. "Get everyone up. The trail leads on ahead. Time to get out of here."

With that, Balless turned and did as he was told.

Borus. He-Dog thought again. No, he wasn't angry at the man. He did pay for them while they were in Sergius' infirmary. As for what was left over, well, they had more than enough now. In his mind, they were even. The thought made him smile a little. Raising his torch, He-Dog walked on into the darkness, following the trail that would hopefully lead them into daylight.

*

The tunnel the Koja followed opened into a larger area, too big to be illuminated by their torches. Axe-Jaw called for his warriors to form a line across the tunnel mouth. Beastmen armed with mauls and greatswords quickly turned and faced the pursing Mar Fahten, snarling at the sounds of their approach. With tidal force, the creatures that existed below Foust burst from the opening and sprang on the beastman line. Shrieks and howls flayed the air. Mauls smashed the life from the charging forms, while greatswords took many a head from grey bodies. The Mar Fahten wave surged against the Koja, but the beastmen held and killed many of the Children. The fighting intensified until the Mar Fahten retreated back the way they had come, mewling and hissing frightfully but respectful of their prey.

Wasting no time, Axe-Jaw cried a command and stole away into the dark, continuing the hunt for the man-things.

*

He wasn't certain he'd caught whiff of it, but then He-Dog paused and decided that he had. A breath of air—fresh air—came from beyond. He didn't know how long he and the others had gone on in the dark, but he knew it was a long time. Perhaps all night. His limbs ached and his body felt weary, which told him that they had gone on a very long time. But smelling the air lifted his spirits. Moments later, he heard people behind him exclaim they smelled the same thing, and one could feel hope growing in the dark.

He-Dog thought it was a nice feeling after the fall of Foust. Up ahead, he thought he saw a ball of light. He led the column toward it, and its size grew until they had reached the exit of the cave. Warm air buffeted his face and he closed his eyes in pleasure. He heard the others behind cry out in joy and that made him suddenly cautious.

"Wait here!" he called and motioned for Balless to follow. Together, the pair ventured out into the sun.

They emerged into a wide bowl of yellow sand and desert rock. Wooden stages used for storing items lay to their left, bare and forlorn. Slopes of yellow stone rose up, leading to mountain tops blazing in an easterly sun. A light wind blew through one end of the rocky formation, the only sound in an otherwise empty grotto. Two roads, parting like a wishbone, lay before He-Dog and Balless.

One road went back, around the mountains they'd just came from, and perhaps led to the husk of Foust. The other road snaked ahead, through hills of rock, in the direction of the coast.

He-Dog stooped and tossed his torch to one side, next to a spent one that wasn't his. He placed a hand to the ground, tracing a finger along the tracks he'd found.

"Wagons," he said. "Or koches. Horses. And boots. Many boots."

"Long gone?"

"Long enough," He-Dog said, taking a deep breath. He squinted into the sun and studied the far off mountaintops. "Get the others."

Balless did just that. Crying out in relief, the refugees of Foust stepped into light they'd thought they would never see again. Some held up hands as if attempting to touch it, others merely wept. Bowlak looked at He-Dog and grudgingly nodded at him, to which He-Dog gave a little smile back.

"We're saved!" some shouted.

"Saved!"

"Wait," He-Dog said in a loud voice, quieting the lot of them. "You're not saved yet. We still have days to go to get to the coast. Only then will you be safe. Look around. See those stages? The tracks on the ground. The Kratoe and whoever he had with him in the keep have come and gone this way, taking whatever was here."

He-Dog suddenly thought of the man called Galt. Another person he would very much like to talk to. In He-Dog's mind, they owed him and his lads some coin.

"He's left you here to rot," He-Dog said. He saw Bowlak's shoulders slump, and those of several of his soldiers as well. He met the face of Borus, staying close with some people who carried the figure of a woman. The one-eyed archer smiled at him, and He-Dog nodded back.

From the depths of the cavern, Chop and the man called Karast emerged. They walked over to He-Dog and

Balless.

"Who are you?" He-Dog asked, his face hitched up and his eyes still squinting in the sun.

"Karast," the other replied grimly, still wearing his black mask. "We have news."

*

Axe-Jaw smelled the air. The torches revealed many signs of man-things. The others saw it too and they grunted their excitement. The hunt would soon come to a bloody conclusion. Axe-Jaw spied the distant light and he gripped his spiked axe. He urged his Koja to follow. He picked up speed, ignoring the straining burn in his limbs and in his chest.

Soon now, very soon.

*

"Are you certain?" He-Dog asked the pair of black-masked men. Chop nodded.

"We could hear something coming in the distance. Far off, but coming," Karast said.

He-Dog looked at the cave mouth. He could form a neck there and make whoever was pursuing them pay in blood if they were hostile. He looked up, and took in the mountain tops. Up one slope, he saw several boulders, large and small, numerous and baking in the sun. He then studied the bowl formation in which they all stood, and a plan formed.

"We'll bury this place."

Balless frowned in confusion.

"The beastmen in Foust will be coming this way soon after they've finished with the city. If we block these roads, they'll have to go around and find another way. More time then. From up there we can tell if that's who's following us, but I have no doubt in my mind. Are you with us?"

He-Dog asked Karast. The big man nodded at once.

He-Dog didn't bother asking the others.

"Listen to me," He-Dog shouted again. "Bowlak will lead now."

The Koor's head snapped up in surprise.

"He'll take you to the coast. We are going to stay here and make sure no one follows. Take that road," He-Dog pointed. "And walk fast. We aren't the only ones coming through the mountain."

People looked fearfully at the cavern opening, understanding filling their faces. Bowlak roared, ordering his soldiers to surround the survivors of Foust, looking in He-Dog's direction.

"Get them moving," He-Dog yelled to him, and the other man nodded slowly. He got to it.

Little Yuti with the heart-shaped face and the straight brown hair stuck out a hand and, fingers wide, waved to Balless. The fearsome man grinned and waved back. He suddenly became aware of He-Dog looking at the exchange in distaste. Balless' smile wilted.

But he gave the little girl a parting wink. And another to Sergius' daughters, Hesel and Samil.

The people filed out of the area much too slowly for He-Dog, but the last of them eventually went around a bend and were hidden from sight by hills of stone.

"We should be with them," Karast muttered.

He-Dog looked at Chop. "Are you certain he's with us?"

Chop and Karast exchanged looks.

"I'm with you," Karast said.

"What are you, anyway?" He-Dog asked, gesturing to the masks.

"We used to belong to Nordun, and the army there. We're True Jackals."

The name meant nothing to He-Dog. "Time to get a move on here."

With that, he turned and began climbing up a nearby

slope. Pebbles rolled from under his feet and it was unsure footing, but he pawed his way upward, the hot air filling his lungs and the glare of the sun in his face. Sweat seeped from his head and body and he thought for a moment that he should've gotten a water skin. Too late for that now. Snarling, he climbed on, moving between rocks littering the slope.

He didn't look behind to see if the others followed.

CHAPTER 35

The Koja spilled out into the clearing and howled at the daylight. Several went to the wooden stages and smashed their weapons into the posts. Axe-Jaw breathed deeply and looked around the clearing. Some of the beastmen crouched to the ground and pointed excitedly. Axe-Jaw saw the tracks they found in the sand and hissed at the two roads leading in opposing directions. He spun about and chose five of his warriors. He instructed them to return to Two-Bite using the road heading back around the mountains. He told them to inform the War Skull that the man-things were moving toward the Big Water, and that they were about to follow.

When he was finished, the five ran off.

The beastmen continued their brutish conversations, when Turn-Bone caught Axe-Jaw's attention. The bare chested beastman pointed up, and Axe-Jaw squinted to see in the sun.

There, halfway up the mountain, like insects scurrying for high ground, were man-things. Axe-Jaw did not think about the tracks on the ground, he only saw the fleeing backs of his prey, and that alone made him give the order for the Koja to go after them.

As one, the beastmen roared back and gave chase, clawing and climbing up the pebbly slope as fast as they could.

*

"Hear that?" He-Dog grinned as he climbed.

"They've seen us!" Karast blurted out.

He sounded scared to He-Dog, and he looked at Chop. "You sure he's one of you?"

"Almost there," Balless grunted as he climbed upward, sweat falling from his thick brow to splash against the rock. They climbed past boulders the size of men, feeling the baked stone slap against their hands and the heat from the sun on their backs.

He-Dog set his eyes on what looked to be a small plateau three quarters of the way up the side of the mountain. A rounded boulder stood tall up there, almost taunting him, begging for a push. He didn't look behind. He knew the beastmen were coming.

The companions reached the lip of the flat outcropping. A huge boulder balanced just at the edge. He-Dog stopped just below the boulder and began driving the edge of his shield into the slabs of loose rock and sand.

"Dig!" he roared.

Balless appeared at his side, winding up and smashing his diamond-headed mace into the stone under the boulder, causing both sparks and rock shards to fly. Chop scrambled up behind the rock, while Karast stood on the other side of He-Dog and smashed his axe into the lip.

"Dig!" He-Dog shouted again. He started to laugh, wondering what it was he found so funny in such a desperate situation. They didn't have much time, but the notion only made him laugh louder. Each strike rang out, and He-Dog listened to the irregular beats, knowing exactly what it sounded like—music for dying. Balless joined in, bursting out between each powerful connection of mace on rock. Above them and pushing from behind, Chop could be heard laughing, causing He-Dog to laugh even more. Perhaps that was the reason he allowed the swordsman to follow them around. In the end, Chop was just as insane as the rest of them.

Karast glanced from He-Dog to Balless and shook his head.

*

From below and only a quarter of the way up, the Koja climbed on, screaming as they came, weaving in and out of the litter of rocks. They saw the figures high above them, but they were unaware of anything else.

Baring his fangs, Axe-Jaw urged them on.

*

Scream! He-Dog thought as he smashed away pieces of rock and sand. It was all they did. He grimaced at the howling from below and stopped digging. He rose and joined Chop at the top. He tossed his shield and helm to ground, and kicked his feet into the ground for sure footing. His hands slapped and pressed against the stone's hard skin. Karast appeared beside them a few moments later, throwing down his axe and bending his back to the boulder. Only Balless continued hammering away at the rock ledge under the boulder. But that suited him fine.

*

The ringing echoed off the mountain and canyon walls and found the refugees hurrying away from the area. Bowlak walked backward, gazing at mountaintops and cringing upon hearing the sound. Oddly enough, he didn't feel so much ill will toward the men any more. In fact, a part of him wished he stood with them.

Back among the moving line of refugees, a little girl with straight hair heard the ringing, and clung to her mother's arm that much harder.

*

Halfway up the mountain, Axe-Jaw looked up at the pounding noise and realized darkly what the man things were trying to do. He quickly looked about and saw that his Koja were on a broad slope, filled with rocks that could potentially come down on them. With a *whuff* he cried out and ordered his minions to split apart. Like a swarm of black insects, the beastmen began to divide to opposing sides.

*

The boulder moved.

"Push!" He-Dog grunted. The men beside him heaved.

"On my word," He-Dog breathed, pressing his shoulder into the jagged surface as much as he could. "Heave!"

It creaked forward, teetering on its tipping point. Balless appeared alongside them, tossing down his mace and placing both his hands against the stone. The four men planted their feet as best as they could and drew breath. They bared teeth with the force of their exertions, summoning the collective power of their backs, their arms, and their legs. Muscles knotted. Flesh went taut.

"Heave!"

The lip crumbled. The boulder tipped as if sick. More rock crumbled from below, sending pebbles bouncing down the slope, the sound of their passage crackling off of the mountain walls.

"*Heeeeave!*"

The boulder creaked and gave way. The men jumped back from its bulk as if frightened it would take them with it. The boulder flipped ponderously over and rolled down the weakened rock shelf. Down the slope, it clacked into two smaller rocks, sending up dust as it went, and urged the two smaller cousins to join the charge. Those in turn rolled down the smooth side of the mountain, knocking into others as they went and raising Saimon's hell faster than anyone cared to think about.

*

Thunder rumbled from above.

Axe-Jaw glanced up to see a wall of dust crashing down. Large bulky shapes moved inside. The speed and violence of the falling rocks coming at the beastmen froze several in place. The Koja leader had just enough time to shout a warning before lunging to safety. Out of corner of his eye, a boulder the size of three beastmen came crashing down. The falling rocks drowned out their shrieks and thunder raged over the slopes, enveloping all in dust.

CHAPTER 36

Dust swirled and rode air currents, hiding the carnage of the rock slide from the four men on the plateau. They stood abreast, breathing hard and quietly marveling at the destruction they had caused. The clouds of sand diminished, and the lower parts of the slopes appeared clawed by the boulders. Figures lay in among the rock, broken, twisted, and unmoving, and covered in splashes of blood tinted sepia by the sand. Boulders filled and blocked both the cave entrance and two roads. No one would be passing that way anytime soon.

"Unfit," Balless muttered.

"Unfit," He-Dog agreed, more than satisfied with the results

Somewhere below, rocks shifted and the clatter lingered on the air.

"That's all then," Karast said, sounding relived. "Now we go?"

He-Dog nodded, but Chop raised a finger, pointing below. He-Dog squinted and made a face. Below and getting to his feet was a beastman. He slowly turned about on the slope, gazing at the fallen rocks. He-Dog wasn't concerned with one beastman.

But two more struggled to their feet. Others stood, shifting and throwing off the blanket of dust and sand covering their dark forms, like insects in a sack of grain. A growl perked He-Dog's ears, and he groaned inwardly upon hearing that sound. He massaged the rubble of his nose.

"They're alive." Balless rubbed at his shaven head.

"Not all," He-Dog corrected him, but he felt disgust all the same. *Beastmen.* He *hated* fighting beastmen. Any moment now...

One of the creatures arched his back and screamed.

Many others answered that call and got to their feet.

"Bastards," He-Dog breathed.

"What do we do?" Karast's black mask faced his new companions.

"Do?" He-Dog asked him in disdain. He pulled out his sword and studied its edge. He gathered up his helm. Balless shook out his arm and sized up his diamond-headed mace. Chop's blades were in his hands and whirling.

He-Dog strapped his round shield to his arm and regarded Karast and his battle axe. Balless and Chop stepped away from each other and took up points along the mountain ledge. He-Dog thought of all the things he could say to the man called Karast. Words might inspire him to do great things. Or perhaps not. In the end, he looked away and watched the beastmen gathered below and adjusted his open-faced helm. He rolled his shoulders. The real work would begin shortly.

"Do," He-Dog breathed to no one in particular, and took up his own place along the ledge.

*

The Koja rose and thickened on the slope under the savage urging of Axe-Jaw. He stepped among the seething survivors, shaking their bodies and weapons free of sand

281

and dust. Some of the Koja were mangled by bouncing rocks, and Blood-Grin fell to smashing their heads in, snarling with each smash of his great maul. Turn-Bone stood and pointed to the mountain heights. He readied his war club. Axe-Jaw stood and peered upward, spying the four who had sent the rocks down on them. Rage energised the Koja leader and his warriors. He screamed at his armored beastmen, his once-mighty force reduced to two score at best. He raged at the ones above, unmoving and watching.

When all the surviving Koja were standing, he waved their swearing, screaming forms onward, to finally meet the man-things waiting for them.

*

They screamed and roared all the way up the slope. He-Dog wasn't particularly surprised, and figured he would be deaf by the time all was done. He watched the snarling faces draw closer, protected by helms of iron. Weapons of barbaric design and power shook and threatened in his direction. The smell of never-washed flesh assaulted his nose. He felt the approaching heat of their anger, and it scalded his contorted face.

Koja. He remembered the name the beastman king gave them.

The armored beastmen, of whom He-Dog and his companions had thoroughly endured enough, were mere strides from the rocky lip of the plateau. They paused on the mountain face for an aching moment, forming up like a black tide as raw and offensive as bloody sewage in a street.

With one last roar, they charged.

And the four men went to greet them.

CHAPTER 37

Balless' mace connected with the nearest helmed head, rocking it one side with a *clang* and breaking the beastman's skull despite the metal protection. Its scream of hate torqued into a squeak as it fell. Three more rushed in to fill the gap it left in the Koja line. He smashed his mace into a sensitive muzzle, halting the monster as if it had slammed into a wall. Balless retreated, avoiding a clash of mauls and war clubs coming down and pitting the rock he'd once stood upon.

He-Dog ran to one side, slashing at heads and upper bodies, ringing his dog skull blade off several iron encased heads and stunning a few. He went to the far side of the ledge and half chopped the leg off the first Koja climbing onto the plateau. He-Dog roared as he shoved the bleeding creature back into the ranks, and stabbed another through the face, feeling the serrated edge of his blade chew into flesh and bone. He deflected an axe with his shield, the impact knocking him back, and jabbed his sword at the owner. The steel tip bounced off an iron chest plate, and the beastman snarled. He-Dog fell back. He saw Karast brain two screamers with quick chops and lop off a hand trying to find purchase. The black masked man stepped back, avoiding greatswords and axes, before leaping back into the action and swinging his battleaxe. He sheared off a Koja's head as the creature attempted to climb onto the ledge.

A bloodthirsty chorus went up from the attacking wave, driven by anger. Jaws slavered and cursed, while a stormfront of crude, heavy weapons lashed, smashed, or slashed at the four fighting men. From the edges, Koja squared off against He-Dog at one end and Balless at the other, forcing them back. In the middle, Chop's blades flashed in the sun like needles, sometimes finding flesh, sometimes deflecting off armor.

A huge beastman barreled forward after Balless smashed aside his companion, raising a heavy maul and swinging for a head. Balless ducked and punched the spike into the creature's gut. The steel spurted out the back of the Koja and he dropped the maul, but his hands clamped onto Balless' head and drew him forward, screaming in his face. Balless cracked his fist into the thing's jaw, snapping the head back. But the creature held on and, while dying, used his bigger mass to carry Balless over the edge of the rock ledge. Two other beastmen followed.

Recognizing the danger of being overrun, He-Dog saw Chop run forward and *jump* over the heads of the beastman trying to climb up on the ledge. Several of their helmed heads arched up and followed the swordsman as he flipped over them, landing hard and slipping on the pebbly slope. Then he was gone from sight. Hate-spewing beastmen lumbered after the man. He-Dog fought on.

*

The bare chested brute known as Turn-Bone sought his chance at a black-masked man-thing wielding an axe. Two beastmen forced the man-thing back. One Koja lunged with an axe and the man-thing blocked the blow. Turn-Bone watched as the black-masked warrior closed and rammed his elbow into his foe's throat, popping the Koja's tongue out at the impact. The man-thing faced the second attacker and cut him open with two well-placed cuts. Turn-Bone grunted and stepped in. He brought his warclub down hard from overhead, and smashed the warrior's axe from his hands. The man-thing wrapped his arms around the bare-chested beastman, seeking to crush his ribs in a hug. Snarling, Turn-Bone dropped his club and returned the embrace, smothering the man's head. Both squeezed at the same time, two monstrous figures momentarily frozen in time, but a sharp crack came from only one. The man-thing's legs danced for a moment and went limp. Turn-Bone squeezed again, crushing the head before dropping the carcass to the ground.

He retrieved his warclub, and spotted a man-thing smashing the life from several Koja with a huge mace.

Whuffing, Turn-Bone walked toward the warrior, lifting his weapon.

*

From the side of the slope, Balless yanked his mace free and faced new attackers. He ducked low and smashed out the knee of one foe, the joint exploding like a rotten apple. As the Koja dropped, Balless parried an axe and spiked the owner through the face. Two more beastmen charged the big man, and Balless brutally killed them both. As an afterthought, he smashed the beastman with the ruined knee. Balless grinned hugely, spread his arms and yelled, catching the attention of a beastman with a dented skull and a warclub.

A *big* beastman. The thing eyed Balless with deadly intent.

In a silent challenge, the two closed.

*

Not seeing Karast die, He-Dog killed two more beastmen before a third lashed down with a greatsword. The weapon's tip grazed off his helm, stunning him, while the steel blade zipped down He-Dog's front, splitting the fine leather cuirass he wore and drawing a spotty red line from chest to belly. He-Dog fell back, stabbing in reflex and punching his sword through his attacker's bicep. The greatsword fell away, and He-Dog kicked the beastman back. He braced his shoulder behind his shield and ran forward, driving into a knot of creatures and slipping his sword into the unprotected guts of one. The beastman fell and blocked the others. One tried to step over his dying companion, but He-Dog clacked his sword off the chest plate before thrusting a second time and killing the beastman through the throat. Blood sprayed through the air and in that shower, a great beastman with a split muzzle rose up before He-Dog. He shield-bashed the wounded Koja. An axe blade took him across his jaw, screeching over the metal of his helm, and he felt the flesh there part. A greatsword deflected off a greave. Another warclub grazed his helm. He-Dog panted, dripping blood, and tore into his attackers— stabbing, cutting, bashing, and leaving a path of ruin among them. He looked up briefly to see Chop still alive and slipping and sliding at the center of a group of attackers, dropping beastman after beastman by simply touching them with his blades.

Sensing danger, He-Dog spun as a spiked axe came down and sheared through part of his shield. The impact spun him toward his attacker, and he stabbed his sword into the belly of the attacking Koja. The creature buckled and He-Dog rammed a greave-plated leg into his face, flipping it over to land flat on its back. He yanked his blade free, and faced a fresh knot of beastmen approaching, catching only a glimpse of Balless at the far end and below the ledge.

Only a glimpse, then he tore back into the Koja.

*

Holding his guts in place with his hands, Axe-Jaw felt his life leaving him. He swore at the man-thing ripping a path of destruction through his last remaining Koja. He reached for his axe, and gripped its shaft. With a grunt and sheer determination, Axe-Jaw got to his feet, staggered, and stalked the man-thing from behind.

*

From the other end, Balless faced off against the silent beastman with the brooding eyes. They swung at the same time, smashed weapons together, untangled themselves, and clashed again. They eyed each other over their weapons, and Balless could see that there were significantly fewer beastmen than before. Even as he watched, he glimpsed Chop blurring through dark figures slipping on the slope and killing foes where they stood or as they fell. The swordsman stabbed one huge beastman up under his jaw, snapping the muzzle shut, and spun to stab his second blade up under the chestplate of a second attacker. The blades flashed in the sun as they withdrew, the beastmen collapsed, and Chop tore into more.

The Koja before Balless lashed for his head. He ducked and smashed the monster's leg, but as the beastman fell, the creature brought his warclub down on Balless' right shoulder, crushing the armor, flesh, and bone underneath. The big man yelped and dropped his mace. The Koja fell forward, his upper body collapsing on Balless. Mighty arms wrapped around Balless' head and he grinned his ruined grin once again.

He had his left arm free, and his left hand still wore a spiked glove.

In one heartbeat, Balless drove his gleaming fist into the bare midsection of the beastman. He struck twice more and felt the arms around his head tighten. He breathed in the savage aroma of his adversary's body. The third punch broke ribs. The fourth punch raked the flesh from the creature's chest. Balless felt the arms seize up, and he looked into dying eyes. He punched the beastman three more times in rapid succession, each impact mashing flesh and crushing bone. With a gasp, the dying beastman let him go and sank to his knees. Balless smashed his spiked fist across the wincing muzzle, snapping it to one side, grimacing as he felt his own ruined arm shake. The creature fell over and Balless raised his fist once more to crush the skull.

The impact of a maul took him off his feet, and drove him to darkness.

*

Battling three beastmen, He-Dog took his share of cuts before he struck them down. He whirled about and crushed the edge of his shield into another's throat. He spun again, seeking the next foe, and saw a single Koja grimacing—the one with the ruined muzzle—and raising a spiked axe. He-Dog bared teeth at the warrior.

From the corner of his eye, he saw Balless go down.

A *wuffing* He-Dog bolted into action, half-decapitating the wounded *Koja* before him with one cut and leaving the creature dead in his wake. He bounded over the carcasses of several Koja, killed three more when they stood between him and his companion, and screamed at the two beastmen standing over Balless' struggling form, smashing him with axe and maul.

The pair looked up as He-Dog flew off the ledge.

His dog-skull blade speared the first Koja through the muzzle, snapping the creature's helm back in a fine spray of gore. He-Dog landed hard and slipped, both of his feet flying into the air and he landed hard on his back. The air left his lungs for a moment, and for seconds, he distantly heard the muted roar and clash of metal. His senses returned, and he rolled over to see Chop, hunched and ragged, standing over a number of dead Koja. One of the masked man's swords stuck up and out from the beastman He-Dog had missed.

With a grunt, He-Dog rolled over. Chop sat heavily on the rocky slope, his head slumped between his shoulder blades. Blood seeped from the man. He-Dog would check him later, but first…

Balless lay on his back with one arm cocked in the air. His chest plates were battered and bloody, and He-Dog wasn't certain of where the metal began and flesh ended. The last two Koja had simply stood over the big man and smashed and smashed and smashed, until He-Dog killed one and Chop the other. Sunlight blazed down, and He-Dog noted that the air had cleared of dust.

"Balless?" he asked, reaching out to touch the man's harsh features. As if sensing him, Balless' eyes opened and shifted to focus on him. One eye was ruined, purpled and bloodied. He smiled weakly, baring his wrecked grin, and He-Dog's throat constricted when he saw the blood seeping from his mouth and smashed eye. He patted Balless' forehead, feeling the grooves of cuts healed into scars, and nodded. Even as he felt the man's flesh, he knew he would be fine. Balless had survived worse in the past. He always survived. He always followed. There certainly wasn't an uglier or tougher bastard He-Dog knew… or cherished more.

Balless chest hitched and he coughed, spitting up dark, dark blood. His battered frame shivered and he blinked at the red-eyed face of He-Dog. A smile appeared once more, the corners of Balless' mouth barely hitching upward. He took in the harsh vibrant blue above.

"Unfit," he whispered.

And died.

CHAPTER 38

They dragged Balless' huge form over and placed him under the broken lip of the ledge. He-Dog and Chop took the remainder of the hot day to cover the big man in slabs of rock and debris, to give him some protection from any scavengers that might be around. Once he was covered in rock, they arranged the dead beastman in a semicircle around the grave, as testimony that Balless didn't die easily. He-Dog stopped several times during the day to rest as he worked, even taking off his remaining armor. Chop stopped as well, twice lying down and simply not moving to the point where He-Dog thought the man had also died. When he called his name, however, Chop raised an arm.

After all was done, they sat on the rocky ledge, and He-Dog's shoulders slumped. He felt the wounds he sustained in the Koja battle, but they would heal. They always did. Grimacing, he regarded the pile of rocks at his feet and stared hard at the pile, as if willing Balless to rise. He did not.

"Unfit," He-Dog muttered quietly. He glanced at the leather armor—once shaped in the guise of a lord's physique—split down the middle. It would be something that could be fixed, he thought, if he could find someone to do it. It looked too good to simply throw away. The Koja had ruined his shield but he didn't mind. Shields were easy to find.

His attention came back to the grave.

"He was… my brother," He-Dog said at last, saying the words and hoping they would alleviate his inner pain.

Chop slowly turned his masked face in He-Dog's direction, his reaction hidden by the stitched leather. The masked man said nothing.

A heavy sigh left He-Dog, and he listened to a wind softly cut itself on mountain's edges. He remembered the man who had found He-Dog and Balless, abandoned on a plain by a mother once raped by beastmen. He never knew her, but he knew his guardian, Rige, shared a dislike for civilization, and raised both boys deep in the wilds, passing on his knowledge where and when he could. Balless was always there for both of them. When their adopted father passed on, they buried him in rocks, and Balless followed He-Dog into the cities. The cities and the people and the unkind welcome. The source of his consuming hatred. All had mocked them both because of their hard looks and gullibility in the ways of civilized men. Difficult lessons learned, and a loathing that grew. But in whatever shadowy holes they found themselves in, they'd always survived. Together.

All over now.

"In the morning, I'll be leaving," He-Dog informed Chop.

The silence stretched on for moments before the black mask dipped in a question.

"To the coast," He-Dog continued. "I want to find the Kratoe. And have a talk with him."

The black mask nodded slowly.

That suited Chop just fine.

*

The people fleeing Foust endured the heat of the sun for three days. They exhausted their water within a day and a half, and baked in the desert until they breached the crest of a sand covered rise, and saw the ocean and the town before it. From where they stood, they saw two high masts over the housetops—merchant ships, someone exclaimed. The sight made them walk faster, as safety lay just before them.

Bowlak halted them just before they entered the town, as the absence of smoke and activity made him cautious. He left ten soldiers with the refugees while he led the rest of his force into the town. The people waited for him on the rise of the land, watching and hoping for the best.

Borus held Mage's hand where she rested on the hot sand, her head in his lap, and wiped the grit and hair from her face. They had both been quite sick the last two days, and Borus feared for the woman's life. Today, however, Mage woke and smiled weakly at him, giving him hope. It hadn't taken as long as he thought it might, but he believed that the worst of their sickness had passed. He hoped.

"Keep her shaded if you can," Sergius had told him a day ago, when the water ran out. Which meant Borus covered her face with the shirt from his back. He didn't like doing that. It made her look dead. The thought frightened the former archer and made him smile. He had once looked for his death, wanted it, and found it in the White Tar—the irony coming when he found a reason to live, right on the very cusp of death, in Mage.

The soldiers emerged from the outer ring of the town and walked back toward the waiting group. Borus watched them.

"See something?" Mage asked him.

"They're coming back."

Bowlak waved for the survivors to come into town.

"I think we have news," Borus told her, and struggled to get both of them to their feet, trying hard to conceal his own budding hope.

Moments later, the Koor met them all halfway and gestured for silence. "There are two merchant ships back there, just arrived this morning. They stayed because of the mystery of the deserted town. Our luck as they were about to leave by mid-afternoon."

"Will they help us?" Sergius asked from the crowd.

To this, Bowlak nodded. "They will. They're Zuthenians by birth, and are more than willing to transport the lot of us to the mainland. Old King Narijo will show us some compassion for what we've endured and for the news we bring, I think. Follow us in. There's a town square with a full well. Drink and rest for a while, but I need whoever is able to help me go through those houses for food. They don't have enough on board for all of us, so we'll have to make do with what we can find. We leave once all is stowed away on board."

The people looked back at him, relief flooding their faces.

And for the first time since they had known him, the Koor called Bowlak smiled. "Let's hurry on, then. The ships are waiting."

He did not have to say it twice.

Borus sat on a pier with Mage in his arms, watching the sun slowly drop into the ocean, as the sky bled great gashes of color. Behind them, the rigging groaned at the oncoming night and the rustle of surf could be heard beyond. The salty air smelled good, and Borus hugged Mage closer as he looked back over the house tops, to the distant ridge.

Behind them, people loaded chickens onto the smaller merchant ship, the clucking of the animals making Mage's head turn.

"I'll see if we can roast one of those," Borus told her quietly.

She nuzzled his chest with her head. "Do you see anyone?"

"No."

"Do you think they died?"

Borus shook his head. He didn't think anything could kill He-Dog, Balless or Chop. He didn't think he knew tougher men alive. Besides himself, his vanity flared, but he kept that thought in his head. Karast, however, was a different sort. He knew Karast had stayed behind, but a part of Borus hoped the man was dead. If the others were also dead, then that meant the end of the White Tar gang. And that was a good thing.

They became quiet, and Borus heard Bowlak and Sergius talking with the captain of the vessel somewhere behind. The people had been split into two groups and assigned ships.

"You two leaving with us?" Sergius asked them from nearby, breaking Borus from his thoughts.

"We are," Mage answered for them both.

"Get on board then, and find a place," the healer told them while looking at the sea. "The captain is nervous about staying the night here. He'll stay, so we can make use of the water in the town's well, but if we have to leave quickly, it's wise that all stay on board."

"We'll do that now, then," Borus said, and got them both to their feet.

"Drink water while you can, both of you," Sergius told them. "You'll recover slowly, but that's better than not at all."

Borus stopped before the man. "Thank you. For everything."

"No need for that," Sergius said. "I've changed my ways in the last few days. Anyway, I'll be going on the same ship as you, so I'll keep an eye on you both."

"Are they stocked up for the trip?"

"As well as they could," Sergius said. "The people living here took what they had, but we've divided up the crumbs."

"Where did they go?"

"We have no idea. Probably the sea."

"Hm."

"Get on board now," the man told them gently. "And find a place to sleep."

Sleep. Borus never thought the word could sound so peaceful.

With the sky lighting up, the two merchant ships cast off and took to deep water. Zuthenia lay four days to the east with good winds to push the ships along. Borus and Mage stood at the railing, while sailors went about their work. The once-champion archer's good eye raked the land in the distance, searching.

"Can you see anyone?" Mage asked.

Borus shook his head.

"I can't see anything at all. You may only have one eye, but it's sharper than both of mine."

He supposed that counted for something.

"Come along," Mage said, "and let's get out of this sun. I've had enough of it to last a lifetime."

Borus turned to leave when, off in the distance, sunlight flashed off something—metal—upon the ridge. It was only a small flicker of light, then it was gone.

He looked, resisting Mage for a moment longer, straining to see anything, but there was nothing to see. Taking a breath, he said a silent prayer for He-Dog, Balless, and Chop, for the best for them, and hoped good fortune would find them somewhere. If it weren't for them, they all would have perished in Foust.

Borus kept the prayer short.

He knew He-Dog hated such.

About the Author

Keith C. Blackmore is the author of the Mountain Man, 131 Days, and Breeds series, among other horror, heroic fantasy, and crime novels. He lives on the island of Newfoundland in Canada. Visit his website at www.keithcblackmore.com.

www.ingramcontent.com/pod-product-compliance
Lightning Source LLC
Chambersburg PA
CBHW031251120726
47906CB00003B/693